Vinnie's Diner

Other Abingdon Books by Jennifer Allee

The Pastor's Wife
The Mother Road
Last Family Standing

A Wild Goose Chase Christmas, Quilts of Love Series

VINNIE'S DINER

Jennifer Allee

a novel approach to faith

Nashville

Vinnie's Diner

ISBN: 978-1-63088-928-9

Published by Abingdon Press, 2222 Rosa L. Parks Blvd.,
P.O. Box 280988, Nashville, TN 37228-0988

www.abingdonpress.com

Macro Editor: Jamie Chavez

Published in association with the MacGregor Literary Agency

Library of Congress Cataloging-in-Publication Data
has been requested.

Printed in the United States of America

1 2 3 4 5 6 7 8 9 10 / 20 19 18 17 16 15

To my son, William, the finest man I've ever known.

Acknowledgments

My thanks to my agent, Sandra Bishop, who actually signed me after reading *Vinnie's Diner*. Several years and seven books later, we finally did it!

To Ramona Richards, who encouraged me way back when she wanted the book but was unable to acquire it, yet continued championing this story until she could give it a home. Thank you so much for believing in Vinnie.

God has blessed me with so many wonderful, supportive people in my life. I want to mention each and every one of you, but I hate the thought of leaving someone out. So, let me just say that every interaction, every relationship, every touch of a hand, every smile, and every tear have shaped the person I am today. For those who have joined me on the journey thus far, and those with whom I continue forward, I give you my thanks and my love.

1

It's a little known fact that flying tire rubber can kill you. But I'm a master of little known facts, and the road I'm on is littered with the stuff.

I grab my water bottle and take a swig while still keeping my eye on the road. Right now, it's pretty much deserted. I can make out a semi-truck in the distance, but other than that it's just me and an assortment of highway litter: Roadside scrub adorned with pieces of paper, plastic bags, and empty snack food wrappers; Crooked signs marking off the miles or announcing how far it is to the next rest stop; A beat up loveseat with one slashed cushion and covered in questionable stains tipped sideways in the ditch between the north and southbound traffic lanes; And a whole heck of a lot of tire rubber.

The theme from *Rocky* starts playing, triggering an automatic smile. That's my aunt's ringtone. I shoot a quick look at my purse out of the corner of my eye. A moment of hesitation, and then I reach over and dig the phone out of the outside pocket. It's illegal in California to talk on your cell and drive at the same time, but who's going to know out here on a nearly empty highway?

My dog, Grimm, sits up in the back seat and barks, chiding me for my reckless behavior.

"Don't worry. I'll be careful." I call back to him, then tap the front of my phone screen. "Hey."

"Hey, sweetie. Have you made it to the hotel yet?"

Aunt Bobbie has attended all my matches until now, despite her illness and work schedule. She loves trivia just as much as I do, so it's no hardship for her, and I think she lives vicariously through my victories. Whether it's local matches in bars, regional competitions in VFW halls, or the semi-finals at the Long Beach University auditorium, she's been at all of them. The only reason she's not joining me this time is because she couldn't get away from work. She's my biggest supporter. Actually, she's my only supporter. But she's enough.

"I'm still in California." I look around for a mile marker, but don't see one. "I passed the big thermometer about half an hour ago."

Her affirmative "ahhhh" makes it sound like she knows exactly where I am. "That's in Baker, so you're out in the middle of nothin' right now. It's a good thing I made you those tapes. They'll help pass the time."

I take in a guilty breath at the mention of the tapes. I haven't played any of them yet, but I don't want to hurt her feelings. "Yeah. They're great."

"They'll keep your mind sharp. Okay, honey, I'll let you concentrate on driving. I just wanted to make sure you were doing all right."

We exchange our mutual goodbyes and I turn off the phone, then toss it on the passenger's seat where it hits an open cardboard box full of cassette tapes. Aunt Bobbie gave them to me the last time I was at her apartment. "To help you keep the gears moving while you drive" she'd said.

Cassette tapes. She must have hunted all over to find those. But if she wanted to record something for me, cassette tapes are the only way. My car is so old, the cassette player is considered an upgrade.

I reach over, grab a random tape, and pop it into the player. After a few scratchy seconds, Aunt Bobbie's animated voice emanates from the one working speaker in the driver's side door.

"What was Whoopi Goldberg's birth name?" There's a pause to give me time to answer.

"Caryn Johnson," I say out loud.

"Caryn Johnson." Her voice confirms that I did indeed answer correctly.

"How old was Stockard Channing when she played 17-year-old Rizzo in the movie version of *Grease*?"

"Thirty-two," I say.

"Thirty-two," Aunt Bobbie says.

"Who was originally cast in the role of Marty McFly in the 1985 movie *Back to the Future*?"

"Eric Stoltz."

"Eric Stoltz."

This goes on for a while, her recorded voice coaching me through overly easy trivia facts that we both know I already know. It's doubtful the drill is helping at all, but it was a sweet gesture, and at least now I can honestly say I used her study aids. Besides, it's a long, boring drive to the city of neon lights, and Grimm is not what I'd call a sparkling conversationalist. At least this provides a distraction.

"Tire rubber."

Aunt Bobbie's voice pulls me back to the moment. I'd zoned out so I don't know what the question was, but the answer sends a chill skittering across my shoulders. It reminds me of the episode of *CSI*, the one where the go-cart driver—who had no business driving that thing on a highway, let alone behind a semi—has his head ripped off by a piece of flying tire rubber. It takes on even greater significance now because, in my desire to hurry up and get where I'm going, I've turned into quite a lead foot and I'm coming up entirely too fast on the semi-truck which is now right in front of me.

Two staccato barks sound in my ear. A quick look in the rearview mirror gives me a glimpse of the ugliest beast in all of California, and most likely the entire West Coast, who is now pacing back and forth across the threadbare backseat.

"Cool it, Grimm."

He whines, definitely not pleased at my indifference to whatever he's trying to communicate. Grimm, so named because he bears more of a resemblance to a creature from a fairytale than a dog, doesn't give a very good first impression. In fact, he looks like he'd be happy to rip a hole in your throat just for the fun of it, which is why he'd been at the shelter so long that he'd ended up on doggie death row. But the minute I saw him, I knew he was the dog for me. You have to really look, but there's a beauty beneath the beast.

If only my excellent judgment of character extended to humans.

"The next rest stop I see, we'll get out and walk. Promise."

The word walk should have gotten a reaction out of him somewhere on the scale between happy and spastic, but instead, he just keeps pacing, a low growl rumbling in his throat.

"Crazy dog." Time to pay attention to what I'm doing.

I lift my foot from the gas pedal and back away from the truck a few feet. Up to now, the traffic has fluctuated from heavy (when in a populated city) to almost nonexistent (when driving through miles of nothing). At the moment, I happen to be in a pocket of emptiness. There's no one else on the desert road between Baker and the Nevada state line. Just me and the pokey truck. This would be a good time to go around the guy.

I'm thinking about the *CSI* episode, when I hear a pop. A puff of smoke shoots out from behind the truck, and it shimmies like Grimm does after a bath.

"Oh no."

A moment later, something big and black crashes against the windshield, and an explosion rocks the car.

Instinctively, I push my body back, yanking the steering wheel hard to the left. At the same time, fifty pounds of Grimm barrels through the front bucket seats and jams himself between me and the wheel. The wind is knocked out of me and I turn my head away, trying to escape even though there's nowhere to go. The whole world looks like some bizarre mosaic through the spider web of cracks spreading across the windshield. The car veers toward the side of the road. Through my window, it looks like a good five foot drop into the wide expanse of dirt and desert scrub between the north and southbound lanes. I've got to stay away from the edge.

Turn into the skid.

The memory of half-listened-to advice plays in my head. You better believe I listen to it now, turning the wheel in the opposite direction, despite the growling mutt in my lap. The car starts to straighten itself. It's working. But then I see a flash of something in front of me.

Something tall with black material flapping around it like the tail ends of an old-fashioned duster. Long, straw-colored hair. A scraggily goatee.

A man?

What's a man doing by the side of the road in the middle of nowhere? And why's he just standing there? Why doesn't he get out of the way? Not that any of it matters. There's no way I can run into him. I yank the wheel back the other way and the car swerves around him.

And heads straight off the road.

For a split second I have the impression of being weightless. Then the front end tips forward and rams into the ground. The glass loses what little cohesion it had left, raining down in silvery shards. The roar of the impact fills my ears as my body tilts sideways. All sense of equilibrium vanishes as the car rolls once, twice . . . I don't know how many times. Grimm's growling has turned to high-pitched whines. My head jerks violently from side to side, then lurches forward, hitting something soft. At the same time I'm pelted with loose objects—CDs, my purse, a water bottle—as if they're all as frantic to get out of the car as I am.

Finally, the world stops bouncing and metal groans as the car settles.

Am I up? Down? I don't have a clue. A weight presses against my chest, and when I reach up to move it, my hand hits stiff hair and a strip of leather. I realize it's Grimm. One of the water bottles must have opened, because his coat is wet. An eerie quiet closes in on me, only to be replaced by a sound like the waves of the ocean amplified a thousand times. I squint, and through the empty place where the windshield should be, I make out the foothills.

But they're all wrong. They're lying on their sides.

The waves pound harder against the walls of my head until the noise is deafening. I try to keep my eyes focused, but everything blurs around the edges. The waves ebb, and I hear a crunching sound, like boots on gravel. Straining to see, I barely make out . . . What is that? A flag? No, it's that flapping black material. I think it's the man I swerved to miss.

A sweet, melodious voice makes its way through the undulating roar in my ears. "Let me help you."

I strain to see. *Help. Yes, I need help.* I lift my hand toward the sound. Then a crash, like the sound of two enormous cymbals slamming together, explodes right above my head. A flash of bright, blinding white light commands my eyelids to slam down against its assault, and my hand jerks back to my chest.

The white light is replaced by black silence.

Then nothing.

2

INTERSTATE 15

My roommate, Sandy, is standing in the middle of our now empty living room. She looks around her at the beige-colored indents on the gray carpet, showing where our furniture has sat for the last four years. Then she looks back at me. "Well, I guess that's everything."

Her voice is drawn out and several octaves lower than it should be, like a sound recording played at super-slow speed. Now her face contorts into an unnatural frown, and she says, "You don't look so good."

Funny, I was thinking the same thing about her. Sandy doesn't look so good. She bends and quivers, becoming a reflection in a disturbed pool of water. She holds up one crooked arm and waves. "Take care of yourself, Allie."

Her image is almost gone now. *Don't go.* I try to call out, but the words stay locked in my head. Thick darkness tucks itself around me, moist and heavy like a wet wool blanket. From somewhere in the distance, Sandy's voice sends me one last warning.

"Watch out for flying tire rubber."

Tire rubber.

I suck in a shocked gasp, but the air is hot and scalds my lungs. Panic prickles across my skin, and my heart pounds so hard it feels like Ricky Ricardo is using my chest for a conga drum.

Think, Allie, where are you? What were you doing?

What was I doing? I packed up my car this morning and left my old apartment for the last time. I was on my way to Las Vegas to compete in the US Trivia Challenge Championship. I was driving behind a truck, and Grimm was going crazy. There was a blow out, and then . . .

This is not good.

I crack open one eye, but the blistering pain that sears through my forehead forces me to squeeze it shut again. That's okay. I can work with this. Maybe I don't need to see to get out of the car. I try to reach out with my left hand, but my arm is pinned against something. I bring up my right hand, and it occurs to me that something is missing. Grimm. He's not on top of me anymore, and I don't hear him moving around. He must have found a way out of the car. Well, if he could do it, then so can I.

Reaching across my body, I feel for the door, but my fingers meet something coarse and dry. I stretch further, hoping to feel air, but it's just more of the same: sand, rocks, and something crunchy. Dry plants, maybe. Nothing is where it should be. After a bit more fumbling, I acknowledge that the Braille approach isn't going to work. I need to see what I'm doing.

I force my eyes open. White hot lasers burn their way through my retinas, drilling into my skull. This kind of pain deserves a scream, but all I can do is whimper.

I want to call for help, but no words will come. Even if they did, what good would it do? I'm in the middle of nowhere, surrounded by a whole lot of nothing. I could very well die out here, all alone. Even my dog has deserted me.

Help me!

"Hold on!" A male voice calls out from somewhere above. Who is that? The overdressed stranger? No, the voice is different than before. Rougher. Maybe it's the truck driver. That makes more sense. Of course he would stop to help me. Relief oozes through my aching body as I force my head in the direction of the voice. It takes way more effort than it should. Above me, the silhouette of a person leans down into the car through the gaping hole that used to be the passenger window. It looks like he's diving straight at me.

"Can you undo your seatbelt?"

I feel around with my free hand until I find the button. I press it, but nothing happens. I give it a few more tries, jabbing at it as hard as I can. The catch finally opens, and the webbed belt snakes lazily across my lap. My hips slide sideways, hitting the door, jarring my body and shooting a fresh wave of pain through my skull. It's like someone decided to use my head for a soccer ball.

The man reaches down. "Give me your hand."

As I stretch my fingers upward, it feels like something slices through my side and between my ribs. My arm falls back down, landing heavy and useless against my thigh. Nausea and discouragement roll through my gut. I can't. This is just too hard. And I'm so tired. Rest. I need to rest. My eyelids drop shut as I slump against the side of the car. My cheek is pressed against the dirt and something sharp bites into my skin. Rocks, probably. Or maybe glass. What difference does it make?

"Stay with me! Grab my hand!"

The man's barked commands cut through the dismay and pain, making me bristle. How dare he yell at me? I'm the victim here. I deserve a little tender loving kindness. I open my eyes and see him leaning farther in, grasping, reaching.

Then he speaks again. "It's going to be all right. I promise." His voice has become soft and comforting, and it turns my reaction around. How can I be angry with the guy who's trying to help me? He just wants to get me out of the car.

Gritting my teeth against the pain to come, I reach out, stretching up as far as I can. His hand closes in above my elbow. His fingers tighten around my arm.

He pulls.

Noises fill the air.

He grunts from the strain of holding all my weight.

I scream as a lightning bolt of pain rips through my spine.

He stops pulling, but doesn't let go of my arm. "I know this hurts, but I've got to get you out."

"Why not—" I force the words through lips that feel like old rubber, dry and cracked. "Why not out through the front?"

He looks at the jagged shards of windshield lining the window frame like broken teeth and shakes his head. "There's too much glass. Besides, I don't know if I could get you out from under the dash that way." He pauses. "It's very important that I get you out of this car. If I can get you out of here, you're going to be all right. Do you understand?"

It's an effort to move my head. The best I can manage is a short, jerky nod. I understand, but I only want to do this once.

"Okay then," he says. "Here we go."

I take a deep breath. The next time he pulls, I tug my left arm free. I twist my body and clutch above his wrist with my other hand. Drawing up my legs, I scramble until I can push my feet hard against the door, all the time groaning and screaming from the effort.

"Now!" He calls out a warning before giving one last, hard jerk that pulls me free.

And then, it's over. I might have blacked out for a second, because when I open my eyes again, I'm lying on the ground, sprawled across my mysterious rescuer.

"Success." He gently pushes me off to the side, then squats next to me on the balls of his feet. "Are you okay?"

I look down at my body, expecting to see a bloody mess or, at the very least, ripped clothing and bruises. But a quick examination of my legs, hands, and arms shows there's nothing like that. Amazingly, I'm in pretty good shape. No blood, no cuts, not even a tear in my jeans.

My car, on the other hand, isn't so lucky. The old, green hatchback lies on its side, the front end wrinkled like an accordion. And it's in pieces. I spot a hubcap over there, a side mirror over here, a license plate way over there, and bits of glass and chrome scattered everywhere.

Yet I've managed to make it through the crash without a mark on me. Not only that, but most of the pain I'd been feeling just moments earlier is gone. It makes no sense, but I'm not about to question it.

I look back at the man. "Yeah, other than a killer headache, I'm fine. Thank you."

This is the first opportunity I've had to really check him out. He doesn't look like any trucker I've ever seen. He's wearing a crazy uniform made up of a white shirt, black pants, striped suspenders and a red bow tie. A paper hat shaped like an upside down banana boat is perched on his head. Pinned to his chest is a plastic oval name tag that reads "Vinnie." The whole getup reminds me of what they make the employees wear at Steak 'n Shake. I look around, as if I'm going to find the restaurant he belongs to, but I know there isn't one for miles. Which brings me back to my first thought about him.

"Are you the truck driver?"

Shaking his head he stands and looks over his shoulder. "Nope."

"If you're not . . . then who . . ." Now I realize what he's looking for. "Hey, where is the truck?" I shift my eyes to the road. No sign of it. "He didn't even stop?"

"He had no cause to." Vinnie is still looking over his shoulder as if he's following the truck's route. "By the time he looked in his side mirror, you'd already hit the ditch. As far as he knows, it was a simple blowout, so he's going to a safe place to take care of it."

I narrow my eyes at Vinnie. "How can you know that?"

He shrugs. "Makes sense, doesn't it?"

I look down the long, empty road. "I guess so."

"Well, sure it does. Any decent person would stop if he knew there was someone behind him who needed help."

Sure, any decent person would. So Vinnie must have driven up right after the accident. But if that's the case, then where's his vehicle? I look around again, swiveling my head like a hoot owl.

Nothing.

Great. He must have broken down somewhere and been walking to the next stop when he found me. Just my luck to be rescued by an on-foot food service worker. Not only that, but I'm stuck in the middle of the desert with a total stranger. I peer down the road in the other direction, but it's empty, too. Looks like it's just the two of us.

Just me and Vinnie. This is an episode of *Criminal Minds* waiting to happen.

He reaches down, holding his hand out to me. I hesitate a second, then take it. His grasp is firm as he pulls me to my feet, grabbing my elbow with his other hand to steady me. But he doesn't need to. I had expected to feel something out of the ordinary, maybe strained muscles or bruised knees, but there's none of that. My legs are only slightly wobbly. Even the pain in my head is subsiding.

Weird.

When he sees that I'm not going to topple over, Vinnie lets go of my hand. I give him a nod of thanks, then wipe my palms against my thighs. "So, what brand of Good Samaritan are you?"

He hooks his thumbs under his suspenders and pushes out his chest, like a proud father in front of a hospital nursery window. "I'm Vinnie. You see that over there?"

He points at a building on the other side of the road. It's flamingo-pink, with palm trees flanking the front door and a big, empty parking lot. A huge neon sign on the roof flashes two different images: first a coffee cup with a pot poised over it, then the pot pouring into the cup. Cup empty, cup full. Cup empty, cup full. It keeps flashing and pouring as I take in the scene and random thoughts zip through my mind.

It's like something from another era.

It's the kind of place I'd like to take my Aunt Bobbie.

It wasn't there a few minutes ago.

I look back at Vinnie. "What is that?"

His smile grows even bigger. "That's my place." With a sweep of his arm he says, "Welcome to Vinnie's Diner."

3

Vinnie's Diner

What I've always loved most about Interstate 15 is all the bizarre roadside attractions.

There's the Mad Greek, which looks like a truck stop but serves authentic Greek food. I stopped in there once. Enjoyed the stuffed mushrooms. Not so much the stuffed grape leaves.

At least half a dozen paint-peeling mini-billboards sport cartoonish drawings of cone-headed green men and point the way to a shop that claims to sell alien jerky—which has always made me wonder, are they saying the jerky would be *enjoyed* by aliens or that it's made *out of* aliens? Is it a kind of extraterrestrial Soylent Green? I never had the stomach to find out.

There's even an abandoned water park sitting back from the road, the huge red slide faded a washed-out pink from years of inactivity under the intense desert sun. It's always reminded me of the kind of place the Scooby-Doo gang would find themselves. Their van would break down, they'd go into the park and think it's haunted, only to find out that some unscrupulous businessman is trying to steal the deed from a bunch of senior citizens. Of course, he'd be foiled in the end by those meddling kids . . . and their dog.

What all these spots have in common is that they'd be totally out of place in the middle of a highly populated area. Some are abandoned. Others just look that way. But out here, in the barren landscape of the desert, surrounded by scrub and sand, they fit right in.

But Vinnie's Diner . . . well, that's different. It doesn't have the wind-battered, sand-blasted look of the other buildings. There are no chips in the paint, no cracks in the windows or missing neon from the sign. The parking lot, though empty, is well kept and ready for patrons. It looks like the kind of place that's been around for a while and has been taken good care of.

Which is why my brain refuses to accept the existence of this diner. Because this isn't the first time I've made this trip. I've driven this road more than once, and I don't recall ever seeing that building before.

Then again, maybe I shouldn't be so surprised. I tend to zone out, especially on long drives. I must have gone right past it and never noticed. Sure, it's possible. After all, I have a habit of letting important information slip by. A fact my mother's shared with me more than once. It's probably why I'm so good with trivia. Useless knowledge seems to stick with me.

Vinnie lopes ahead, and I have to jog to keep up with him. At the edge of the highway, I stop and carefully look both ways before crossing. It's more out of habit than necessity, since my car is still the only vehicle on the road. Which is another odd thing. Even though it's a weekday, there's usually a lot more traffic.

"Wait a minute." I stop at the edge of the road. "Have you seen Grimm?"

Vinnie turns around. "Excuse me?"

"Grimm. My dog."

"Big black mutt? Not winning any beauty contests anytime soon?"

There are some dog owners who would be offended by that remark, but I can't fault the guy for speaking the truth. "That's him."

"Yep, I saw him. He ran into the diner when I came out." He turns around and resumes walking. "Follow me."

Once we're at the building, Vinnie opens the door and stands aside, ushering me in with an extended palm. Cool air rushes out to greet us and I lift my face to it, taking in big, greedy gulps.

He laughs and gives me a gentle push between the shoulder blades. "If you go have a seat I can shut the door and stop air conditioning the desert."

Embarrassed, I take a step forward, far enough inside for him to enter the building and close the door behind us. But then I stop again. The place is full of people. Customers sit at tables, perch on counter stools, lean against the wall. One man chews on a toothpick as he talks to a circle of friends, then takes it out of his mouth and pokes it in the air to emphasize his words. A young waitress, her hair framing her face in tight, brown ringlets, is at the service window picking up more plates of food than it seems possible for one person to carry. On the kitchen side, a round-faced cook with huge, bushy sideburns offers her a lopsided grin.

"How did all these people get here?" The question sputters out of me as I turn back to Vinnie.

He shrugs. "Same way you got here, I suspect."

He's kidding, right? "They walked in here after rolling their cars in the middle of the road?"

Vinnie raises an eyebrow in amusement, but he doesn't say anything else.

"Your parking lot is empty," I continue. "These folks sure didn't walk in off the street. So how did they get here?"

He twists his mouth and leans his head to the right. "That's a good question. What do you think?"

Normally, I'm all about figuring out the answers to word puzzles and brain teasers. But this isn't a normal day, so I'm less than excited about playing Twenty Questions. Despite my lack of enthusiasm, I think going along with him is the smart thing to do. When it comes right down to it, I have no way of knowing if I can trust Vinnie. This isn't the reaction you'd expect after someone saves your life, I know. But I've learned the hard way that people who do good deeds usually have an ulterior motive. Besides, this guy's still a stranger to me. How do I really know what I'm dealing with? Sure, he looks harmless enough, but so did Ted Bundy until he let you see the real him. For all I know, he might be the type with a hair-trigger temper. It's probably best not to do anything that could possibly antagonize him.

I consider his question and try to work out a plausible explanation for the crowd. There are no cars in the parking lot, but all these people had to get here somehow. Most of them have plates of food sitting on the tables in front of them, so it seems likely that they arrived as a group and placed their orders at the same time. And the diner is on the way to Las Vegas. So . . . "They were dropped off by a tour bus?"

Vinnie taps the tip of his nose twice with his index finger and then points at me. "That makes a lot of sense. The driver could have dropped them off to eat while he went to gas up the bus."

Sure it does. Except that any exit with a gas station has at least one fast food place nearby, so why go out of the way to drop all these people off here, go get gas, and then come back? But bringing that up would probably just mean more questions, so I keep the idea to myself.

The familiar sound of panting followed by the clacking of toenails on tile draws my attention. Grimm saunters around the end of the counter, ears perked up as if he's taking in the entire conversation. He's my ugly, loveable mutt, but something isn't right. He's way too calm. Before the wreck, he'd been edgy and bristling. Now, he's downright placid. And he's much too clean. Shouldn't he show some evidence of fleeing the site of an accident?

Vinnie moves behind the counter. "Sit." He pats the open spot between two customers.

Grimm plops down on the floor as I hitch myself up on the red vinyl stool and rest my elbows on the counter. While Vinnie messes with something on his side, I let my gaze wander the diner, checking out the décor. It's an amazing mix of entertainment memorabilia. Movie posters from just about every decade share wall space with black and white publicity photos and prop replicas. I'm pretty sure that's supposed to be the Maltese Falcon peering down at us from a shelf in the corner. Off to the left is a poster for the final episode of the Star Wars saga. I stop, squint, look again. *Revenge of the Jedi.* Wow. I've heard about those posters. George Lucas changed the title to *Return of the Jedi* because revenge is not a quality that's associated with The Force, but not before a first run of posters had been printed. Most were pulled, but some with the original title survived. I've never seen one up close and personal before. I wonder if Vinnie has ever been tempted to sell it on eBay. Or maybe that's where he got it. My eyes continue to sweep the walls. This place is paradise for a trivia buff like me.

Trivia. *Shoot.* The realization smacks me hard like a face palm. The trivia contest. If I don't check in by five o'clock, they'll disqualify me. I need to let someone know what happened and where I am. I reach for my cell phone, but it's not there. Neither is my purse. *Double shoot.* They're both still in the car.

"Vinnie, is there a phone here I can use?"

Instead of answering, he sets down a tall glass sporting the Coca-Cola emblem on the counter. "Here you go."

I look at the drink I didn't ask for. "Thanks, but I really need to make a call. You don't understand how important—"

"I think you'll agree that nothing clears the mind and revitalizes the spirit quite like a Vanilla Coke."

A Vanilla Coke? The mention of what's in the glass manages to ease my anxiety over making contact with the contest officials. He's got a point. A few more minutes won't hurt anything.

The first time I tasted a Vanilla Coke was when my Aunt Bobbie took me on an old-fashioned Hollywood sightseeing trip for my tenth birthday. We saw everything: the hand and footprints in front of Grauman's Chinese, the star-studded walk of fame (and the pan handlers who worked the crowd along the walk of fame), the Capital Records building, the Pantages Theatre, Hollywood and Vine. We'd ended up at an old-fashioned diner not far from Farmer's Market. When the waiter came to take our drink order, my aunt spoke for both of us.

"We'll have two Vanilla Cokes." She promised me it would be the best thing I'd ever had to drink. And she hadn't oversold it.

After that, Vanilla Cokes were our special thing. Some of the nicest memories of my life include my aunt's eccentric wit and an ice-filled, condensation-beaded glass like the one in front of me. My throat is so parched, and the memories are so strong, I let it slide that Vinnie still hasn't told me where the phone is. I guess I can wait a few minutes to make that call. "Thank you."

He pushes the glass closer to me. "So what's your name, Miss?"

The fizzy liquid pricks pleasantly at my throat as I swallow. I take another drink and smack my lips before answering. "Allie."

Vinnie nods gravely, as though I just gave him the correct answer to a very difficult question. "Nice to meet you, Allie."

The smile returns to his face, and he slaps a menu down in front of me. "In case you want to eat something."

The waitress hustles around the back of the counter and stops next to Vinnie. Her uniform is nothing like his. While his unique, quirky outfit seems to complement his personality, her dull brown dress is completely at odds with her full-lipped smile and sparkling blue eyes. And it's much too tight. The buttons up the front are straining, particularly where the dress pulls across her generous hips and chest.

"What'll you have, honey?"

There's something familiar about the tone of her voice. It's rich and smooth, but breathy at the same time. I feel like I know her, but I can't imagine where we would have met. She holds an order pad in one hand and a stubby pencil in the other, ready to scribble down my order. Absently, she reaches up and uses her pinky to tuck a lock of hair behind her ear, revealing an enormous rhinestone drop earring. At least, I think they're rhinestones. Nothing that large could be real.

I don't know if my eyes got big, or I gasped, or what, but she can tell I've noticed her jewelry. Her smile is shy and hesitant. Her eyes dart from me, to Vinnie, then back to me. She flicks the earring with the pencil eraser, making the stones flash as it swings from her lobe. "You like?"

Since we just met, I doubt she cares about my approval in particular, but approval in general must be important to her. I nod. "It's beautiful. Gives your uniform a little extra zip."

Her smile unfolds like a time delay shot of a blossoming flower. She shakes her head, setting both her earrings to dancing. "You know what they say, honey. Diamonds are a girl's best friend."

A shrill *ding* cuts the air and plates clatter as the cook sets them on the edge of the serving window. He leans out as far as he can, nearly laying one sideburn-covered jowl in a plate of chicken fried steak. "Norma Jeane, quit your cluckin' and get over here. Your order's up!"

"I'll be right there," she calls over her shoulder. She looks back at me and sighs. "Men. They're impossible to please. But it sure is fun trying." She gives an exaggerated wink before flouncing off toward the kitchen.

I stare at her as she walks away, trying to make sense out of what I've just heard. *Norma Jeane?* The earrings, her voice, her shape . . . all the pieces come together, forming one unfathomable conclusion. It's impossible. It can't be true, but at the same time, it all fits. It explains why she looks so familiar and why I feel like I know her.

Norma Jeane Mortenson, baptized as Norma Jeane Baker, married name Norma Jeane Dougherty.

More commonly known to the movie-going public as Marilyn Monroe.

A chill permeates my body. I reach for the Vanilla Coke, try to grab it, but my fingers have become stiff and clumsy, like fat tubes of raw, overstuffed sausage. I can't bend them, and instead of gripping the glass, I push it over, spilling the contents across the counter. I watch as the liquid pours out. It moves slower than it should. More like molasses than soda.

Vinnie's right there with a rag. He wipes it up, his movements so casual it's as if he'd been waiting for me to knock over my drink.

I grab his wrist, stopping him in mid-wipe. "What's happening?" The words come out of me, thick and weighted. "What is this place?"

My head spins. Without letting go of Vinnie, I lay my forehead down against the counter, letting the feel of the cool surface sink into my skin.

I need a minute.

Just a minute to collect myself.

I close my eyes. Just for a minute.

4

Nine years earlier

"Marilyn Monroe had it made."

I lift my head and open my eyes, expecting to see Vinnie, but he's not there. Neither is the diner. I'm not sitting on a stool anymore, either. I'm on a carpeted floor, knees drawn up to my chest, my back pressed into a corner. I look around, taking in the entertainment center on one wall, the tall bookcase beside it with shelves bowing under the weight of hundreds of DVDs and VHS tapes, the framed family photos on the walls, and it slowly dawns on me where I am.

It's Aunt Bobbie's apartment.

And if that's not shocker enough, I realize that the person I heard talking is none other than a younger version of me.

There I am, sitting on the blue and white striped couch, stacking up empty bowls on the coffee table. I'm wearing baggy gray sweatpants and an oversized, faded t-shirt with a cartoon cat on the front. From my place on the floor, I wrinkle my nose. It's hard to believe I ever dressed that way. And my hair. It's pulled up into a high ponytail, but from the frizzy ends, I can tell this is during my "home perm" phase. What was I thinking?

Letting go of my knees I lean forward and raise my hand, just a little, hoping to get my own attention, but afraid at the same time. What will happen if past-me becomes aware of future-me? Will we rip a hole in the space-time continuum? Or will I just quietly lose my mind? But past-me is oblivious. When nothing happens, I become bolder, raising both hands and waving them frantically. Still no response.

It would appear I'm nothing more than an observer here, like Ebenezer Scrooge being forced to relive his history. But a look to my left and right reveals there's no Ghost of Christmas Past along for the ride. I'm on my own.

Aunt Bobbie comes in from the kitchen and looks at the girl on the couch

"What did you say?"

"That Marilyn Monroe had it made." I . . . she . . . oh, heck . . . *Allie* hands her aunt the bowls and tops them off with two empty soda cans.

Aunt Bobbie's hand shakes, just a little, as she reaches for the trash. Then she looks over her armload, one eyebrow cocked. "How do you figure?"

Allie shrugs as she digs a few stray popcorn kernels out of the cracks between the couch cushions and wraps them in a napkin. "Guys thought curves were sexy back then."

Laughter trails behind Aunt Bobbie as she heads into the kitchen. "Honey, guys will always think curves are sexy. The challenge for us women is having those curves in the right places."

Allie picks up a few more used napkins, follows Aunt Bobbie into the kitchen, and tosses them in the trash can.

I'm starting to remember the details of this particular day. It was during the week I stayed with my aunt because my mother had just gotten married and was on her honeymoon. Again.

I watch Allie walk back into the living room. She scoops the remote off the coffee table and hits a button. The credits for

Some Like It Hot disappear from the TV screen. In their place is a commercial for Slimfast. Image after image flashes by, "real people" morphing from pasty, flabby *before* to tan and tone *after.* As the chatty women talk about how easy the program is, and all the ways it changed their lives, almost microscopic print appears at the bottom of the screen: *Results not typical.*

Which had pretty much been my point all along.

Allie looks down at her torso and sucks in her gut. At the same time, she tries to push out her chest. Nostalgia and regret ripple through my mind. I know exactly what she's feeling. I remember the thrill I felt when my flat chest was finally starting to blossom, and the irritation that my stomach never would be teen-model flat. It was as though my body was playing some ironic joke, and it caused me no end of frustration. Now, I want to tell the girl in front of me to slow down, not to worry about the outside so much. Enjoy being a kid while you can.

She pokes her stomach with one finger. "But how do you get the curves to go in the right places?"

Aunt Bobbie comes back in the room, wiping her hands on a paper towel. "Honey, you're only fourteen. You should thank the good Lord you don't have to worry about any of that yet." She turns off the TV, pops out the DVD, and puts it back in its case. "If you ask me, curves are nothing but trouble. Look what they did to poor Norma Jeane."

"What do you mean, poor? They made her famous."

"They made her miserable." She shoots the DVD case into an empty spot in the entertainment center, then turns back to Allie, shaking her head. "People saw her as an object, a sex kitten. They didn't care about how smart she was, or how much pain she was in. They just took what they wanted."

"But didn't she use that to her advantage?" Allie flops down on the sofa, propping her bare feet on the coffee table. "I mean, she didn't really have a career until she stopped being Norma Jeane and started being Marilyn."

"That's because they didn't give her a choice. She did what she had to do to survive." Aunt Bobbie's eyelashes flutter like crazy, and for a second, it looks like she's going to burst into tears. Instead, she takes a deep breath and shakes her head. "I know you think it's important to be attractive, sexy even, but trust me . . . physical beauty is really a curse."

Looking at my aunt now, with the perspective and distance of the last nine years, it strikes me that Aunt Bobbie has lived her life by that belief. A thick woman, I suspect her measurements are the same for bust, waist, and hips. She's always been neat and clean, but I've never seen her wear makeup or nail polish or do anything to her low-maintenance hair other than cover it with a scarf when the Santa Ana winds start blowing. She's the exact opposite of the flashy celebrities she's so in love with.

Still, underneath all the dowdiness I can see the possibility of who she could be: her wide smile, bright green eyes, expressive hands. She bears enough of a resemblance to my mother—who can only be described as gorgeous—for me to guess that Aunt Bobbie has worked pretty hard over the years to exorcise the curse of beauty. But why?

I'd wanted to ask her about it then. Not because I understood her as well as I do now, but because I couldn't understand why anyone wouldn't want to be beautiful if they could. But there was no way to ask that question without insulting her appearance. And I would never do anything to hurt my aunt. So I went at it from another direction. "Mom says the only thing a woman can control is her own body. She says it's never too early to learn how to use it to get what you want."

The smile slips from Aunt Bobbie's mouth and she gives her head another shake. "My sister is one of the smartest people I know, but that's surely the dumbest thing I've ever heard."

34

Even though I agreed with her, I remember feeling like I should at least try to stick up for my mother. After all, that's what a good daughter would do.

"Well, she must be doing something right or else she wouldn't keep snagging husbands."

Aunt Bobbie snorts. "If that's so, then why isn't she able to hold on to any of them?"

Good question. A better question might be why she chose those particular husbands in the first place, but that wasn't any of my business, which had become painfully clear after the few times I'd tried to talk to my mother about it.

The whole reason I was with Aunt Bobbie that week was because mom and hubby number five, which made him step-dad number four, were in Mexico on their honeymoon. At that point in my life, I shouldn't have had any more expectations. But Ethan had seemed different than the others. I found myself hoping he'd stick around for a while, even though I knew the chances were slim.

How I wish I could drag the younger version of myself away by the arm and tell her a thing or two about expectations. And fashion.

"What do you want to do now, Aunt Bobbie?"

My aunt taps her temple, then with a snap of her fingers she turns, making an awkward dash for the hall closet. "I know! I found a great board game at the thrift store last week. It's brand new. Whoever donated it hadn't even taken off the plastic." The rest of her words are muffled as she digs for her new found treasure. When she comes back into the living room, she holds out a gray box. "See. Trivial Pursuit. Silver Screen Edition!"

As Aunt Bobbie sets up the game, I see it again. That tell-tale tremor in her hand. But the young version of me doesn't notice. She's picking at the fuzz pills on the arm of the sofa, absorbed in her own troubles.

She's wondering what mom and Ethan are doing right now. She's wondering how long this one will last.

In my corner on the floor, I wrap my arms tight around my legs, drawing them back to my chest, drop my forehead on my knees, and squeeze my eyes shut. Why should I have to relive the past if I'm unable to change it? My chest is tight, and it's becoming harder to breathe.

Run, Allie. Run to someone you trust. Save yourself.

Even if I could make the words leave my throat, she wouldn't hear me. And if she heard me, she wouldn't believe it. She has no idea what's coming, and there's no way I can protect her.

5

VINNIE'S DINER

"Allie?"

Vinnie's voice cuts through my haze, pulling me back to the present. Or what I assume is the present. I raise my head, slowly, and look around. I'm back on the red vinyl stool, my arms crossed on the cool Formica counter top. I have returned to the diner.

I open my mouth to speak, but no sound comes out. My throat is so dry and scratchy, my tongue is literally stuck behind my teeth, unable to form words. Vinnie lowers his chin, his forehead creased with concern. He pushes a glass of water toward me but instead of taking a drink, I grab his wrist again, almost toppling the glass before he can save it.

I swallow once, twice. I force my mouth to work. "Where am I?"

He covers my hand with his, gives it a reassuring squeeze, then peels my fingers off him. "You're in my diner, remember? Are you sure you're feeling okay?"

I wave away his concern and grab the glass, gulping the water down until my throat no longer feels like the bottom of an old, dry terrarium.

"That waitress." I point to the woman who is now on the other side of the room and has three plates balanced across the length of one arm. "Your cook called her Norma Jeane."

"Of course he did. It's her name." Vinnie laughs and shakes his head. "She's really something. Have you ever seen anyone carry so many plates at one time and not make a mess out of any of them?"

My eyes dart from Vinnie, to the waitress, and back again. He can't be so oblivious. Doesn't he see it?

"But . . . she's . . . I mean, look at her. She looks like . . ." I cover my face with my hands. This can't be happening. She can't be who I think she is. It's not possible. What am I supposed to say to him? *Hey Vinnie, did you know you've got a dead movie star working in your diner?* It's too stupid. The dream, or hallucination, or whatever it was I just experienced, is making my mind jump to bizarre conclusions.

Stop. Think. There has to be some kind of reasonable explanation. Could she be a celebrity impersonator? It's possible, especially considering how close we are to Las Vegas. But based on what little experience I've had with female impersonators, I don't think so. Most of them are men, and the waitress I'm looking at can't possibly be a man in drag. There's not enough makeup or prosthetics in the world to create a getup that convincing. Besides, I've never seen anybody impersonate the pre-Marilyn Norma Jeane before.

Even if my wild thoughts are wrong and she turns out to be just another impersonator, why would she be waiting tables in character? Is she simply part of the diner's entertainment theme? But if that's the case, wouldn't she want to look more like the Marilyn everyone's familiar with? And wouldn't Vinnie have acknowledged that?

I've got to get out of here. At the very least I need to make contact with somebody outside of the looking glass I've fallen into. "I need my phone."

Vinnie takes a box of paper wrapped straws from beneath the counter and starts dropping them into a glass jar. "What you need to do is sit and relax. You still look a bit pale."

One of my hands balls up into a fist while the fingers of the other nervously play the counter top as if they are sliding over piano keys. "You don't understand. If I don't check in with the contest officials, they'll think I'm a no-show. I'll be disqualified."

"Contest?" Vinnie glances at me briefly, his look only mildly interested. He's much more fascinated by the straws he's fiddling with.

"Yes, a trivia contest. It's why I'm going to Las Vegas."

Vinnie makes a sound in his throat, but says nothing else. It's a good thing there's no silverware on the counter, because I'm frustrated enough to throw it at him. Or worse. He doesn't understand how important this is. There's more at stake than just winning a contest. I need that money. Aunt Bobbie needs that money.

A hand rests firmly on my shoulder. I jump and spin around on the stool, accidentally jabbing my knee into the man sitting next to me.

"Sorry," I mumble.

The man turns slightly, brushing his hand across a white pant leg, his mouth curving up beneath a fat, gray walrus mustache. "No need for apologies. As I don't believe in accidents, then surely Providence meant for the collision of our limbs. In time, when the pain has subsided and the bruises have dissipated, all will become clear."

He turns back to his coffee, and I stare at the back of his white suit jacket. Who's this guy, a Mark Twain impersonator? If so, it's a first for me.

"Excuse me."

Now what? Is Frank Sinatra going to croon me a song? I look up at the fellow in front of me. He's tall with weathered skin and a shadow of stubble dusting his cheeks. His brown hair curls up at the ends, against his neck and around his ears, making it look like he's gone a few weeks too long without a trim. His eyes are chocolate-milk brown and the corners crinkle up when he smiles at me.

My heart jumps a little. I look at him more closely, try to place him. But nothing comes to mind. In his long-sleeved, denim work shirt and clean but slightly wrinkled Dockers, there's nothing special about him. He looks like any other average guy you might pass on the street. I relax as I realize that I've never seen this man before in my life. Thank God. I don't think I could have taken another famous person look-alike.

He puts his hand back on my shoulder. "Since you're going to be here for a while, I'll get your things out of the car for you."

Now we're getting somewhere. "Thank you."

It's not until he walks out the door that what he said hits me. "What did he mean I'm going to be here for a while?"

I spin back around on the stool and look for Vinnie. The straw holder is completely full, but he's not behind the counter anymore. I reach for my glass of water, which is right where I left it. My stomach growls. When was the last time I ate? Oh yeah, I'd picked up a bag of overpriced nacho cheese Doritos when I gassed up in Victorville. What's left of them must be strewn in broken, bright orange bits all over the highway.

My stomach rumbles again. As if on cue, the beefy cook pushes his way through the swinging kitchen door and sets a plate of food in front of me with a *clunk*.

He leans his elbows on the counter and lets his head bob up and down, back and forth, like one of those tacky bobble headed dogs some folks put on their dashboards. "You've got to keep up your strength, little darlin'. I didn't know what you were hungry for, so I fixed you up my personal favorite."

With a wink and a dip of his shoulder he turns and propels his portly body back through the door. My eyes drop to the plate and my stomach lurches. Not because the food looks gross, which it does, but because of what it is.

A fried peanut butter and banana sandwich.

It can't be.

The edges of my vision start to fuzz out, and the diner begins to fade around me. Aunt Bobbie's voice echoes in my ears, bouncing around inside my skull like a Ping Pong ball in a bingo cage.

"It's no wonder Elvis got so fat at the end. All his favorite foods were fried."

Elvis?

Brakes squeal, the sound loud and sharp in my ears. My body starts to tip. I grab at the counter, but it's not there anymore and I fall from the stool.

A scream shatters the air as I land hard on my side. My head bounces against the ground with a dull thud, igniting a thousand sparks inside my brain.

Pain shoots through every part of my body. The air around me is hot, thick with the smell of dirt and burned rubber. I try to move, but my left arm is pinned again and hurts so bad it feels like it's on fire. A crushing weight pushes down on my chest

I force one eye open and try to determine where I am but it's like looking through a kaleidoscope smeared with bacon grease. Blurred colors and shapes melt and merge into each other. It's no use. I squeeze my eyes tight and something warm and wet slides down the side of my cheek and into my ear.

"Hold on! I'm calling 911! The ambulance is on its way!" A frantic man calls to me from somewhere far away.

Who does that voice belong to? I know it's not Vinnie.

Where is he?

Where is the diner?

Where am I?

6

VINNIE'S DINER

I'm having one of those weird dreams. The one where I'm falling, falling . . . I flail my arms, my hands clutching, trying to grab something so I can pull myself to a stop, only there's nothing but air all around me. I just keep falling.

Down . . .

Down . . .

And now, a new sensation. Something warm and rough, rubbing rhythmically against my cheek. Something like wet sandpaper . . .

"Allie!"

My body jerks as though I've been jabbed in the ribs with a light saber. My eyes pop open. A crowd is gathered in a half-circle at my feet. Standing in front of everyone else, waitress Norma Jeane and Elvis the fry cook look particularly concerned. Vinnie is kneeling beside me, holding my hand, rubbing it gently. Beside him sits Grimm, his shoulders hunched and his head hanging down. I assume he's the one that licked me, but then I realize that another dog sits beside him and is closest to my face. It's a big, fluffy collie, head cocked sideways, tongue lolling out so it's almost smiling.

Lassie.

43

My heart soars and relief washes over me. I'm back in the diner!

But then my heart does a one-eighty and plummets to my toes. I'm back in the diner. And instead of being licked back to consciousness by my own dog, I get Lassie.

I struggle to push myself up into a sitting position. "What's going on?"

Vinnie puts his arm around my shoulders for support. "What do you mean?"

His question is cautious, guarded. Like he knows the answer, but he needs to know that I know it, too, before he'll confirm anything. I'm so not in the mood for these games.

"I was just outside again."

"You were?"

He's not contradicting me. More like he's checking. I stop. Think. Had I dreamt the whole thing? The pain, the sensations are all still fresh in my mind. I shake my head. No, it had been real.

"Yes, I was out there. I could smell the dirt. I think I was back in the car and my arm hurt like it was broken." I squeeze my forearm, but as far as I can tell, it's fine. "I could barely breathe, and I heard some guy yelling about calling 911." I glance toward the front door, but it's heavily tinted, so I can't see anything through it. There are two big windows on either side, but the shades are drawn, blocking off all view of what might be on the other side. I look back at Vinnie. "He said he was going to call an ambulance. Why would he do that? I need a tow truck and a lift to Vegas, not an ambulance."

Norma Jeane and Elvis exchange uneasy glances. Mark Twain smoothes down his enormous mustache with the thumb and forefinger of his right hand. In the far corner, Judy Garland, whom I'm noticing for the first time, puts a bejeweled hand to her middle-aged throat and looks to the ceiling, eyes darting left and right.

Vinnie just keeps looking at me with that same calm, understanding expression. Right now, he's probably the only one in the diner who fully understands what's going on. I mean, it's his place, it's named after him, so he must have some answers. I'm certain he could clear all this up, but instead he's making me pull the information out of him bit by torturous bit. And knowing that makes me want to slap him silly.

I squeeze Vinnie's hand and stare into his eyes, hoping to get across how serious I am. "Why is that man outside calling an ambulance? I need you to tell me."

His eyelids droop and he does that slow nod of his: once, twice. "There's something you need to see."

He stands up, then holds his hand out to me. I hesitate. For no good reason, fear, cold and irrational, wraps itself around me. What if I don't like what he's about to show me? But then an image of my aunt pops into my head and pushes the fear away. Not so far that I can't feel it anymore, but far enough that it no longer paralyzes me. I've got to know what's going on so I can get out of here and get to that contest. And as far as I know, Vinnie is the only one who can help me.

I grab Vinnie's hand and he pulls me to my feet. About twenty pairs of eyes follow our movements as we cross the room and stand in front of the window. He reaches for the cord, ready to pull up the blinds, when another hand shoots out and stops him.

Norma Jeane looks straight past Vinnie and her doe-like eyes lock onto me. "Are you sure you want to know what's out there, honey? There's no going back once you know."

What she doesn't understand is that I don't want to go back. Not unless I can go all the way back to the beginning of this nightmare and prevent the accident, and that doesn't seem to be an option. I need to push on and figure out what all this means. Maybe then I can get out of this place and get back to my carefully laid out plan.

My fingers circle her wrist. She's wearing a garish diamond bracelet now, and the stones cut into my palm as I pull her hand away from Vinnie. "I'm sure. I need to know. I need to do this."

Norma Jeane steps away. Behind me, I hear the click-clack of toenails on tile. I turn to see Lassie—the boy dog that always had to play a girl—trotting up to me. He stops at my feet and gives two loud, sharp barks. Crouching down, I bury my fingers in the silky fur behind his ears.

"It's okay, girl . . . uh, I mean, boy. Go save Timmy from the well. I'll be fine."

The collie trots off to join Grimm who is begging table scraps from a group in the far corner. I stand, go back to Vinnie, and give one quick, decisive nod of my head.

Vinnie tugs on the cord, pulling the blinds up with a whoosh. He takes a step back and motions me forward.

There's my car, just like I expected, lying on its side in the dirt between the northbound and southbound traffic lanes. A big black SUV is stopped a few feet in front of it on the northbound side of the road. A man wearing a baseball cap and khaki shorts is pacing back and forth, a cell phone pressed against his ear, the tail of his tropic print shirt flapping in his wake. He keeps looking at his watch. He must be late for something.

As if he heard my thoughts, Vinnie says, "He already called for help. Now he's trying to convince his fiancée that he's not backing out on her."

"Excuse me?"

Vinnie points at the man. "He was on his way to Las Vegas to get married. Coming across your accident has thrown him off his schedule."

I want to ask Vinnie how he knows all of this, but if I do, I might miss what's going on outside. My eyes are pinned to the man. He started out right next to the car, but now he backs away. Then he moves in close again, but quickly does a hop-skip backwards. Finally, he gets even closer than before and squats down, looking through the empty windshield hole into the depths of the car. He seems really nervous.

Still looking at the scene outside, I ask Vinnie, "So what's he waiting for? If he's late, why doesn't he just get back in his car and drive to his wedding?"

"He doesn't want to leave you."

I'm about to point out the obvious, that if the anonymous groom-to-be is so concerned about my welfare, he should be in the diner with me, not walking a rut in the dirt outside. But right then, the man jerks himself up, stumbles backward with his hand covering his mouth, and hurries away from the car. A moment later, he's doubled over, puking his guts out.

"Oh, that's pretty," I mumble to myself.

Vinnie doesn't seem to notice the man's gastric distress. Instead, he's got all his attention focused on the road and what lies beyond. "Here they come."

At first, I have no idea what he's talking about. But then I hear them, too. They start out low, then increase in intensity, until they slice through the air, thin and sharp as Errol Flynn's fencing foils. Sirens, and lots of them.

Two fire trucks, a police car, and an ambulance screech to a stop by the SUV. They move slowly down the road to a spot that's not so steep, then they drive down into the dirt and surround my car, kicking up a cloud of dust. Talk about overkill. It reminds me of the time I saw a fire truck speed up to a Walmart store. Turned out there was no fire then, either, just a little old lady who had slipped on a busted bag of elbow macaroni in aisle three.

The emergency workers spring from their vehicles, making me think of circus clowns pouring out of a Volkswagen. These fellows are going to feel pretty silly when they find out I'm safe and sound inside the diner, sipping on Vanilla Cokes and chatting with celebrity look-alikes.

Within seconds, uniformed people are everywhere. The frazzled motorist sits on the bumper of the police car, his head hanging between his knees, while one of the policemen squats in front of him, waiting to take his statement. A herd of firemen surround the car, peering through the broken out windshield and making lots of hand motions. Two EMTs, a man and a woman, pull a gurney out of the ambulance.

The sight of the gurney is the last straw. This has really gotten out of hand. "I'd better go out there and tell them to save the stretcher for someone who needs it."

I step around Norma Jeane, who looks terrified, go to the front door, and push it open.

Vinnie is right behind me. He puts his hand on my shoulder, stopping me before I can cross over the threshold. "You don't want to do that." His voice is low and serious.

A blast of hot air hits me, scalding my cheeks and stealing the moisture from my lips, but I somehow feel cold at the same time. Frozen. I can't move, can't blink, can barely even breathe. All I can do is stand in the doorway and watch.

The firemen put some kind of pads or blankets down around the edge of the windshield frame, covering the remains of the broken glass. One of them, wearing heavy overalls and gloves, crawls into the car until only the soles of his boots are peeping out. My ears are assaulted by a garble of voices as the rescue workers shout questions and orders to each other. Then, above them all, I hear one voice, strong and loud, as though it's right beside my head.

"She's still alive."

Excuse me? Yes, she's still alive, and she's standing right here. Shocked out of my statue-like state, I lift my hand in a half-hearted attempt to flag them down, but no one looks my way. In fact, no one has given the diner so much as a passing glance since this fiasco started.

A movement catches my eye. Something black that's flapping by the side of the fire truck. Squinting, I try to see what it is, but the heat's coming in waves now, distorting the picture. Even though I can't fully make it out, it seems familiar, like I've seen it before.

I turn to Vinnie, open my mouth to ask him about it, but he just motions back to the open door with a jerk of his head.

The fireman is backing out of the car now. He's struggling with something, making his movements slow and awkward. His head emerges, but his arms are still stretched out in front of him. He's pulling something out of my car. He stops, takes a breath, and then continues his slow, steady backward crawl. As soon as he's clear of the vehicle, the other firemen move in to help him, blocking my view, but not before I see what he's dragging out.

It's a body.

It's me.

7

VINNIE'S DINER

The rescue workers are a source of nonstop movement, like dancers in an intricately choreographed jazz routine. One wipes blood off the young woman's face, then steps to the side. Another swoops in, covers her mouth and nose with an oxygen mask, then steps to the side. The first cuts back in and puts some kind of brace around her neck. Then both close in together for the grand finale, and the firemen step closer to get a look. I wish they'd all get out of the way so I can see her.

Wait, not *her*. Not *her* face, *her* neck . . . but *my* face, *my* neck.

They're working on me.

One of them calls out, "She's stable."

I'm stable. Stable is good.

The voice again, "She's non-responsive."

Well, that doesn't sound nearly as good as *stable*.

"The dog probably saved her life."

Grimm? If my body was still in the car, does that mean Grimm's body is in there, too? And if he is, why aren't they getting him out?

Instinctively, I take a step backward, out of the doorway. I don't want to be the woman on the gurney, and I don't want to have anything to do with the people outside. Outside, I'm a battered, bloody, nonresponsive mess, and my apparently heroic dog is still trapped in the wreck. Things are much better inside. Inside the diner, Grimm is chowing down on pieces of leftover steak being fed to him gingerly by a man who looks an awful lot like Harpo Marx, and I'm safe, clean, and pretty darn responsive.

"Are you okay?"

I turn my head slowly, piercing Vinnie with my best are-you-kidding glare.

"Peachy." The word shoots out of me in two bullet-like syllables, *bang bang*, aimed right between his eyes. I wait for his reaction. A wince, a frown, a grimace. Anything to indicate that I've wounded him. But he doesn't even blink. I'm getting the idea that Vinnie's a pretty unflappable guy.

He nods his head, pulls the door shut, and moves to the window. He gives the cord a hard, quick jerk, and the blinds fall shut with a snap.

A great sigh moves through the building. It's as if everyone around me had been holding their breath, waiting to see what I would do. Which is ironic, because all these people are dead, aren't they? They shouldn't even be standing here, let alone breathing. I look from one face to the other, and the truth of my situation sinks in, saturating my consciousness like sticky syrup into a pancake. I can't deny it anymore. I can't make up any more excuses. These people aren't impersonators. With the exception of Vinnie, every single one of them is a deceased personality. So what are they? Figments of my imagination? Ghosts?

Hysterical laughter begins to bubble up inside me. I see dead people.

And if they're dead, then what does that make me?

"You're not dead, you know."

Vinnie's words bring an abrupt halt to my near mental melt-down, but they don't surprise me like they would have twenty minutes ago. Of course he knows what I'm thinking. Why wouldn't he? He seems to know everything, even though he only shares what he wants to. Vinnie is the Head Honcho of Crazy Town.

I stalk across the room and let myself fall onto the shiny red vinyl cushion of the booth by the far wall. Vinnie follows me and sits on the opposite side of the table. "You're not dead," he repeats.

"I know. I'm just nonresponsive."

"Only as far as they can tell." He smiles, looking almost mischievous. "You seem to be responding pretty well to me."

I narrow my eyes at him, and a niggling little pain starts in my forehead. Pressing my thumbs against it, I push it away with sheer force of will. He can't charm me into submission. I'm going to make some sense out of all this if it kills me.

"No more games, Vinnie. I want the truth."

"I'll tell you what I can." He draws his finger across the table as if he's drawing a line that can't be crossed. "There are some things, though, that you have to figure out for yourself. Trust me, it's a lot better that way."

"Better for who?"

"You, of course. This whole thing is about you."

It's all about me, but I can't get a straight answer to a question. I have to figure everything out. If I have to figure out one more thing, I just might hurt somebody. I open my mouth to say as much, but the door swings open and music starts playing. Weird, I don't remember any tunes playing when I opened the door before.

Everyone in the diner turns to wave or shout hello to the man who walks in. It's the guy who said he'd get my things out of the car. A little spark of hope ignites in me but is quickly blown out. He didn't get my purse like I wanted him to. Instead, he's carrying what looks like a miniature treasure chest. The dark wood is trimmed with metal studded strips of leather. Near the top it has an ornately carved piece of brass above a thick latch which is secured with a fat iron padlock. It looks like something straight out of a pirate movie.

There's absolutely nothing fair about this. If I have to be losing my mind, why oh why can't it be Johnny Depp strolling in with this chest?

Oh yeah. Because he's not dead. Silly me.

The boringly nondescript man walks up to the booth and sets the chest on the table with a dull thud.

I frown and press back into my seat as if he just dumped road kill in front of me. "What's this?"

"It's all your stuff."

It's been one heck of a hard day. I've been thrown around in my car, stranded in the desert, befuddled by Vinnie, traveled back in time, and watched myself in an out of body experience. I'll be the first to admit my memories might be a little like Swiss cheese. But I know what I packed in my trunk when I left this morning. I packed the same two things I always pack when I go on a trip: my black pull-along suitcase with the florescent yellow tape wrapped around it to make it easier to spot in a crowd, and my small bright blue bag containing my blow dryer, hair care products, makeup, and other essential toiletries. I am one hundred percent sure that I did not pack this chest. So there's no way it could have come out of my car.

I shake my head. "That's not mine."

The unknown man scratches the stubble on his chin. "Oh, it's yours all right. You've been lugging this stuff around with you for years."

He's so certain it belongs to me that I can't argue with him, even though I want to. So I look down at the thing sitting on the table in front of me. It's hard to explain how an inanimate object can taunt a person, but I feel like it's daring me to figure out a puzzle. *Because I haven't had enough of those today.* With a sigh, I decide to give it a go.

Okay, so what would a person keep in a locked chest? Something valuable. Something you want to keep safe.

Or something you want to keep hidden.

My stomach flips, and something clicks into place. I look at Vinnie. This can't be right.

Vinnie reaches across the table and pats my hand. "I'm afraid you're going to have to open it and go through what's inside before you can leave here."

I stare at the chest. In the background, the music that came on when the stubble-faced stranger walked in the door is growing fainter and fainter. But before the last notes fade away, I'm finally able to name the song.

"Here Comes the Sun."

8

Vinnie's Diner

In my trivia studies, I've read a lot of weird stories about a lot of weird people. Including those "walking into the light" kind of stories. Some people claim when you experience a traumatic event that brings you close to death, your life truly does flash before your eyes. Lots of them say it reminded them of random images flashing on a movie screen, similar to early eighties music videos. But others report having much more detailed experiences. A poet in Moose Lake, Montana, said her loved ones appeared to her one at a time and spoke in nonsensical haiku. A third grade teacher in Wichita, Kansas, who happened to moonlight as a square dance caller, said everyone he'd ever known had gathered together in a barn for a hoedown.

Now, sitting here in this unreal diner, those stories don't seem quite as weird as they used to. Maybe this is how it works. My accident induced, nonresponsive state certainly qualifies as a life-endangering trauma. Apparently, all those trivial facts I've absorbed over the years have reduced my life to this: a room filled with entertainment memorabilia and a flock of dead celebrities.

It's sad, really, that not one member of my family is here. Not that there are many to choose from. My family is small and just barely classifies as functional. Still, it's too bad Aunt Bobbie couldn't have shown up for this party. She'd be in her element hobnobbing with Elvis and Norma Jeane.

Of course, I still don't have an explanation for Vinnie. Or the guy who brought in the mystery chest.

I look at the thing, sitting innocently on the table, varnished wood glowing warm, polished brass shining. It's not big enough to contain very much. Still, I don't think the old saying that "good things come in small packages" holds true here.

I lean across the table toward Vinnie, making sure I don't accidentally brush against the chest, as if the mere act of touching it might set some terrible events in motion. "Are you absolutely certain I'm not dead?"

"Yes." His answer is so quick, he almost speaks over me. "I'm certain. You're not dead yet."

I jump in my seat like he shot me with a Taser gun. "Yet?"

Vinnie shrugs and lifts his palms to the ceiling. "Sure. Everyone dies. You will, too. The question isn't *if.* It's *when.* And how."

Irritation builds and bubbles like the contents of a soda bottle that's been shaken with gusto. "I know everyone dies. And if I could decide when to go, I would. But it's not like I have any control over it."

Mr. Twain slips from a stool at the counter and walks over to the booth. With his arms hanging straight at his side, he looks down at me, a rascally expression on his face. "Am I to understand that you are not a believer in free will?"

I shake my head. "That's not what I was saying. I—"

"So then you do believe we have the power to make choices in this life?"

"Yes, but—"

"Then you concur that your destiny resides squarely in your own hands and is not left to the whim of fate." He looks very pleased with himself. "As a matter of fact, you could say that—"

"Just a minute!" It's my turn to grab the reins on this conversation. "What I'm saying is that I don't believe there's a plan in the grand scheme of things. Sometimes you get to make choices, but other times there's no choice to make. Life just dumps on you, and if you're lucky, every once in a while you can jump out of the way before you get too dirty."

Twain puts his hand to his chin. "So what you are saying is . . ." He holds out his hand, palm up, inviting me to finish the sentence.

"I'm saying that life sucks. I can do everything I know to do to stay out of trouble. But if someone decides to kick me, there's not a lot I can do to stop him."

That answer seems to satisfy Twain and gives him something to think about. He walks away with his hands clasped behind his back, nodding his head and making "mmm hmm" sounds.

The unnamed man sitting next to me moves his mouth into a sad smile. "You have control over more than you think."

I twist my body on the cushion so I'm facing him dead-on. "Look . . ." This is ridiculous. I'm talking to a man who's part of my near-death experience, and I don't even have a name for him. Well, since I'm in control of so many things, I'll just take care of that. "Look, Joe . . . you don't mind if I call you Joe, do you?"

His smile becomes amused, and he shakes his head. "If that helps you, go right ahead."

"Great. Joe, if there's one thing I'm sure of, it's that my life has been a long string of uncontrollable events. If I'd had the ability to change most of it, I would have. But when you're a kid, adults make the decisions and you have no choice but to go along for the ride."

"True, you can't control the actions of others," Joe says. "But your response is another thing. You can always control the way you respond."

My breath catches in my chest. I can control the way I respond? So what is he saying, that my life is what it is because I didn't respond in the right way? Who does this jerk think he is?

"You have no idea what kind of things I've been forced to respond to." It's surprising how calm and even my voice is since my insides have turned into a quivering mountain of angry Jell-O. Still, I lean forward until less than six inches of space separates us. "You don't know me, so don't pretend you can understand me."

Joe doesn't back down. In fact, he leans closer still, crossing the invisible boundary line into my personal area. "You'd be surprised."

The empathy in his voice pushes me back in my seat. Is it possible that he does know about me? About my past? About the choices I've made? The thought scares me more than anything else I've encountered so far.

I don't want to talk to Joe about this anymore.

I turn back to Vinnie. "What's going on in the real world right now?"

It's obvious from the frown tugging down his eyes and mouth that he'd rather stay on the current path. He looks at Joe. Joe nods. Then Vinnie looks back at me.

"You're being taken care of." Vinnie lifts his chin, looking past me and motions with his head. "Norma Jeane, would you be a dear and turn on the radio?"

"Sure thing, honey."

I crane my neck and see Norma Jeane mince her way to a huge radio on a table against the wall. It's an old Philco, the kind with glass tubes inside and a polished wooden case with a rounded top. I've seen one of these in person once, when my mother took me to my grandma's house after she died. Mom said we were going there to clean it out, but she didn't keep anything. Instead, she made lists, threw out trash, and put

Post-It Notes on things for the estate sale people she'd hired. I have no idea what happened to the radio. It probably ended up in the home of some antique lover.

Norma Jeane turns a knob, and the radio hums for a few moments before coming to life. At first, all I hear is scratchy static and a high pitched whine, but she turns another knob and soon something different is coming out of the speakers. Hissing. Electronic beeps. The sound of rubber soled shoes squeaking on tile. A far off voice on a PA system paging Dr. Roberts.

I look back at Vinnie. "I'm in a hospital?"

He nods.

"But how did they get me there so fast? It can't have been more than fifteen minutes since I saw them pull me out of the car." Now there's a bizarre sentence.

A man with a wild shock of white hair pops up from the opposite side of the booth and leans over, almost resting his chin on Vinnie's head. "Time is relative, my dear. We all have our own perception of time and its passing. You perceive it differently here than you would in another plane of existence."

I pinch the bridge of my nose and squeeze my eyes shut. Of course. I shouldn't need Einstein to help me figure that out. I'm about to say something cutting and witty when I hear a man's voice coming through the radio.

"I'm here, Allie. I'm not leaving you. You're going to get through this. I'm praying." There's a long pause. "I love you."

I stare at my hand. It tingles.

I feel the warmth of skin on skin, pressure on my fingers.

I gasp.

Even though I'm sure he already knows the answer, Vinnie asks me, almost in a whisper, "Who is that?"

"It's my boyfriend. I mean, my ex-boyfriend, Jake." I almost can't get the rest out. "And he's holding my hand."

9

Vinnie's Diner

Norma Jeane has been staring at the radio, listening along with the rest of us. But now she whirls around and exclaims, "Ex-boyfriend?" She seems amazed that anyone sweet enough to stand by my death bed could be an ex anything.

I look down at my hand. The moment's over. The feeling's gone now, so I wiggle my fingers at her instead. "It's a long story."

She pouts, but doesn't press the issue. Joe is not as considerate. "We've got plenty of time."

"Do we, now?" I spit back at him and twist around in my seat, away from the hospital noises that still come from the radio. But now I'm facing the ill-named treasure chest. I am so sure there's nothing good in that thing.

Einstein wags his head, making his hair dance. "Of course we do. Remember—"

"Time is relative." The two of us say it together and are joined by most of the people in the diner. Lassie barks, providing the punctuation mark at the end of the sentence. We end up sounding like a bizarre Greek chorus. "Yes, thank you professor. You may go." He nods again, smiling, hair jerking, and disappears back behind the booth.

"Soooooo," The word stretches out of Vinnie like taffy being pulled on a hot day. "What about Jake?"

I want to put him off, jump to another subject. But one look at Vinnie and I can tell he's not going to let it go. There's no way I'm getting out of this without saying something. Besides, if I talk about Jake, it means he won't be pressuring me to open the chest.

"Jake and I dated for about six months. And things just didn't work out. So I broke up with him."

The order-up bell dings from the kitchen window and fry cook Elvis leans out, waving a big metal burger flipper in the air. "Was he cruel to ya?"

I laugh, both at what I'm seeing and the mere idea of Jake hurting anybody. "No. Not at all."

"Did he take you for granted?" Norma Jeane stands behind Joe, eyes wide. She's nodding, as if she fully expects me to start rattling off a list of all the times Jake stood me up or used me for his own nefarious purposes. She must be drawing from her own experience. But that's not how things were between Jake and me.

"No."

From the counter, Mr. Twain spins around on his stool, holding a coffee mug aloft. "Was he not in possession of his mental faculties?"

I shake my head. "Jake is very smart. And completely sane." Other than the fact that he fell in love with me.

Vinnie cocks his head to the side. "So what's wrong with him?"

I sigh. Why am I even bothering with this? They will never understand. The problems between Jake and I hinge on too many other things. Things that have nothing to do with him and that I refuse to talk about. But one look at their expectant faces tells me they're not going to drop the subject. I have to tell them something, so I offer up the easy, surface explanation. "It's not what's wrong with him. It's what's wrong with me."

"Ahhhhh." The syllable vibrates through the air as it simultaneously escapes from the lips of everyone in the diner. Apparently, they think they *do* understand. Their reaction makes me want to laugh and cry at the same time. Story of my life.

A commotion of sounds comes from the radio, dragging my attention back to it. Being that I'm from a generation that's always had television, I'm used to seeing who's doing the talking. But now I find myself listening to an old time radio show without a narrator. At first, it's just a jumble of anonymous voices. Even though there's nothing to see, I stare at the speakers as I strain, listening carefully, trying to pick out anything familiar. Finally, I'm able to make out who's who.

Aunt Bobbie: "Who are you?"

Wait a minute, if Aunt Bobbie didn't call Jake, then what's he doing there?

Jake: "I'm Jake. Her boyfriend."

And why is he still calling himself my boyfriend?

Aunt Bobbie: "She told me about you. She said you broke up."

Good for you, Aunt Bobbie. Let's see what he has to say to that.

Jake: "She had me in her cell phone as her only ICE person, so I'd like to think she still has feelings for me."

Okay, that explains why he's there. He must have been called by the EMTs, or whoever it is that gets saddled with that lousy job.

Aunt Bobbie: "Maybe she does." Pause. "How did you know to call me?"

Jake: "She talked about you all the time. But I didn't have your number, so I called Sandy."

My now ex-roommate. Who should have been on a plane heading for her new career at the same time I went rolling across the road.

Aunt Bobbie: "I thought Sandy was flying to London today."

Jake: "She is, but she got bumped off her flight and was waiting in the terminal for the next one."

And that explains how he was able to get a hold of Sandy. Lucky for me she was able to get the call.

Jake: "If I hadn't gotten in touch with her, I wouldn't have known how to contact you."

Aunt Bobbie: "Thank God."

Jake: "Exactly."

Mom: "Wait a minute! How do you know so much about Allie's life?"

Ah, so my mother *did* make it.

Aunt Bobbie: "We talk. A lot."

Mom: "And why didn't she list me as her emergency contact? Why was I the last to be called?"

This is typical for my mother. She hasn't yet asked how I am or what happened to me. Nope, the most important thing is to find out why she isn't the center of attention.

I turn from the radio and am surprised to discover everyone else is staring at it, too. Elvis leans out the kitchen window. Norma Jeane sits nearby, her elbow on a table and her chin propped against her fist. Everyone is leaning forward, totally caught up in the verbal soap opera emanating from the radio speakers. When they realize I've caught them eavesdropping, a few have the good graces to look embarrassed, but most just turn to me with the same expressions of rapt interest. I can't say I blame them. If I hadn't lived with that kind of drama my whole life, I might be interested, too.

With a wave of my hand toward the radio, I say to everyone around me, "Welcome to my family."

10

*V*INNIE'S *D*INER

When I was a little kid, I used to sit cross-legged on the living room floor in front of our square box TV, watching black-and-white reruns of the old Felix the Cat cartoons on PBS. Felix had a big black bag of tricks, and he could pull just about anything out of it, from a monkey wrench to a jet plane. Whatever Felix needed was right there at his fingertips. His bag was much bigger on the inside than it was on the outside. I always wished I had a bag like that.

And now that I do, I don't want anything to do with it.

Nobody has said so, but I have a feeling the chest on the table is my own personal bag of tricks. I'm afraid that once I open it, there will be too much stuff inside for me to ever get it closed again. There's no good reason I can think of to go near the thing. Because really, does a person who's in stable—but I'm guessing, critical—condition need that kind of stress? I don't think so.

Not that the drama playing out in the hospital room is any better. Through the radio speakers I can tell that all three of them are talking at once. The female voices are getting faster, higher-pitched, and slightly frantic. I hear Jake, who manages to sound calm and controlled in the middle of the commotion, say the words *driving* and *flipped*. He must be telling them what happened.

An unexpected wail pierces the air, and I pull my shoulders up to my ears in an automatic cringe. I know that sound. That's my mom's *how could this happen to me* sound. She uses it whenever she feels that she's being treated badly, whether by people or by life in general. I've heard her use it when a husband walked out on her, when she accidentally broke her pinky finger in the process of slamming the door on a boyfriend she never wanted to see again, when the toaster caught on fire, and when she found out one of her favorite TV shows had been cancelled. It's a multipurpose sound.

Mom: "How could this happen?" The words are delivered in a kind of sob that removes almost all the consonant sounds.

Aunt Bobbie: "Calm down, Georgie. At least talk to the doctor before you go to pieces."

Good advice, but Mom goes on like Aunt Bobbie hasn't said a thing.

Mom: "What am I going to do?"

Aunt Bobbie: "What are you talking about? You don't have to do anything but stand here. Or go sit in that chair. And pray, if you can remember how."

Ooo, nice dig from Aunt Bobbie. As usual, Mom continues to ignore her sister.

Mom: "But she's been unconscious for so long. What if the doctor makes me decide?"

Aunt Bobbie: "Decide what?"

Mom: "About pulling the plug. What if it comes to that? How can I do it? How can I make that kind of decision?"

"*What?*" I propel myself from the booth, scrambling for the radio. My toe catches on something and I almost fall, but I jerk my body upright and regain my balance. I end up hunched over the radio, screaming into one of the speakers. I really hope this thing works both ways.

"Don't touch the plug!" I've got one hand on top of the radio, the other on the side. It's the closest I can get to making physical contact with the crazy woman standing next to my body in some sterile hospital room that I can't see. "Stay away from the plug!"

Aunt Bobbie: "For heaven's sake, Georgie, get a grip. Why would you even say such a thing?"

Jake: "Both of you, stop. I think she can hear us."

His voice is low, but his words have the same effect on the women in the room as if he'd pressed a mute button. The only thing I hear for the next few moments is the monotonous background noise of the medical equipment. When Mom and Aunt Bobbie do start talking again, they're practically whispering.

Mom: "What?"

Aunt Bobbie: "Why do you think that?"

Jake: "Because right after you talked about pulling the plug, her heart rate spiked."

A little glimmer of pride sparks to life in my chest. Jake is pre-med, but even so, he has to be paying pretty close attention to me to notice something like that. Then I remind myself that I cut Jake loose, so I have no right to have any feelings about him anymore, proud or otherwise. Like a candle doused with water, the spark fizzles, crackles, and dies.

There's more jumbled conversation coming out of the speakers. *Watch what you say* and *How was I supposed to know?* They're speaking in hushed, almost reverent tones now. I guess none of them wants to be the one responsible for pushing me over the edge.

I turn back to Vinnie. He has that "I told you so" look on his face. He doesn't need to say a word for me to know what he's thinking. *See, you can control more than you think.*

I raise my hands in surrender and take a step toward the booth. "Okay, so I can make my heart rate spike. Good for me. If I ever get out of here, I'll have another skill I can list on my resume. Or maybe I'll pull it out at parties. It oughta be a real crowd pleaser."

"You are a very sarcastic young woman." He looks at me through narrow eyes, but his voice is warm. He reminds me of a grandfather who knows he should be scolding his grandchild, but he's just too fond of her to do so.

I stare him down, waiting for him to give me more information about what's going on at the hospital, but I can't intimidate him. He simply stares back, unblinking and unfazed. Eventually, I'm the one who has to look away. And my eyes fall right on that blasted chest. I sigh. There's no escaping it.

The thing is almost glowing. It seems to pulsate, inviting me, calling me to take a look. *Come on . . . one look won't hurt.* No matter how certain I am that I don't want to open it—and I am one hundred percent certain—it sucks me in. I move forward, like a cat inching in, whiskers flicking and muscles twitching, trying to get as close as possible without actually touching it, and curiosity gets the best of me. I need to see what's in there. I start to put my hand out, but I'm frozen where I stand. Like I stepped into wet cement at Grauman's and let it harden around me.

"I'll bet this is how Pandora felt," I say under my breath.

"It's probably how she would have felt," Joe says from behind me, "if she'd been a real person."

Right. Lucky Pandora was just part of a Greek myth. But here I am, part of a . . . whatever this is.

Joe puts his hand lightly on my shoulder. "Don't be afraid. You can do this. You're not alone."

At the touch of his fingers, a sensation slides through my being, flowing from limb to limb, until it permeates every part of me. It's something I'm incapable of explaining. It's more than warmth. It's more than peace. It's a certainty that even though I'm about to embark on a very rocky road, I will make it through to the other side. But just as soon as I grasp the feeling, it starts to fade. I close my eyes and soak up as much of it as I can before it totally slips away and leaves me empty again.

Joe gives my shoulder a squeeze. "You can do this," he repeats.

I believe him. Even though I don't want to do this, now I know I can. And even though I don't understand why, I know I have to.

There's nothing left now but to face the chest.

I take a step toward the booth. Another. Another. I ease myself down onto the vinyl seat. It squeals and squeaks as I slide myself over. I place a hand on either side of the chest and let out a long, steady breath.

Vinnie still sits in the seat across from me on the other side of the booth. Joe grabs a metal chair with a red and white striped seat and pulls it up to the edge of the table so he's sitting between Vinnie and me. I look around the diner. Norma Jeane is standing behind Vinnie, her lips pursed and eyes expectant. On the other side of Vinnie, Einstein leans his elbows on the back of the booth's high seat, his hair shaking every time he takes a breath. Across the room, the kitchen door swings open and Elvis saunters out. He takes off his apron, balls it up, and throws it in the corner. Almost before it hits the floor, Judy Garland dives on it in a swoon and clutches it to her bosom.

This is my support team: concerned, attentive, and highly dysfunctional. They don't exactly engender great confidence.

I close my eyes again, just for a moment. Take a few steadying breaths, fill my lungs with air, and then empty them. There's no way I can put it off any longer. I steel myself, open my eyes, and reach for the chest. Then I stare at it.

Wait a minute. . . .

Relief floods through me and I fall back against the booth's padded backrest. "I can't open this."

"Why not?" Vinnie asks.

I'm almost giddy, grinning like an idiot and waggling a finger at the front of the chest. "Because it's locked."

This revelation makes me a whole lot more comfortable with the article on the table. Since the chest is impossible to open, I'm not afraid to touch it anymore. I turn it around so Vinnie and Joe can get a look at the fat padlock secured on the latch. "See? Locked."

"That's okay. You can still open it." Joe's voice is indulgent, like a teacher gently leading his student toward an answer.

I frown at him. "What do you want me to do, rip the lock off?"

"You have the key, Allie."

"No I don't"

"Yes you do." His tone remains gentle. "Look in your pocket."

This is crazy. I'd know if I had a stray key on me, wouldn't I? I'll just have to prove that he's wrong.

I stand up and start jamming my hands into the front pockets of my jeans. "I'm telling you, I don't have the key for this thing. I've never even seen—" My frantic movements stall as my fingertips brush against something hard and thin and warm. Slowly, I pull it out. Gripping it between my thumb and forefinger, I hold it out in front of me as far away as I can, like it might be radioactive.

It's a long key made of some kind of dark metal with a loop at one end and two big, uneven teeth at the other.

"How did this get in my pocket?" I look from Joe to Vinnie.

Joe smiles. "You've always had the key."

My eyes return to the mysterious piece of hardware as I drop back onto the seat. What he's saying makes no sense. How did this key get into my pocket?

Vinnie turns the chest back around so the lock is facing me again. His simple act speaks volumes: *No more excuses. It's time for you to open it.*

I don't have the strength to argue anymore.

I slide the key in the hole and then stop. I grab on to a new hope. Maybe this won't work. Maybe it's the wrong key. Or maybe the lock is so old that it's rusted shut. I hold my breath. Then I twist the key.

The movement of the tumblers is smooth and fluid, almost as if the lock has been well oiled and maintained. With a clunk the body of the lock falls free from the hooked piece of metal at the top. It's cold and heavy in my hand as I turn it sideways and slide it out of the latch. I lay it on the table and stare at the chest. There's nothing keeping me from looking inside now.

Still, I hesitate. It brings to mind all the summers I'd spent swimming at the public pool near my mother's house. I was always the girl who lingered at the steps on the shallow end, putting in first a toe, then my whole foot, then stepping in up to my knees, then my waist. Each new step brought a renewed shock of cold that I had to get used to before going in any further. While other kids were jumping into the deep end, taking the full force of the cold water at one time then getting right to the fun, splashing and chasing each other, I would drag it out, making myself miserable until I was finally in all the way. How many hours of summer did I waste because I was afraid to jump into the water?

The fast approach would probably be a lot better now, but I still can't do it. I undo the big, metal latch on the front, letting it fall with a clank. Next, I ease my hands up the side of the chest's smooth, varnished surface until I get to the lid. With my thumbs at the corners, I give it a push and slowly lift it up. The hinges creak in protest and I freeze, bracing myself for whatever pestilence is going to fly out and ravage the earth. But the only thing that escapes is a slightly musty smell. Exhaling a breath, I push the lid up the rest of the way, up and over, until it's all the way open. I move forward in my seat, spine a little straighter, and crane my neck to look inside the box.

A sob catches in my throat. I reach in and my fingers grasp soft fur, worn bare in spots. It used to be white, but as I take it out and hold it in front of me, I see it's now mostly pale yellow with darker patches of brown here and there. The paint is almost completely rubbed off of the once-shiny black plastic nose, and one ear is missing, the rip mended haphazardly with thick, dark thread.

Peppy the Polar Bear.

I hold him in both hands, my fingers digging into his lumpy softness, unable to tear my misty eyes away from his cloudy brown glass ones.

"That must be a very special bear," Vinnie says.

I nod. "It was a gift from my father."

"When did he give it to you?"

"The day he left me."

"Tell us about it." Joe's voice, soft and encouraging, finally gets me to look away from the bear. Now I'm locked on Joe. For the first time since I entered the diner, someone's asking me to do something that I wish I could do. But I can't.

"I was only a year old," I say, shaking my head much longer than necessary. "I don't remember it. I just know what my mother told me." And when it comes to the men in her life, I have serious doubts about most of the things my mother has told me. I'm not even certain that the bear came from my father. For all I know, she picked up the toy at a thrift store and just told me it was from him.

Joe leans in closer to me. "But you were there the day he gave it to you. You've got it in your mind somewhere."

He puts his hand on my wrist, and something sizzles up my arm as if I just brushed against an electric fence. His eyes are clear and bright, and as I look into them, they swallow me up. And I know he's right. The memory of that day is part of me, buried to be sure, but solid and unseen like the foundation of a house. I can't deny it's there, whether I want to remember it or not.

I bring the bear to my face, my nose pressed deep in its fur. Smells of talcum powder, men's cologne, apples, and other things I can't distinguish imbue me with a sense of time and place. The diner becomes hazy, fading into muted colors around me. I shut my eyes and let myself be carried along by the strength of the memories building inside my head.

11

A SMALL APARTMENT—CALIFORNIA—TWENTY PLUS YEARS EARLIER

I open my eyes.

I'm standing in a small living room. The walls are painted a neutral cream. There's a squatty entertainment center and television on one side of the room. The other two free walls are lined with a loveseat and a sofa, both in the same shade of coconut shell brown. There's no other furniture in the room: no coffee table, no bookcase. The middle of the room is taken up by a mesh-sided playpen. The baby inside it is yapping to herself and playing with her toes, but no one's around to see.

Muffled voices come from another room. I turn my head in their direction.

The voices get louder. A door opens at the end of the hall, and a man walks through it. His jet black hair is so short it stands up by itself, and his jaw is clenched so tightly I'm afraid he might bust off a tooth. He leans forward under the weight of the duffle bag slung over his shoulder. The woman who follows behind him is animated, her arms flailing, hands drawing pictures in the air to match the words that erupt from her lips.

My mother. Even though she's over twenty years younger than the last time I saw her, she looks pretty much the same. She certainly sounds the same.

She grabs the back of the man's collar and yanks him to a stop, nearly toppling him.

"You can't just walk away. How can you do this to me?"

Now things start to click. The baby, my mom, and the man she's got by the collar . . . his eyebrows are drawn together. They're thin for a man, and they become even thinner on the outer edges. They almost seem to disappear. I know those brows. I've seen them for years, every time I look in the mirror.

For the first time in my adult life, I'm looking at my father. On the day he walks out of my life forever.

He drops the bag, and his arms fall limp at his sides. I see him clench and unclench his fists, trying to get himself under control. After a moment he turns around to face her.

"I'm not the only one doing this. You had a part in it, too."

Her cheeks flame, and she jumps at him. "Don't you dare. After all I've done for you!" She jabs her finger into his chest, punctuating each statement. "I cook! I clean! I take care of your kid!" Her arm swings like the grim reaper wielding his scythe as she points an accusing finger at the playpen. The oblivious baby is on her hands and knees now, nose right up against the mesh side, pressing herself toward the adults.

The man's shoulders slump in defeat. "I know having a baby wasn't part of the plan, but she's here now. She's your kid, too, you know. She belongs to both of us."

The woman's eyes are wide, almost wild. "Yes, she does belong to both of us. But you're walking out on her. You're abandoning your own child. What kind of a man does that?"

He frowns, his eyebrows drawing together in a V. He hesitates. "You know it's not like that."

Uh oh. He showed some weakness. And a tiny bit of self doubt. No way will my mother let an opening like that go by. As I watch her, I can almost see the wheels of her mind turning, the gears shifting. "How can you do it? How can you walk out on her? On your own flesh and blood?"

I roll my eyes to the ceiling. She's laying it on a little thick with the melodrama. But then I look at my dad. She's obviously hit a nerve. Maybe she's on to something after all.

The muscles across his jaw line tense. "I'm not leaving my child," he says slowly, deliberately. "I'm leaving you."

Nope. She lost. Her pretty face contorts into a mask of anger and, in his face, she spits a string of profanity worthy of a Bruce Willis movie.

He drops his chin and takes a step back, but he stands up under the brunt of her tirade. When it seems like she's run out of ways to tell him how awful he is, he looks up at her again. "I'm sorry, Georgie, but I can't live like this anymore. I've tried. I really have. But you've changed so much. I don't know what happened to you, but you're not the same girl I fell in love with."

The transformation in her expression comes so quickly, it's as though someone flipped a switch. She steps to him, her face soft and sweet, and puts her hand lightly on his arm. "I can change. I can be that girl again." Her other hand curls around the side of his neck, her fingers stretching up to touch his hair. "I can be any way you need me to be. Just don't leave."

The room is silent. He looks at her closely, eyes narrowed. The temptation is clear on his face. Should he believe her? Should he give her another chance? But he finally shakes his head. "I wish you could, but I don't see how things can get any better. You've been like this for over a year."

He doesn't say it, but the implication hangs in the air between them. *You've been like this since the baby was born.*

She yanks her hand away from his neck, letting her nails dig in and rake across his skin. He grimaces, and I can see the three red welts she left behind. But that's not enough. Her arm pulls back, and she slaps him hard across the face. The sound echoes in the small room as she whirls around and runs back down the hall. A wail pierces the air as a door slams, and the pictures on the cream walls shake.

My father blows out a hard sigh and runs a hand down his face. Nonsensical syllables draw his attention to the playpen. The baby has pulled herself up into a standing position and is slobbering on the padded railing with toothless gums.

A giant fist squeezes my heart as I watch him lift her up and hug her tight to his chest. She tries to grab handfuls of his hair, but it's too short and she can't hold on. He kisses her cheek, breathing in deeply as if trying to memorize the smell of her. Then he puts her back in the playpen and squats down in front of it.

"I wish I could take you with me, but they don't allow little girls in the Air Force, not even ones as pretty as you."

He pauses, takes another long breath, and glances in the direction of the hall. "If I didn't have to leave you alone with her, I wouldn't." He looks back at the baby, forcing a smile. "But don't worry. She's your mom, and she loves you. All mothers love their kids, right? Besides, she needs you. She just doesn't know it yet." He's rambling, talking more to himself than the baby, working through his guilt in the guise of talking to his daughter.

The baby holds onto the rail with one hand and waves an open-palmed hand in the air while bouncing up and down on rubbery legs. She looks like she's practicing to be a bareback rider in the rodeo. The man laughs and shakes his head. "Hey, I got you something."

He digs in the duffle bag and takes out a white stuffed bear. "Something to remember me by." He holds it out to her, but rather than grab it, she swats it with her free hand and it falls to the playpen floor. "I'm sure going to miss you. But if I come back around, your mother will just make us both miserable. So it's best if I keep my distance. But your bear will keep you company."

His voice has grown thick and his eyelids blink rapidly. He ruffles the girl's hair and presses another kiss against her forehead.

"I love you, Allie."

He stands quickly, scoops up the duffle bag, and walks out the door. He pulls it closed behind him, careful not to make it slam.

I watch the door, wondering how he was able to convince himself that leaving was the best thing for everybody. Hoping he'll change his mind and come back. But the past is the past.

He won't come back. He never did.

I slide down the wall until I'm sitting on the floor, eye level with the baby. Little Allie bounces a few more times before she drops to the bottom of the playpen. She rolls from side to side, then pounces on the bear and wraps herself around it, making baby sounds that no one is around to hear.

12

I'm still holding on to the bear, clutching it so tight my fingers hurt. According to my mother, I never let the toy out of my sight. I treated it the way some kids treat their blankets or their pacifiers. It wasn't until I went to kindergarten and she made me leave it at home that I finally detached from it. The promise of having other children to play with overrode my affection for my old friend. But it was never far away. I slept with it for years, then, sometime in sixth grade, I gave it a place of honor on top of my dresser. That's where it stayed, all through high school. The last time I saw the bear was when I put it in a storage box before leaving for college. It's a treasured memento that I'll never part with, but haven't looked at for years.

But now here it is, in my hands. I run my fingertips over it one more time, then start to put it back in the chest. At the last second, I change my mind and set it on the seat beside me. Something tells me that once and item is out of the chest, it probably shouldn't go back in.

I shake myself, trying to let loose of my trip to the past. Where did all that come from? Of course, I'd already known part of the story. I knew about the bear. I knew my dad joined the Air Force. I knew I had never seen him again. But I knew all that only because of what I'd been told by my mother. I'd never had any real memories of it.

Until now.

But this had been more than a memory. Even the strongest memories I possess have holes in them, lacy doilies of connected thoughts, feelings, and images. But this had been like watching a movie unfold in front of me. A very vivid, 3D movie, complete with ambient sounds and smells. It was unsettling, to say the least.

Vinnie and Joe are still sitting with me at the booth. They gaze at me, waiting for me to say something. Did I describe the story as I saw it happening? Did they see it with me? I don't have a clue. But I can tell they know what happened. More than that, they understand it.

I look down at the bear. It's forlorn and bedraggled lying against the bright red of the cushion. "I always wondered how he could leave me with her. And why he never came back."

"People always have a reason for the things they do," Vinnie says. "It doesn't mean the reason is good or that it makes any sense, just that it's there."

I pull a napkin from the silver holder at the end of the table and start fiddling with it, drawing it through my fingers again and again. "So, he found a way to justify leaving me behind. And he really trusted her to take care of me, despite the way she was acting?"

"Yes."

"And he convinced himself that it would be better for *me* if he never came back?"

"Yes."

I look down at my hands. The table top is littered with the now mangled and shredded remnants of the napkin. I push them off to the side, shaking my head. "You're right. Just because he had reasons didn't make them good ones."

"Was he wrong?" Vinnie asks.

My head bobs up and down. I'm a marionette and someone's jerking on my strings. "Oh yeah, he was wrong. On both counts. Way wrong."

"How so?"

"That whole spiel about not coming back because it was better for me? Baloney. That was nothing but a huge cop out. And the innate love of a mother for her children?" I let out a very unladylike but completely appropriate snort. "No such thing. Just because a woman's had a kid doesn't make her a nurturing caregiver."

I shift my eyes to Joe. He's been quiet through this whole exchange. Something in the way he looks at me says he's got the answers to any question I could ask. But I figure there's no point in asking. He won't just hand over the information. Instead he'll say "The truth lies within you" or something else equally as Yoda-like.

"Okay, that was fun." My gaze darts from one man to the other, and I purposely put on an over-exaggerated smile. "Now that we're done with that, how about we work on getting my consciousness back into my body, or however it works."

"You're not done." Vinnie gives the side of the open chest a pat. "It's not empty."

Of course it's not. But after what I've just gone through, I don't think I want to scrutinize any more of the stuff Joe claims I've been carting around wherever I go. There's plenty of crud in my life that's better ignored than examined. I'm not one hundred percent sure what all is in there, but I'm positive that I don't want to find out.

I lean toward them, hoping to reason my way out of this. "Look, as far as I can tell, I'm supposed to learn something about myself from going through this box. Fair enough. So what did I just learn? That my mother was a shrew, and my dad was an idiot. Satisfied?"

Vinnie winces. "Don't you think that's a little harsh?"

No, I really don't, but I'll play his game. "Gee, I'm sorry. Let me rephrase that. My mom was extremely upset and emotional, and my dad was naïve and just a little bit selfish." I wave my hands in the air as if I'm trying to see through a cloud of smoke. "Put it however you want. Bottom line, I didn't enjoy that little trip into my past, and I don't want to take another one. I don't see how any of this is supposed to help me."

"Quit whining and look in the box."

I turn my head slowly in Joe's direction. I'm shocked. This is the advice he gives me? Quit whining? Not very Yoda-like at all. But strangely, I find it a lot more helpful. I could probably avoid gentle prodding all day, but a direct command is something else. And the tone of his voice doesn't leave any room for argument. But that doesn't mean I have to act happy about it.

"All right, fine. I will."

With a frown I reach into the box. I feel a stack of something tied together with ribbon. I pull it out.

"Pictures?"

I tug on one of the loose ends, and the ribbon falls away. Since the first image is of my father, I can't say I'm completely surprised when I fan the photos out in front of me and get a look at the rest of them.

Vinnie cranes his neck to get a better look at what I'm holding. "Who are they?"

I'm pretty sure he knows already, but I appreciate him trying to make this an interactive experience. I turn the pictures toward him, feeling like I'm holding up the world's worst hand of playing cards. "Mom's husbands and boyfriends. It's the cavalcade of men that have paraded through my life."

A quick glance tells me they're already in order from oldest to newest. I straighten the stack, then look from Vinnie, to Joe, and back to Vinnie again. I hold up my father's picture and wiggle it in front of me. "My dad. You already know about him." I put it on the table and tap the remaining stack of pictures with my finger. "So, I guess you want to know about the rest of these guys, huh?"

They both nod. Around the edges of the diner, heads turn in our direction. Norma Jeane gets up from the table she's been sitting at and moves closer. Grimm pads his way across the floor and sits next to my side of the booth. He rests his massive, battle scarred head on the seat and prods me with his cold, wet nose.

I look down at my dog, and for the first time I notice the similarities between him and my love-battered, stuffed bear. "Et tu, Grimm? Okay. I guess there's no way out of this."

I lift my head and lock eyes with Joe. His expression is intense, almost as if he's offering to help me call up the memories again.

I shake my head. "Thanks, but I've got this covered."

I wish I needed help. I wish I could look at Joe and say, "You know, I don't remember much about these guys. Why don't you give me a jolt to get me started?" But that's not the case. Unfortunately, each one of these losers is ingrained in my brain.

No matter how much effort I've put into trying, they are impossible to forget.

13

VINNIE'S DINER

"Stanley Gaebler." I slap down a photo of a man wearing black parachute pants and a multi-zippered, red leather jacket straight out of Michael Jackson's "Thriller" video. Stan knew every word of that song and every step of the dance routine. This man had enjoyed the eighties so much that he stayed there, even when the rest of the world moved on without him.

Vinnie looks down at the photo. "Nice pants. Who is he?"

"Stepdad number one. And don't let his outfit fool you. I was five when mom and Stan got married, so that puts this somewhere in the nineties."

Mom's voice is shrill in my head. *I've gone too many years without a man.* I don't know why she waited until I was five to start dating again, but she did. Maybe it was too hard to date with a little kid hanging on to her ankles. Maybe it just took her that long to decide she wanted to put in the effort where men were concerned. But one day, she made her declaration, dropped me off at Aunt Bobbie's for the night, and hit the dance clubs. That's where she found Stan.

Stan unleashed my mother's inner performer. To hear her tell the story—and I've heard it more than once, because she loves to tell it—Stan was mixing tunes in the DJ booth when he saw my mom out on the dance floor. He left the booth and by the end of the song, Stan had boogied his way between mom and her partner of the moment. His stellar pickup line had included something about her booty and the way she shook her groove thing. I've banished the exact words from my mind.

Six months later, they got married right there in the club. I was the flower girl and so proud of the pink rose petals I threw across the dance floor. But as soon as the ceremony was over, someone came through with a broom and a long-handled litter pan, the kind you see used at amusement parks, and swept the petals away. They didn't want anyone to slip and fall when the dancing started.

Mom and Stan did a lot of dancing. I remember the two of them practicing their moves in the living room. They even competed in a retro-disco competition, and I think they came in second. Stan was a good dancer, I'll give him that. He just wasn't good for much else.

"Mom thought it was funny that marrying Stan made her initials G.G. She started calling herself that. She'd say, *Hi, I'm Gigi.*" I imitate her, making my voice high-pitched and exaggerated. It sounds nothing like my mother, but I've managed to capture the essence of the moment.

"Stan lasted a year and a half."

Vinnie tilts his head to the side. "What happened to him?"

I'd been sick that day, so when Stan said he was going to the club to check out the new lighting system, Mom reluctantly decided to stay home. But she couldn't stand missing out on the fun for too long. By ten o'clock, Aunt Bobbie had responded to her emergency call to come stay with me, and mom headed out the door with a finger-wiggled wave goodbye. She was all smiles when she left. But finding Stan doing a slow grind on the dance floor with a young blond waitress wiped the smiles away.

"Stan got tired of having only one dance partner."

I push his photo off to the side.

"When things didn't work out so well for my mother at the dance clubs, she moved on. To biker bars." I slap down the next picture and let everyone get a good look.

"Shooter Williams. Stepdad number two." He's wearing a Harley jacket and has a mustache thick enough to hide things in, which he often did. Not on purpose, but pieces of breakfast or dinner could routinely be seen falling out of that hank of hair when he talked. It was pretty disgusting. How mom could stand to kiss him remains a mystery to me.

Vinnie makes a face. "Shooter?"

I nod. "Because he could down more shots of tequila than anyone else in Buzz Kill." All the faces around me wrinkle up in varying shades of confusion and revulsion. "The bar he hung out in. The name was Buzz Kill."

"Oh."

"Ahhh."

"Ewww!"

So many drawn out sounds fill the air, I feel like we're on an episode of Sesame Street, the one where we're all learning how to pronounce our vowels.

I point back to the picture, to what's standing next to Shooter. "And this is Butch."

My mother never wanted to have animals in the house. Whenever I asked for a pet, she always said no. Even to goldfish. "You'll just get bored with it," she'd say, "And then you know what will happen? I'll end up having to take care of *it*, too." But when Shooter moved in, his dog, Butch, moved in with him without a word of argument from my mother. Butch was as ugly as he was bad tempered, but Shooter loved that dog more than his own mother,

From his spot next to me, a low growl rumbles in Grimm's throat. I smile down at him and scratch the top of his head. "My feelings exactly." Grimm may not be a beauty, but he's got a good soul. My personal belief is that Butch was black-hearted and soulless.

Vinnie taps the picture. "Was he an alcoholic?"

I jerk my head up and raise my eyebrows. "Butch? Naw, but he did like to drink out of the toilet."

Vinnie stops just short of an eye roll. "You know what I mean. Was Shooter an alcoholic?"

Yeah, I knew what he meant. "Well, that depends on who you ask. Not when Mom met him. Not technically. He was a *recovering* alcoholic. Sober for a whole ninety days." I frown at the memory. "Then they got married, and he un-recovered real fast."

"That's terrible!" Norma Jeane squeals.

"Yes, it was." Sober, Shooter had been rough around the edges, but nice enough. Drunk, Shooter went beyond any reasonable definition of *rough*. Alcohol chased all the nice out of his body, leaving a pretty unpleasant person behind. "He was a mean drunk, too. Yelling, throwing things. And I'm pretty sure he hit my mother more than once." As skilled as my mom is with a makeup sponge and concealer, she never could completely erase all the bruises.

"Did he ever hit you?" Norma Jeane's voice escapes from her lips in a whisper, so thin and airy the question almost evaporates before it reaches my ears.

This isn't something I like to think about, and I sure don't want to talk about it. Maybe I should just move on to the next picture—

"Did he?" Joe speaks up. I should have known he wouldn't let it go.

"Once." I made the mistake of changing the channel when he was out of the room. I don't know for sure what he'd been watching . . . a rerun of *Cops*, I think. And what eight-year-old girl likes *Cops*? I just wanted to see what else was on, but he came flying at me like I'd insulted his mother. Or kicked his dog.

Mom saw it all. She told me to get ice for my face, then she sent me to my room while they yelled at each other. Even though my head was under my pillow, I could hear them scream. Then something crashed. The next day, my lip was split, my cheek was purple, a lamp was in the trash, and Shooter and Butch were gone. Which proves that even my mother has her limits.

"That one lasted six months. Good riddance." With a flick of my wrist, Shooter joins Stan.

I look at the next picture and can't help but laugh. Poor Morris.

"I've gotta warn you, this next one is going to be a surprise." I look around at the expectant faces and then put the photo on the table. "Ta da! Here he is. Stepdad number three."

Complete silence. This was not an unusual reaction when people first met Morris. His extraordinarily long face, prominent front teeth, and gangly limbs gave him a strong resemblance to a horse. And not a particularly handsome one.

Vinnie clears his throat. "She decided to go another way, huh?"

"Yep." Mom met Morris Singleton at night school in a class called Tax Preparation for the Mathematically Illiterate. He was the instructor. She dropped the class, but picked up a new boyfriend. "I guess she thought it was time to try a calm, stable life."

Behind Vinnie, Einstein shakes his head, setting his hair to bobbing to and fro. "It certainly does not take a genius to figure out why that did not work."

No, it doesn't. Morris went way beyond calm. He was closer to comatose. And extremely practical. He didn't like a fuss being made over him. He thought money belonged in the bank or invested in the stock market, not being spent on frivolous things like birthday celebrations or Christmas presents. Since this made perfect sense to him, he expected it to make perfect sense to his wife, as well. Unfortunately, Mom and Morris didn't talk about fiscal responsibility until after they were married. Once she understood his family spending policy, his days with us were numbered.

I put his picture gently on the stack. Morris wasn't a bad guy. He was just from another planet.

There's still a good sized stack of pictures in my hand. I look up, my gaze moving across the faces of the people who surround me. "Should I go on?"

Norma Jeane's eyes are round as film cans as she points at the stack. "She didn't marry all of them, did she?"

I shake my head. "No. Mom went on a lot of dates after she showed Morris the door."

"Oh, good." Norma Jeane fans herself, then waves at me. "So what are you waiting for, honey? Keep going."

I quickly flip through a dozen or so photos, all of different men. Mom isn't one to discriminate so they come in all manner of shapes, sizes, ethnicities, and professions. There's Lance the cable installer, Raul the bartender, Max the corrections officer, and Alexi, who had a promising career in animal control until he had to endure a round of rabies shots after that crazed squirrel took a chunk out of his finger. This one liked jazz music, that one liked classic rock. Most of them were older than Mom, but at least one was so young he couldn't buy a six pack of beer without showing his fake ID. If you put them all in a room together, chances are they'd have nothing to talk about. But there is one thing that they all have in common; all of them said they loved my mother, but none of them found a compelling reason to stay with her. Some were around for months, others for just weeks, but in the end, they all left.

"Let's see," I say, wiggling a photo back and forth, "this is Jin, the female impersonator." I wave the picture at Judy Garland to get her attention. "He did one heck of an impression of you."

She puts her hand flat against her chest and starts to laugh, a wavering warble that seems to get stuck and circle around and around in her throat. I think that means she's pleased.

"How old were you when he was dating your mother?" Vinnie asks.

I think back. I remember it was after the movie *Chicago* had come out because Jin tried to put together a Catherine Zeta-Jones impression. It wasn't bad, but it was no Judy. "Hmm, I think I was about fourteen."

Fourteen. A chill runs through my body. I let go of the photograph and watch it fall in slow motion from my fingers, hanging in the air for a moment before it lands with the others.

"What's wrong?" Joe asks me this, even though we all know he doesn't need to.

"That's the last of the boyfriends." Suddenly, it's become very hot in the diner. Perspiration pools under my arms and slides down my back. Even my hands are sweating. "Is anyone else hot?"

They all ignore the question. Joe points at my hand. "You've got one picture left."

I start fanning myself with the photo, wanting to do something constructive with it. Wanting to do anything but talk about it. I look at Vinnie. "Can you turn down the thermostat or something?"

He shakes his head slowly. Then he reaches across the table and grabs my wrist, stilling my frantic movements. He pulls my arm out with a gentle tug and looks down at the photo. I'm holding it so tight, the bottom edge is creased.

"We're coming up to another stepdad, aren't we?" he asks.

My whole body tenses. I want to pull my arm away from Vinnie, jump out of the booth and run out the front door. I want to get away from this crazy diner, away from all these questions. All these memories.

"Please." My eyes squeeze shut as I shake my head in quick, sharp movements. "I don't want to see him again."

Vinnie's thumb rubs across the top of my wrist in a comforting gesture. He doesn't speak, but when I open my eyes and look from Vinnie to Joe, I know that begging won't get me anywhere. I can't run away from this.

My eyes drop back to the photograph of Ethan Lansing and I draw in a long, deep breath.

"Yes, it's another stepdad. The last one, actually."

And this one's the worst of the bunch. Because this is the one that broke my heart.

14

SOUTHERN CALIFORNIA

This time, it's different.

This time, I'm suspended in a foggy, swirling vortex of images and thoughts. I'm like Dorothy Gale, sitting on the bed in her Kansas farmhouse, caught up in the eye of the tornado, and watching out the window as pieces of her life fly by.

And the first thing to fly by is Ethan.

Mom met him at church, if you can imagine that.

My Aunt Bobbie had recently had a come-to-Jesus moment, and she thought it would be good for me to have some kind of spiritual upbringing. Mom said no to the idea, of course, and continued to say no every time it came up. But Aunt Bobbie refused to back down, which was totally out of character for her. Not only does Aunt Bobbie do everything she can to avoid confrontations in general, she also tends to defer to her older sister. But in this case, she was like one of those annoying little rat-dogs, always yipping about church, nipping at my mother's ankles, tugging on her sleeve. It finally wore mom down. In a moment of weakness, she caved and we ended up at Blessed Redeemer Community Church.

I liked the idea of going to church, but the reality was a whole other matter. At fourteen, I was already feeling unsure about myself. My body was changing, but not in the way or at the speed I wanted it to, and my emotions were all over the place. Stepping into a new setting, with kids who had mostly known each other forever and were happy with things the way they were, was difficult. There was little room for a new girl trying to make friends. So I sat in the corner during the youth Bible study hour, trying to keep to myself, and observing the other teens as they interacted. I felt like Jane Goodall studying the social interactions of gorillas.

See how the male puffs out his chest and struts for the female while she pretends to ignore him? Fascinating.

The worship service itself was a mixed bag. Sometimes the sermon was interesting and made me think about how I could apply it to my life. Sometimes I zoned out and found myself pondering other important things, like what I should wear to school the next day, how I'd look with a French manicure, or whether I should grow out my bangs.

Out of the whole church experience, my favorite part was the music. The BRCC praise band was really good, and the songs were much more interesting than the hymns I had expected to be singing in church. Somehow, the words and the music began working together, speaking to my heart in a new way. I started to feel that when I was singing about God, he might actually be out there, and he might even start to notice me.

As it turned out, the singing is what made Ethan notice my mother. He came up to us after the service one day, smiling warmly and reaching out to shake our hands, first mine, then Mom's. He held her hand longer than I thought he needed to, and looked into her face as he talked.

"I was sitting behind you during service and couldn't help but notice what a beautiful voice you have. Have you ever thought about joining the choir?"

Mom did have a nice voice. Whenever we were in the car, she'd crank up the radio and sing along. And from her dancing days, I knew she had rhythm. But she was strictly a casual vocalist. As far as I knew, she'd never tried to read sheet music before, couldn't tell one note from the other. That wasn't enough to stop her, though. Not when a nice looking man showed some interest.

Ethan was a tenor. The following Wednesday, Mom found out she was an alto when she showed up at her very first choir practice.

Mom and Ethan dated for six months. At first, I treated him the same way I treated all the other men in my mother's life. I was pleasant, but distant. Never rude, I still didn't let myself get too close. There really was no point when I knew he was just a temporary fixture, like a lamp she'd get tired of and replace when it was time to mix up the décor.

Most of the men who'd visited our apartment in the past were fine with my approach. They weren't any more interested in a kid than I was in them. But Ethan turned out to be different. He actually talked to me. At dinner, he'd include me in the conversation. He'd ask me about school and my friends. He enjoyed it when all three of us played board games or watched movies together.

And he never spent the night. Not that he didn't have the chance. One time, he'd taken both Mom and me to the San Diego Zoo. By the time we got home, it was well after midnight. We were all exhausted, but Ethan still had to drive across town to his place.

"I hate to think of you getting back in that car. Why don't you stay here?" Mom suggested.

He smiled, but shook his head. "We've talked about that, Georgie. You know I can't."

"No, I meant on the couch." She dipped her lashes and, for a moment, she actually looked innocent. That's an expression I wasn't used to seeing on my mother.

"Thanks for the offer, but it just wouldn't look right. Besides," he gave me a gentle chuck under the chin, "we don't want to set a bad example for this one."

That night, he impressed me on two levels. First, he made it clear to my mother that they wouldn't be sleeping together. Then, even more miraculous to me, was the fact that he thought about how it would make me feel. I was absolutely sure none of her other boyfriends had ever let my feelings come between them and their male urges.

Little by little, Ethan was winning me over, and I was starting to think that having him around was a pretty cool thing.

The grainy mass of memories swirling around me slows. It dissolves until there's nothing left and I drop with a thud. Looking around, I realize I'm in the apartment my mother and I lived in while she was dating Ethan. And there I am, the fourteen-year-old version of me. Just an oblivious teenager doing homework at the kitchen table.

The doorbell rings. She goes to the door. Looks through the peep hole. Then she takes a step back and opens the door. Ethan's on the other side.

"Hey, Allie." He looks over her shoulder, past her and into the little apartment. "Did I beat your mom home?"

She nods. "She's still at work. She probably won't be here for another half hour at least."

"Good." A slow smile spreads across his lips. "Because there's something I want to ask you."

She sits on the couch and he sits beside her, close enough to talk but not so close that it would make anyone feel uncomfortable.

"Here's the thing. I love your mother." His voice wavers a little. He sounds nervous. "And I think she loves me. I want to ask her to marry me, but before I can do that, I need something from you."

Allie's forehead wrinkles in confusion. "What?"

"Your blessing." When Allie doesn't say anything, he just goes on. "I want to marry your mom, but only if you think it's a good idea."

I remember how I felt that day. Shocked. Surprised. And strangely powerful. I held my mother's future in my hands.

"Why does it matter what I think?"

He smiles. "Because you and your mom have been a team for a long time. If you're not happy, she's not happy. And I want to make sure you'll be happy if I'm your stepdad."

Clearly, he had no understanding at all of how my relationship with my mother worked, but that wasn't important. At that moment, the only thing that mattered was that a really nice guy was asking if it was okay to be my stepdad. It was almost like he was proposing to me.

He puts his hand on Allie's leg, just above her knee. His thumb moves back and forth, slowly, once, twice.

As I watch him, cold anger spreads its sharp fingers across my body. I should have known right then. It's so obvious now. But then, all I could think about was that finally, *finally* here was a man who loved me enough to talk to me, to ask me how I felt. A man who made my mother happy and wanted to take care of her. And if mom was happy, maybe some of that would spill over to me and I really would be happy, too. All I could see was that this man might be the answer to the hesitant prayers I'd started praying to a God I'd just recently considered might actually exist.

On the couch, Allie is smiling. "Of course I'd be happy. You'll make a great stepdad."

"Great!" He gives her knee a final, quick squeeze and pulls his hand away. "So, how was school today?"

We sat and talked until Mom got home twenty minutes later. She seemed suspicious, almost wary when she first discovered that Ethan was alone with me. But when he asked her to marry him, she cried and laughed and cried some more. She even smiled at me. Then Ethan took both of us to Sizzler for a celebration dinner.

The scene around me fades. The fog swirls. I catch glimpses of my life after that. Mom in a wedding dress. Me being part of the wedding party. Again.

Mom had previously been married in a night club, in Las Vegas, and in two different courthouses. Her wedding to Ethan was her first in a church, and it was beautiful. While they were on their honeymoon, I stayed with Aunt Bobbie. And when they got back, the three of us started our new life together in Ethan's house. Only now, it was *our* house. I finally was part of a normal family, with a mother and a father, and it was wonderful.

Until two months later.

On a Thursday.

On my fifteenth birthday.

The world around me becomes sharp again. I'm standing in our house, by the front door. Across the room, Ethan stands on a folding chair, taping party decorations to the ceiling.

The door beside me opens. Teenage Allie walks in and looks up at the balloons and pink and purple streamers hanging above her. She shuts the door and Ethan looks over his shoulder at her, eyebrows raised and eyes wide.

"Hey, you caught me!" He steps down and walks over to her.

I had always liked Ethan's smile. But that day, there was something wrong about it. It was a little too wide, a little too stiff. And why did he sound surprised that I was home? He knew what time school got out. Even then, not knowing everything I know now, the situation made me uneasy.

"Why aren't you at work?" she asks him.

"I told my boss I had something very important to take care of. And what could be more important than celebrating my favorite girl's birthday?"

He pulls a small, wrapped box out of the front pocket of his khakis. "Here. This is for you."

She looks at the gift, then looks back at him. Then she looks over her shoulder, expecting to find her mother somewhere nearby. But she and Ethan are alone. "Shouldn't we wait for Mom?"

He licks his bottom lip and gives his head a sharp shake. "Not this time. This is a special gift." He hesitates, his mouth curling up every so slightly at the corners. "Just from me to you."

Something is very wrong. Allie knows it. A voice inside her head says to stay as far away from Ethan as she can. But it makes no sense. He's only trying to give her a gift. It would be rude if she didn't accept it. So she ignores the voice.

Allie takes the present from him. She carefully peels the tape off each end of the box, removes the paper, and lifts up the lid. It's a delicate gold cross necklace, very pretty and sweet, lying on a bed of stark white cotton.

"Thanks. I love it."

It's a lie. She doesn't love it. It's nice, so she likes it. But she can see it's really important to him that she loves his gift. So she tells him what she knows will make him happy.

Allie starts to put the lid back on the box, but he catches her wrist and stops her.

Watching the scene unfold in front of me, seeing the look of fear etched in Allie's face, I want to do something to stop it. I want to hurl myself at Ethan, pull him away, tell him to leave and never come back. But all I can do is watch, ghostlike and ineffective, unable to change the events that are coming.

Ethan leans down, his face close to hers. "No, don't put it away. I want to see how pretty my present looks on you." He takes the box from her, removes the necklace, and opens the clasp. Holding the ends of the chain apart with the cross dangling in the middle, he says, "I'll help you put it on."

He moves behind her, draping the necklace around her neck. "Pull your hair back," he says, his lips so close to her ear that she can feel the heat from his breath. She does as he asked. He fastens the chain. Then his hands slide down either side of her neck to her shoulders. "So beautiful." And then his lips are on her skin.

I can't stand by and watch anymore. I hurtle forward, my hands outstretched. I try to pull him off, but it's no use. My fingers grasp nothing but air. And then I collide with myself.

The whole scene shifts. I'm not watching from my safe, detached vantage point anymore. Now, I'm in it. Reliving every repulsive sensation, every emotion.

I pull away and twist, but he grabs me. Tugs me hard against him. Smashes his lips down on mine.

His breath pours over my face, sour and hot. "I've been waiting for this since the first day I saw you."

The first day. In church.

"What about Mom?" The question tears out of me, ragged and raw.

"Mmm, she's a sweet one. But what man can resist two helpings of sweet meat under the same roof?"

My stomach lurches, and I wish I could throw up all over him. Instead, I fight him, struggling to pull free. But he jerks me sideways until I fall over the arm of the couch with him on top of me. I'm pinned beneath him, unable to breathe, unable to believe what is happening, as he touches me in places no one has touched me before.

I claw and kick, but he just laughs. He's enjoying it. My shirt rips, and a guttural sound gurgles up from somewhere deep in his throat.

Discouragement weighs down on me, heavier than the weight that already presses me into the couch. It's useless. I can't fight him off. In fact, the more I fight, the more he seems to like it. It crosses my mind that, maybe, if I stop fighting, it will take the thrill out of it for him. Maybe he'll get bored and let me go. So I let myself go limp. And without even meaning to, I pray.

Please, God, help me. Make him stop.

But he keeps at it. And I lay there, just wishing for it to be over.

He doesn't notice the squeal of the screen door. The scratch of a key in the lock. But I do.

My mother is home.

A burst of adrenaline shoots through my veins. Screaming as loud as I can, I flail my arms and bring one knee up hard, catching him in the groin. He grunts and falls forward, crushing me. I turn my head and bite down on his ear. He wails, jerks to the side, loses his balance. His hand flings out, grabbing for something to hold on to. His fingers slide through the chain around my neck, and I feel a hard tug. It snaps as he falls to the floor.

"What the hell is going on!"

For years, I've tried to erase the image of my mother standing in the doorway, but it's a memory that has never left me. Her face is white as the china plates she called "the good dishes." She looks at me, as I clutch the front of my blouse together, knees drawn up to my chest, pushing myself into the corner of the couch. Then she looks at Ethan, pulling himself up from the floor, blood oozing from between the fingers he holds over his ear. Her mouth moves, but no sounds come out. The shock of what she sees has left her speechless.

With a groan, Ethan gets to his feet and stumbles over to her. "Georgie, sweetheart, it's not what you think. I can explain this."

"Explain?" Her lips form the word slowly, like a foreign exchange student speaking English for the first time.

It's no surprise that Ethan tries to throw the blame on me. "She's been coming on to me for weeks. I didn't want to say anything because I thought she was just acting out and I could handle it. But she seduced me."

Mom knows better. I can see that she does. But I can also tell that she still wants to believe him. She's desperate for him to say something that makes sense and will explain away what she just saw so she can continue living in happy, marital bliss. And it might have worked. If he talked long enough and said the right things, Ethan might have come up with some way to sway her. But then, when he sees she's not buying his story, he says the absolutely wrong thing. The thing that seals both our fates.

"Come on, Baby, I'm just a man. How can you expect me to resist the temptation of someone so young and pretty in my own home?"

Her face turns to granite, and even though she knows I'm the victim, I've also become her enemy on this particular playing field.

She swears at Ethan. Tells him that if he leaves and never comes back, she won't call the police.

Any remnant of Ethan's nice guy persona disappears. He mutters and swears on his way to the door, throwing some choice words in my direction, as if I'm the one who destroyed everything. Once he's gone and it's just Mom and me left in the room, she looks at me for a long time. I clench my jaws together and bite down on the inside of my lower lip, trying not to cry, trying to hold it together. I pull what's left of my blouse around me. I try to tug down my skirt, even thought it's already as far down as it will go. And she just keeps staring. Finally, I can't take the silence anymore. I reach out my hand.

"Mom." The word quivers in the empty space between us.

Now she looks away. She looks toward the kitchen. She looks up at the decorations on the ceiling. Then she looks back at me.

"Are you okay?" Her voice, cold and hard, doesn't match the concern in the question.

I nod my head.

"Did he . . . ?"

"No. He tried . . . but no."

"Good."

She nods her head once. Then she turns and walks quietly into her bedroom, shutting the door behind her.

I want my mother to hold me, to tell me everything will be all right. I want her to say that she loves me, that we'll get through this thing together. But I guess she needs someone to tell her those things, too. Someone other than me.

I don't let myself cry until I'm alone in the room. Streamers and balloons move gently on the ceiling above me, swaying from side to side as if sharing in my grief. I have no idea how long I stayed like that, balled up on the sofa, weeping against my knees, but it seems like hours. Finally, when there are no tears left and my mouth is devoid of any moisture, I stand up. I don't know where I'm going, but I have to go somewhere.

I take a step away from the couch.

And I feel something beneath my foot.

It's the cross. I bend down and pick it up. The delicate chain hangs from the top of it, limp and broken. I stare at the pendant, at its shiny golden surface reflecting the light. My fingers close tight around it and it bites into the flesh of my palm.

Why did Ethan do it? Why did he give me a cross? It was supposed to be a symbol of hope. A symbol of love. But for me, it has just become a symbol of depravity and betrayal.

A scream rises from a pit of white hot anger in my core. I pull my arm back and hurl the revolting thing across the room, into the shadows by the tall entertainment center.

15

Vɪɴɴɪᴇ's Dɪɴᴇʀ

My head is on the table. I lift it slowly and wait for the diner to come back into focus again. I'm getting used to the process, but I don't think I'll ever get used to the experience. My whole body is quivering, shaking as though it's encased in ice.

There's still a photo pinched between my thumb and fore-finger. It's Ethan, smiling up at me. He looks like the perfect image of a God-fearing family man.

What a joke.

I want to spit on the photo, destroy it, grind it under the treads of my dirty tennis shoes. Instead, I tear it in half, slowly, relishing the sound of the paper splitting and ripping. I lay both halves face down on top of the other pictures.

"That's the last one," I say to Vinnie. "She never brought another man home after that. Not until after I moved out to go to college."

I push the stack of pictures as far away from me as I can, sending them dropping through the crack between the wall and the table. They cascade to the floor like some kind of dys-functional waterfall.

My mother's voice crackles out of the speakers of the radio behind me.

"I need to get some coffee."

Of course she does. Because ever since that day, she's found it difficult to be in the same room with me for very long.

I drop my head and stare at my fingernails. They're ragged around the edges from me picking at them. I used to be a nail biter, which drove my mom nuts. One day, when she caught me gnawing on my thumb, she'd had enough. "You might think it's old fashioned, but men notice hands. What are you going to do when you go on a date, and a boy takes your hand and you scratch him up with these things?" She'd held up one of my hands, bending the fingers down so they were practically touching my nose. I was only ten, but I got the idea. Men were important, and men noticed nails, therefore, nails were important. So instead of biting them, I started filing them, painting them, spending extra time on my nail grooming. For years, I had the best looking nails in the school district.

That day, on my fifteenth birthday, I broke off two of my beautiful, perfectly shaped Pink Pearl colored nails as I scratched and clawed and fought off Ethan.

I don't bother with polish anymore. Now I'm a nail picker, and they look worse than ever. But at least I didn't go back to biting them. Very often.

"Things between my mother and I were never the same after that." *Pick. Pick. Pick.* "Not that they were great before."

Vinnie's hand covers mine, stilling me. I look up into his face and I can tell. He gets it.

With a smile, he pats my hand twice, then pulls back. "Tell us about your Aunt Bobbie."

This is an unexpected surprise. I was sure he would ask me more questions about Ethan. That he'd probe into the deep recesses of my mind. Want to know how it made me feel to be attacked and rejected all in one birthday afternoon. But instead, he wants to know about my aunt.

And thinking about my aunt reminds me of the trivia contest.

"Look, I appreciate your help, but I've got to get back to my body so I can get to that contest." I stretch my arms across the table, holding my hands out to Vinnie, imploring him to help me. "You have no idea how important it is."

"And you have no idea how important *this* is." He motions around him, and I assume he's talking about my diner experience.

My fingers curl in on themselves forming tight fists. "You're right, I don't know how important this is. Because no one will tell me." A little droplet of spit flies out of my mouth and lands on the table. I need to calm down. I slide back in my seat, breathe in, hold it, then slowly let it out. Then I continue.

"You want to know about my aunt? Fine, I'll tell you about her. She's the most important person in my life. She's more of a mother to me than the woman who gave birth to me. And she's dying."

Joe reaches out and puts his hand on one of my fists. "You're all dying, Allie."

I jerk my hand away. "Yes, I know. But she's got Parkinson's. And it's going to steal everything that makes her who she is. She'll be dead long before her body goes. But there's a drug that could give her more productive, happy years. Only it's expensive and her insurance won't cover it because they say it's still considered experimental. That's why I need to get to the contest. If I win that money, I can pay for her medication."

Joe folds his hands together in front of him. "You're trying to save her."

My eyes burn, and I know if I open my mouth I'll start bawling. So I just jerk my chin up and down in response.

Joe looks at Vinnie, who nods back. "Allie," Vinnie barely touches my hand with the tip of one finger, then points at the radio. "There's something you need to hear."

I turn in my seat, angling toward the radio. The volume increases even though no one is standing anywhere near it.

There's a knock, like someone rapping on a door. Then a whoosh.

"Excuse me. Can I come in?" It's a male voice I don't recognize.

"Sure." That's Aunt Bobbie.

"I've seen you around the hospital the last few days."

Days? I turn to Vinnie. "It's been days?"

He points again. "Just keep listening."

"Is this your daughter?" the unknown man asks.

"My niece. But she's the closest thing to a daughter I'll ever have."

There's nothing for a moment, then the man clears his throat. "I'm Dr. Hoffman."

"Bobbie Burton."

Another pause. "I hope I'm not being too intrusive, but as I said, I've noticed you, and . . ."

"And . . ."

"You have Parkinson's, don't you?"

Aunt Bobbie and I gasp at the same time.

"How did you know?"

"From the way you walk. And I noticed the tremors."

"You sound like an expert."

"Yes, I suppose I am. I'm head of the hospital's Parkinson's research unit." His voice is gentle, not at all like some of the doctors I've visited with Aunt Bobbie. I wish she'd met this guy a few years back. "We ran the clinical trial here on Betricept."

I'm feeling a little light headed. Betricept is the drug I'm trying to get for Aunt Bobbie.

Aunt Bobbie laughs, but it's not a particularly happy sound. "The world's a tiny place, doctor. I tried to get on that drug, but my insurance company refused to pay for it. Said it was too expensive for something that wasn't proven to be effective."

"Really? Well, I guess that's why I'm here." She must be looking at him funny, because he makes a nervous laughter kind of sound before going on. "I just felt like I was supposed to talk to you about your condition and . . . well, to cut to the chase, I'm still involved in an ongoing study with Betricept. Even though it's FDA approved, we want to keep an eye on long-term effects. I believe I can get you into the program, if you're interested."

I nearly jump out of my seat. "Did you hear that?" I whirl around, grabbing Joe by the arm, since he's the closest. "She might get the drug after all."

Joe laughs, hearty and full throated. "Yes, I heard. But there's more."

My jaws ache from the intensity of my smile. But I can't help it. My aunt might get the help she needs. I look back at the radio, wondering what more this wonderful doctor has to say.

But it's my aunt that speaks next.

"That would be fabulous, but . . ." Her voice trails off, and I hear snuffling.

"But what?"

"I just wish we'd known sooner. Before Allie left for that contest. She was trying to win money to pay for my medicine."

I press my forehead against the back of the seat. She knew. All this time, I thought it was my big secret, but she knew. And she never let on.

Aunt Bobbie begins to cry. There's a rustling sound I can't identify.

"This is all my fault." Aunt Bobbie's voice is muffled. Is the doctor hugging her? Trying to comfort her?

"But if you hadn't been here, in this hospital, you probably would never have known about the study. I think this is a case of good coming out of tragedy. Besides, I know your niece's doctor. She's one of the best in her field."

"She is?" Aunt Bobbie's voice is clear again, and she's sniffing. The tears are almost done.

"Yes. Your niece is in very good hands."

A long silence, then Aunt Bobbie speaks. "Are you a believer, doctor?"

"Yes, I am."

"Would you pray with me?"

"I'd love to, Mrs. Burton."

One short, tiny giggle comes out of my aunt. "Miss."

"I'd love to pray with you, *Miss* Burton." And now, I hear a smile in the doctor's voice.

It's the last thing I'd ever expect. But I think my aunt may have just received medical help and the personal interest of a physician all at the same time.

16

VINNIE'S DINER

I turn back to Joe and Vinnie. They both look rather pleased with themselves.

"I'm not getting to the trivia contest, am I?"

"No," Vinnie says.

I let it sink in. No contest. No shot at the game show job. No chance of winning the $100,000. I'll admit, I'm disappointed. I would have liked that job. And if I'd been able to use the money on myself, I could have paid off my student loans. But now that I know Aunt Bobbie's got a chance of getting her medication, I can get over it.

Which brings me back to the task at hand: getting out of this diner. And the only way to do that seems to be by doing what my booth mates tell me.

I tilt my head at Joe. "Where were we?"

"You were going to tell us about your aunt."

As far as I'm concerned, they've just heard the most important stuff about her. But I'll tell them whatever else I can. "Aunt Bobbie is my mom's younger sister."

"Are they close?" Vinnie asks.

I grin at him. "That depends on the day. They don't agree on much, and they argue a lot." Over the years, mom has spent a lot of time on the phone with Aunt Bobbie. When something great happens, she calls my aunt to gloat. And when she's in the midst of another heart-wrenching breakup, Aunt Bobbie is the one she turns to for comfort. So I guess, when it comes right down to it, Aunt Bobbie is really my mom's best friend.

"Yeah, you could say they're close. But they're nothing alike."

"Really? How so?"

It would probably be easier to tell him what they *do* have in common, like the crazy custom in our family of naming girls after men. My mother is named for her Uncle George. Aunt Bobbie is named for her Uncle Robert, who had the misfortune of dying of pneumonia before she was born. I, of course, am named after my father, Alex. If Aunt Bobbie had had kids, she probably would have followed right along with the tradition. Not me. I've already sworn to myself that if I ever have a daughter of my own, I'll name her something girly and unmasculine, something like—

I cut the thought off before my mind can complete it. Out of the corner of my eye, I glance at Joe, wondering if he was following my train of thought. If so, he's doing a great job at hiding it. I'd better just concentrate on answering his question.

"How are they different? Well, you already know my mother's been through her share of men. But Aunt Bobbie has never been married. She says she has too much fun on her own to be tied down with just one man."

Vinnie nods. "Then she dates a lot?"

I have to think about that for a minute. "No, I don't think so."

I shuffle through my memories like CDs in a bargain bin, trying to pinpoint one time when I've seen Aunt Bobbie with a date or heard her talking about anyone special. But I can't. All I can come up with are memories that make me pretty sure she doesn't much like men, let alone trust them, which makes her tiny flirtation with the doctor by my hospital bed all the more perplexing.

I remember her saying things like, "Don't ever turn your back on a man, Allie." Or, "Most men are only in it for what they can get. And after they get it, they're gone." I've had some experience with that particular sentiment. Too bad I didn't pay closer attention the first time she shared it with me.

I look over Vinnie's shoulder at one of the movie posters on the wall. *Love Me Tender.* It's Aunt Bobbie's favorite Elvis flick, and the first time I ever watched it was with her.

"I won a Golden Globe for that movie."

Elvis pushes himself from his spot at the counter and walks closer, keeping his eyes on the poster.

"Yes, I know. Most Promising Newcomer."

"It was the start of my film career. The Colonel said it would make me a big star. That I'd do important things." The pride on his face melts away, leaving him sad and disillusioned. His shoulders sag, and he walks back to the swinging doors and disappears into the kitchen.

Poor Elvis. People used him for what they could get and told him what he wanted to hear even if it wasn't the truth. Just like Norma Jeane, they turned him into a well-paid, extremely talented pawn.

Bringing my attention back to Joe and Vinnie, I point my finger at the poster. "Aunt Bobbie told me all about the movie. She said it was the only one of his movies where he got second billing, but that it was worth it because of the Golden Globe. She considered it a highlight of his career. Once she told me, 'Sure, there's more flash in some of his other movies, but he gets to die at the end of this one.'" A light comes on in my head, something that had never occurred to me before. "Huh. Now that I think about it, the fact that the character dies before he can screw over the woman he loves is probably a real selling point for her."

Vinnie looks over his shoulder at the poster. As he turns back to me, he says, "Sounds like your mother and your aunt both have issues with men."

"I guess that's true. But they approach them in totally different ways. My mother manipulates men and uses them for what she can get. When she stops enjoying herself, she's done. And when she's done, they're gone. But Aunt Bobbie doesn't want anything to do with them." I look back at the poster and smile. "Well, except for totally inaccessible, movie star men. Those she drools over."

Vinnie chuckles. "So what else is different about your mom and your aunt?"

I start picking at my thumbnail but stop and pull another napkin out of the holder instead. "Mom is obsessed with her looks. Aunt Bobbie couldn't care less."

If you saw my mother walking down the street, you might wonder if she'd been a fashion model in her younger days. She takes exercise classes at the Y to stay in shape. She's mastered the art of discount shopping and knows exactly what colors and cuts best play up her features. She keeps her hairstyle modern and free of gray. She hasn't had any "work" done, but that's only because she hasn't been able to afford it. If the money was there, she'd be nipped, tucked, sucked, and lifted in a heartbeat.

Aunt Bobbie, on the other hand, is soft and round and all about comfort. It doesn't matter to her that her clothes aren't trendy, or even that the colors and patterns don't usually match. If the material feels good against her skin and they don't bind at the waist or chest, she's happy.

Joe shifts in his chair. "What about deeper things?"

"Like?"

"Are they spiritual women?"

Joe doesn't say a lot, but when he does, he gets straight to the point.

"Not always. When I was young, Aunt Bobbie wasn't religious at all. But somebody at work started talking to her about Jesus and invited her to church. She still doesn't go to church much, but she talks about faith a lot. She believes God watches everything we do and looks out for us." I look down at the napkin in my hands. Darn it. Shredded another one.

I push the bits of paper aside and continue. "Mom tried the church thing, and you see how great that worked out. Now, she believes only in herself. She says nobody is going to take care of you, so you've got to do it for yourself." This is the one area where I'm more like my mother than my aunt.

Joe folds his hands on top of the table. "So you don't believe God watches out for you?"

I lean away from Joe, angling my back to the corner of the booth. "You have got to stay out of my brain."

He shrugs and smiles. "I wouldn't be here if you didn't want me to be."

I shake my head. I still don't see how I have any control over what's going on. And trying to make sense of it only frustrates me more. I'm done answering questions. "You know what I want right now? I want to find out what else is going on in the land of the living." I scoot out of the booth, knocking against Joe's knees in the process. I don't say I'm sorry. It doesn't seem to bother him.

"Norma Jeane," I call out to the waitress and circle one finger in the air, "crank up the radio."

She gives one of the knobs a twist. Ambient sounds come through the speakers: The snap of magazine pages being flipped too fast for anyone to actually be reading them. The slurping sound of someone drinking coffee through a protective plastic lid. The door opening and slowly hissing shut.

"Hey." That's my Aunt Bobbie.

"Hey." That's Jake. He pauses, then asks, "Where's Mrs. Burton?"

I lean over the radio, my mouth close to the speakers and yell, "She went to get coffee."

"She had to take care of something at work," Aunt Bobbie sounds tired. "She'll be back here for the night shift."

She went to work? I turn to Vinnie. "I thought she just went to get coffee?"

"A little more time has gone by than you think." He waggles a finger at the radio. "Keep listening."

I turn back and hear metal chair legs rasp against the hard floor and the squish of someone sitting on a plastic cushion.

"Okay, Jake. Now that it's just the two of us, there's something I've been meaning to ask you."

"Shoot," he says, not sounding worried.

"How did you get the nurses to let you into the ICU? They have a pretty strict family-only policy in there."

She makes it sound like I'm not in the ICU anymore. How much time has gone by? When Aunt Bobbie was talking to Dr. Hoffman, it had only been two days. If I'm not in the ICU, then where am I?

Jake takes a moment before he answers. "I told them I was her fiancé."

He what? I'm speechless. Apparently so is my aunt, because it takes her a while to respond.

"Is that so?" She sounds skeptical.

"It's a little complicated." There's another long pause. I can imagine Jake leaning forward in the chair, scratching the back of his head, looking sheepish. "I asked Allie to marry me about three weeks before the accident."

Norma Jeane sucks in a shocked gulp of air. "He asked you to marry him?"

I shush her and point to the radio, not wanting to miss the rest of the conversation.

"I don't understand," Aunt Bobbie says. "She told me the two of you broke up."

Oh boy. Yeah, I did tell her that. And I told her why, which I hope she remembers to keep to herself.

"After I proposed, she said she needed time to think it over. I think the whole thing freaked her out because she never did call me and she wouldn't answer when I called her. She did a great job avoiding me. Even at graduation. But there was no official break up."

Aunt Bobbie makes a sound resembling a snort. "She thinks there was."

Yes, she does.

"I'm getting that idea." Jake's voice sounds sad, tired. "But unless she tells me differently, I say we're still together. I love this woman, and I intend to marry her."

This is like a scene from one those movies Aunt Bobbie loves. It's *While You Were Sleeping* in reverse. Even though I can't see her, I know my aunt is melting under the warmth of Jake's sincerity.

"That's the most romantic thing I've ever heard." There's sniffling. Aunt Bobbie's crying. "And I'm sure you think you mean it."

"I do mean it."

"But what if . . ." She snuffles a few more times. "I mean, I've been praying. Every day. But what if she never—"

"She will. She's going to come through this." Jake sounds so sure of himself he almost has me convinced that everything's going to be all right. The thought sparks an idea, igniting a new hope in my head. Maybe I will be all right. Maybe I already am. Maybe this is just a dream and I'm going to wake up soon. Maybe . . . I pinch myself hard on the arm. Other than hurting like the dickens, it doesn't do any good. I'm still in the diner, and Norma Jeane is looking at me like I'm a loon.

A garble of noises comes through the speakers. It sounds like someone's gotten out of a chair and is walking across the room. A warm whisper of air brushes against my cheek. My fingers tingle. It's Jake. I don't know how, but there's a connection between us that bridges space, time, and the insanity of all this. He's standing next to me, close enough I feel the warmth of his body.

In the background, I hear the door open and close.

"I'm going to be here when you wake up." His voice is soft coming through the speakers, yet it's loud in my ear. "If you tell me to go then, I will. But I'm not leaving until I hear it from you."

There's a soft smacking sound. The flower petal softness of lips on skin. I put my fingertips to my forehead. Has anyone ever loved me like this before? Will anyone ever again?

Norma Jeane looks like she's about to melt into a puddle at my feet. "He's so dreamy. How could you have dumped this guy? Are you nuts?"

Maybe. I certainly feel like I'm losing my mind right now.

"You really love her, don't you?"

I gape at the radio. That's my mother. She's the one who just came into the room.

"Yes, Mrs. Burton, I do."

"Even when she's like this? Even when she's all banged up, and you don't know what's going to happen . . . you still love her?"

"I love her because of who she is, not what she looks like or how her body functions."

Silence. Then, "Huh."

That one syllable says it all. It's beyond my mother's comprehension that love doesn't hinge on what the other person can get from you. Come to think of it, it's beyond mine, too.

"Do you mind if I read to her?" Jake says to whoever else is in the room.

"Not at all," my Aunt Bobbie answers him. "I like it when you read. It gives me hope that things really will turn out okay. Georgie, is that all right with you?"

"Sure. Go ahead."

I see they've done this before. How long has it been? How long have they been sitting by my bed, taking turns watching over me? I hear pages rustle. The rattle of a throat being cleared. Then Jake starts to read.

"The Lord is my shepherd; I shall not want."

He goes on, reading the psalm about a shepherd who looks after the sheep, takes care of them, protects them. It's a spiritual metaphor about a God so big and so great that he wouldn't let harm come to one of his children.

A shiver shimmies its way from my scalp to my toes. I had a very good reason for running away from Jake. And I can't afford to forget it, not for a minute.

I turn down the volume and turn my back on the radio, looking straight at Norma Jeane. "No. I wasn't nuts to leave him."

In fact, it's probably the sanest thing I've ever done.

17

If it hadn't been for Hamlet, Jake and I might never have met.

The library was the last place I wanted to be on a Friday night, especially during winter break, but there I was. As I made my way down the literature aisle, I saw a guy walking toward me from the other end. He was cute, in a bookish kind of way. Like Clark Kent, with dark, slicked back hair and sensible looking glasses. I started to smile, but stopped myself. It was time to focus. I wasn't there trolling for guys. I was there to study. There was no way I was going to fail a lit class. Not this close to graduation.

I stopped in front of the Shakespeare section. So did the guy.

I looked up and down the shelves. So did the guy.

Finally, I saw the book I wanted. I reached out for *Hamlet in Modern English*. So did the guy. But at the last minute he pulled his hand back and looked at me.

"Are you here for the Hamlet book, too?" he asked.

I should have taken the opportunity to grab the book and run. But instead I crossed my arms over my chest and nodded. "Looks like we've got a problem. There's only one copy left."

123

He nodded back and folded his arms, just like me. I learned about that in Intro to Psychology. It's called mirroring. People usually do it when they hope to gain your trust. This guy was going to try and sweet talk me into letting him have the book. I lifted my chin. Fat chance.

"I've got an idea," he said. "How about we share it?"

My chin fell. "Share it?"

"Sure. I really only want to read a few passages. You can check it out and we can go get coffee somewhere and look it over. When we're done, you can take the book home with you. What do you think?"

What did I think? I thought it was one of the more original pickup lines I'd heard. I thought he had one of the most engaging smiles I'd ever seen. I thought a cup of coffee sounded pretty good, especially if I got to look at that face across the table. But I didn't want him to know I was thinking any of those things.

So I played it cool. "I guess we could do that."

"Great. I'm Jake, by the way." He held his hand out.

"Allie." I took his hand and pumped it once, twice. He had a nice handshake, firm, but not bone crushing. And he didn't try to hang on longer than necessary. "Do you have a car?"

He pulled a ring of keys out of his pocket and jingled them in front of me.

"Okay, then. Let's go." I took the book off the shelf, and we headed for the checkout desk.

Of the three Starbucks near the university, he chose the one that was the farthest away. The place was crowded, so I snagged a table while he got our drinks. I opened the book in front of me, but instead of reading it I watched Jake. He slouched a little as he stood in line, hands hanging in the pockets of his jacket. When he got to the front, he smiled at the girl behind the counter and she smiled back. She was clearly flirting, but I could tell Jake was simply being polite. A little zap of happiness skittered up my spine when he took his change and moved on with no further banter, no over-the-shoulder smile. The barista appeared mildly disappointed, which just zapped me again.

When Jake sat down with two tall cardboard cups, I expected him to go straight for the book. But instead, he asked about me. Where I was from, what my major was. How I ended up in a Shakespeare class in the last semester of my last year.

"Desperation. I was going over my transcripts with one of the counselors and realized I was short a couple of English credits. This class was the only one I could work into my schedule. How about you? What drove you to Hamlet?"

He took a drink and set down his cup before answering. "I thought it sounded interesting."

"Really?" I knew there were people who studied Shakespeare because they wanted to, not because they had to. I'd heard of them. I had just never met one before.

He laughed. "Weird, I know. But I had a hole in my schedule and this class caught my eye." He picked up the cup again and swirled around the liquid inside. "So did you."

"I what?" I asked, fiddling with a packet of Sweet 'N Low.

"You caught my eye. I noticed you in class."

I dropped the sweetener and sat up straight, as though someone had pushed a button and made a steel rod shoot through my spine. "Have you been stalking me?"

His eyes got wide, and he put his hand in front of his mouth to keep from spewing coffee. "No, I have not been stalking you. Am I sensing a little distrust here?"

"Maybe. But you're getting away from the point."

He nodded. "I did notice you in class, but I never followed you around outside of it. I sure didn't expect to find you in the library this week."

Not many students hung out on campus during winter break, especially those who had family in the area. But I had my reasons. There was the Shakespeare book. And there were other, more complicated reasons. Reasons I usually kept to myself. "I've got an apartment nearby."

"Ah. You've got a roommate, I hope."

"You hope?" I thought it was an odd thing for him to say, but he acted like it was perfectly natural.

"Sure. I don't like the idea of anybody living alone. Too many weirdoes out there. I'm a big fan of the buddy system."

"I see. Well, you'll be happy to know that I have a very nice, perfectly sane roommate. And a dog who strikes fear in the hearts of men."

"Good." He put his cup to his lips, then lowered it. "Female?"

"No, male." I said as innocently as possible. "You meant my dog, right?"

"Uh, no." His eyes narrowed. "I meant your roommate."

"Yes," I answered with a laugh, "she's female."

"Even better." He crossed his ankles under the table, accidentally bumping my foot. We both pretended like it didn't happen. "Do you have any family in the area?"

I nodded. "My mom and my aunt. I'll see them on Christmas day." He gave me a look, as if he wondered why I wasn't going to spend more time with them, but he didn't want to come out and ask. Normally, I'd let that kind of thing pass. But for some reason, I felt like Jake could be trusted with a little personal information. "My mom and I don't get along all that well. And my aunt's a little under the weather." That was my euphemism for *Aunt Bobbie's in the hospital after a bad reaction to Parkinson's medication and is too weak to spend much time with visitors.*

He didn't dig for more details. Didn't pry. But I could see that he was processing what I'd told him. "That's hard," he finally said.

Empathy. That was interesting. Did he know how I felt? Did he have a similar experience? "What about you? Why are you spending your Christmas vacation in the library?"

He fiddled with his cup. "Money, pure and simple. Otherwise, I'd be on the farm right now."

Now it was my turn to choke back coffee. "You're kidding. You're a farm boy?"

He gave his head a slow, languid nod and slid down slightly in his chair. "Yes ma'am, I am. The family farm sits on three hundred acres just outside of the hickest hick town in Kansas."

I tried to imagine living out in the country, surrounded by nothing but fields and sky and animals. Even though I'd gone through a Laura Ingalls Wilder phase in grade school, I couldn't fathom it. I'd been a city girl all my life, and the thought of anything else, even a farm in Kansas, was sort of exotic and interesting.

I leaned forward, just a little. "Do you miss it?"

He dropped the country boy act and leaned forward, too. He was mimicking me again. "Most of the time, I do. If I could get home for the holidays, I would. But it was a choice between me going home now, or mom and dad coming out here for graduation. There will be other Christmases, but graduation only happens once. Until I graduate from med school, that is. Anyway, it made the choice seem obvious. I was pretty bummed out about it this morning, though." He grinned, and his eyes crinkled behind his Clark Kent frames. "But now, being trapped in California doesn't seem like such a bad thing."

We talked so long that the staff started cleaning up around us. They swept, picked up trash, straightened chairs. Finally, the girl that had served Jake earlier turned the sign around in the window, closed-side out. Cupping her hands around her mouth, she called out through the make-shift megaphone, "Closing time! Sorry, folks, we've gotta go."

Jake looked down at the book. "We didn't read any of this."

"No, we didn't. But I've got an idea." I pushed it toward him. "How about you take it home tonight, and I can get it from you tomorrow?"

127

He dipped his chin, looking at me over the top of his glasses. "Tomorrow?"

I nodded, smiling slowly. "Umm hmm. How do you feel about pizza?"

"I have very positive feelings toward pizza." Jake picked up the book, stood, and held his hand out to me. "It's a date."

18

VINNIE'S DINER

I shake my head, bringing an abrupt end to the film that's been unspooling inside my brain. If I go back to the beginning, it's easy to see why I fell for Jake. He was handsome, charming, smart . . . but in the end, it hadn't been enough. Bigger things stand in our way. There is no way Jake and I can ever be happy together.

"I don't get it," Norma Jeane says, winding a chocolate brown curl around her finger. "If you didn't want to marry him, why not tell him so? Why just leave him hanging and never give him an answer?'

I stare at the brunette waitress in front of me, thinking of the woman she becomes. If Marilyn were standing here right now, she would get it. More than anyone, Marilyn would understand that sometimes it doesn't matter if you love someone. She would understand that sometimes, being in love only makes things worse.

The sad truth is, I *did* want to marry Jake. But I couldn't. And it scared me to death to tell him the reason why.

"I didn't give him an answer because then he'd want to know why I wouldn't marry him. I was afraid if I did that, he might

129

talk me into changing my mind." Or hate me, but I keep that part of the thought to myself.

My answer is firm and direct, so I hope this will be the end of the discussion.

Norma Jeane glances at the radio, then looks back at me, equally as determined not to let it go. "It doesn't sound like that would have been so bad."

She's a tenacious one. But I'm done talking about this. In fact, I'm just plain done. "Enough about me." With my hands on my hips I stroll into the middle of the room. I don't want to talk about myself anymore. I'm sick of picking apart every little piece of my life. Turning slowly, I look at the eclectic cast of characters surrounding me. "What I really want to know is why are *you* all here?"

Vinnie, still sitting in the booth with Joe, shakes his head. "You figured that out already. We're the equivalent of your life flashing before your eyes. Remember?"

I let my chin fall to my chest and roll my head from side to side. I should have known I wouldn't get a straight answer the first time out.

"Yes. I did figure out that much. But what I want to know is, why *this* bunch? I've studied all kinds of trivia about all kinds of people. So why did I wind up here with only dead people?" Lassie barks at me. "And a dog," I add. Then Grimm barks and I huff out an exasperated sigh. "Yes, and you too."

There's a roar in the diner as everyone starts talking at once. The room is full of shouts, exclamations, and denials. Oh boy. Apparently, whoever put this all together hadn't thought to let the people in the room know anything about their own destinies . . . or histories. I'm not sure which one you'd call it.

Either way, none of them know they're dead.

Looking around at the shock and dismay on their faces, I feel bad for hurting them and guilty for dropping this huge bombshell in such an untactful manner. But then I pull myself together. These people aren't real. They can't be. They're all dead, for crying out loud. They ceased to be a long time ago. I know that, so I guess it's time they know it, too.

I lift my hands, flapping them like I'm a bird trying to take off, until I restore some order. "Yes. I'm sorry to tell you, but where I come from, you're all dead."

"I'm not dead," says Joe.

"Neither am I," says Vinnie.

Ah, now we're getting somewhere. It makes sense that Joe and Vinnie aren't dead celebrities, since I don't recognize them from anywhere. So why are they here, and who are they, really? Are they figments of my imagination? Time travelers? Aliens? The by-product of too many nacho cheese Doritos? I want to pursue this thread of conversation, but everyone else presses in around me, cutting me off from the two not-dead people. Ironically, this is the liveliest I've seen this bunch as a group since I got here. They all want to know the same thing: What happened to me? How do I—*did I*—die?

If I hope to get to the truth behind Joe and Vinnie, I'm going to have to deal with the peanut gallery first.

"Okay, okay. One at a time." They back off, giving me a little breathing room. I start with the burly cook standing next to me. "Elvis, you overdosed and died at home in a bathroom."

His usually smiling lips turn down, and he shuts his eyes for a moment. Then he looks back at me, his head cocked. "When?"

"Too young." I reach out and squeeze his shoulder. "August 16, 1977. You were forty-two."

"Everyone wanted a piece of me." Then one side of his mouth curls up, and I see a miniature version of his cocky grin. "Guess I showed them."

He walks away, and I can't help but feel sad for him. Being found unconscious in a pool of your own vomit after falling off the toilet isn't what I'd consider a victory.

I turn to Judy Garland. She can't seem to hold her head still. "You overdosed and died at home in a bathroom."

She doesn't ask when. She doesn't even look surprised. She just walks away, following unevenly behind Elvis.

Norma Jeane grabs my arm. "What about me?"

I've very rarely seen motivation or true emotions reflected in a person's eyes, but Norma Jeane is one of the exceptions. I remember once Aunt Bobbie and I were watching a documentary on Marilyn Monroe. There was a clip of her being escorted out of her home by her lawyer. She'd just announced that she was filing for divorce from Joe DiMaggio. Flashbulbs were popping, microphones were being stuck in her face, and she looked like she might collapse. Her eyes were completely raw, full of pain and disillusionment. They told the whole story.

Looking at her now, a crazy amalgam of the girl she was and the woman she became, she's still the most tragic person I've ever seen. The last thing I want to do is bring more pain to those eyes, but there's nothing I can do about it. The past is the past. It's her history, and she has a right to know.

I lay my hand gently on Norma Jeane's shoulder. "You died of an overdose."

Her eyes are wide. Her hands are clasped together and pressed against her lips so that when she talks, it's a challenge for me to make out what she says. "Please. Please don't tell me it was in the bathroom."

I give her shoulder a squeeze. "No. Not in the bathroom. In your bed. Naked."

She lets out a sigh of relief and backs away. My hand falls from her shoulder and slaps against my side. Huh. I guess dying naked in bed beats keeling over in a bathroom.

Mark Twain waves an unlit cigar in my face. "After hearing the fates of these poor souls it seems they are following a pattern of self-extinction. However, I refuse to believe that I would in any way consider the taking of my own life."

I smile. "You don't have to believe it because you didn't do it. You died of natural causes. A heart condition." But he wasn't a very happy man when he died. Despite all the wit and wisdom he's known for, Twain was deeply depressed after the deaths of two of his daughters and his wife. I've always thought that his was the case of a man truly dying of a broken heart. But there's no point in telling him that.

Einstein runs a hand quickly over his wild shock of hair as he looks down on me. "And in your slice of time and space, how do I meet my demise?"

I tilt my head back a bit, surprised to realize how tall he is. After all his hiding behind the booth, I thought he was a shorter man. "You also had a heart condition."

He nods, accepting the answer, and moves away, hands in his trouser pockets.

There's a bit of a commotion across the room. A man gets up from a stool at the end of the counter and makes his way to me. His dark suit is neat, as is his trimmed beard and mustache and the snow-white crown of hair that starts three-quarters of the way back on his scalp. He's been sitting in the corner the whole time, observing, taking everything in, and occasionally scribbling down notes on a lined yellow pad of paper.

"Hello, Dr. Freud." He seems even taller than Einstein, and I couldn't remember if that's right or not. Trivia was failing me a bit. But I had to tilt my head back to look up at him.

He doesn't return my greeting. Instead, he pinches his chin, looking at me closely. "Very interesting. Of those you've spoken to, three have killed themselves, and two have died of natural causes. Which leads me to wonder, which group will I fit into?"

It's the kind of observation I'd expect from Dr. Freud. "Actually, you kind of fit into both groups. You were dying of cancer, so you asked a friend to help you end it. He gave you three doses of morphine, and you died of an overdose."

"So in point of fact, I did kill myself."

"Yes."

He purses his lips, pulling his mouth to the side as he ponders this revelation, "But only after living with the pain until it became too much to bear."

"Yes. It was an assisted suicide."

He nods, rubs a hand over his bald pate, and walks back to his seat, muttering the whole way. "Interesting. Very interesting."

Yes, it is interesting. But what does it mean? Norma Jeane, Elvis, and Judy . . . they'd all had difficult lives. Although it was never proven that any of them meant to commit suicide, they'd chosen to dull their pain through drugs. It was their attempt to escape from reality and deny the ache of their existence that ultimately killed all of them.

Then there were Twain and Einstein. Neither one had lived an easy life. Twain had lost just about every person he ever loved. And Einstein was so consumed with his work that he was writing a speech in the hospital when he died. But both had continued on, pushing through their suffering. Both had died when it was their time to go.

And finally, there was Freud. He was a mixture of the other five: a man who suffered for years and finally gave in to the pain. When he knew he was close to death and couldn't take it anymore, he decided to end it himself. He made a conscious decision.

I walk over to Vinnie. He's turned sideways facing out of the booth, one elbow on the table, the other at his side, his hands clasped in front of him.

I motion back at the others. "This is all supposed to mean something, isn't it?"

He nods slowly. "Yep."

"You're not going to tell me what, are you?"

His head moves slowly in the other direction. "Nope."

Fine. Then I'll try something else. I look at Joe. "Who are you?"

A glimmer of a smile plays across his lips. "You know me. You just don't recognize me right now. But you will."

He gets up and walks to the front door. As he pulls it open, "Here Comes the Sun" begins playing again. He starts to go outside, but turns around in the doorway and looks back at me. "By the way, my name's not Joe. But you can call me that until you're ready to use my real name. I've been called worse."

19

VINNIE'S DINER

The door swings shut. The music stops. Empty air presses in on me from all sides. The diner feels a little smaller now that Joe—or whoever he is—has gone.

Wait a minute. The diner is smaller. It seems to have shrunk, closed in on itself. And it's a lot less crowded than before. Norma Jeane hovers by the radio. A deep-throated hum rattles out of Elvis as he wipes down the counter, which is now half the size it used to be. Across from him, Freud sits on a stool, intent on scratching his chin. A couple of stools away, Einstein is using toothpicks and sugar cubes to create what looks like a model of an atom. Back in the booth, Vinnie is still sitting sideways, still looking at me, one elbow resting near the open chest.

But everyone else is gone.

My legs wobble and exhaustion pushes me down into the seat across from Vinnie. "Who are you?" I need to know before he vanishes like the rest of them.

He shifts his body until he's facing me again, but he doesn't say a word. Just smiles that irritating it's-for-me-to-know-and-you-to-find-out smile of his. My patience is stretched long and tight, like the strings on a violin. Buzzing fills my ears. Finally, a string in my head snaps with a nearly audible twang

137

"You told me I have more control than I think I do. So okay, I'm ready to take control. Tell me who you are. *Now.*" I pound my fist on the table for emphasis, making the salt and pepper shakers hop.

The last reaction I expect from Vinnie is a smile. But that's what I get. He almost looks proud. "I knew you could do it." He takes hold of the chest by its base and turns it so it's sideways between the two of us. He reaches in, takes out something the size and shape of a baseball card, and hands it to me. "What do you know about this?"

The card has seen better days. It's old and faded with bent, split corners and a tear on one side. It has the Lord's Prayer printed on it in intricate, faded calligraphy.

"It's a prayer card."

"Yes, it is." He taps the top of the cardboard. "You've prayed that prayer before, haven't you."

He's telling me, not asking. "You know I have. And if you know that, then you should also know how long it's been since I prayed it."

He nods. "Yes, I do. But to quote your wild-haired friend, time is relative."

Einstein remains bent over his arts-and-crafts project, but bounces his head up and down, shouting out, "Yes! Yes!"

"Besides," Vinnie continues, "You're not the only one who's ever said that prayer. Or prayers in general."

I look down at the card and then back at Vinnie. "So you're here because I prayed once, a long time ago?"

"Partially. Other people have been praying for you, too." He points toward the radio. "I'm sure you know that Jake's been praying for you since the day you met."

Truth is, Jake's been praying for me since before we met. But that's a whole other story, one that I don't want Vinnie nosing around in. So I just nod.

"And don't forget your Aunt Bobbie. She prays for you every day."

My eyes sting, and my throat tightens. I know my aunt is a praying woman. I've seen her pray before meals, when she's seen an accident report on the news, and for Brad Pitt to win an Oscar. And I know she's been praying for me while I've been in the hospital. But it never occurred to me that I might have been the subject of her prayers on every other normal day. "She does? She prays for me?"

"Absolutely. The morning you left on your trip, she felt a particularly strong urge to pray for your safety. The woman literally fell to her knees and called out to God. I think her exact words were, 'Lord, send your angels to protect her'."

My nose starts to tingle like a thousand little pins are sticking it from the inside. "How do you know that?"

Vinnie's face softens and light spills in from a tiny window high up on the wall by the ceiling. The area behind him is illuminated, making his paper hat glow. George Lucas and all the computer wizards at Industrial Light and Magic couldn't have created a better effect.

He gently pulls the prayer card from between my fingers, turns it around, and gives it back to me. "How do you think I know?"

The picture on the other side of the card is stunning. The background is a mosaic of sun rays hitting a bright stained glass window. In the foreground is the face of a man, beautiful in its calm peacefulness, yet at the same time strong and commanding.

It's a picture of an angel.

It's a picture of Vinnie.

What I wouldn't give for a Vanilla Coke right about now. Or maybe even something a little stronger. Even though the inside of my throat feels like it's been glued together, I force myself to speak. "You're . . . you're an angel?"

He dips his head. "At your service. Guardian angel, first class."

My head is spinning. I've seen lots of angels in lots of movies, and Vinnie doesn't remind me of any of them. Nor does he look like any of the angels I've seen in famous paintings. I've seen tall, Viking warrior-type male angels with flowing blond hair, white robes and enormous wings. I've seen female angels who looked more like fairy princesses than heavenly beings. And then there are the little chubby baby angels wearing strategically placed cloth coverings and perched on clouds. But not a single angel I've seen represented in any form of media wore suspenders and a banana boat hat.

"Am I your project?"

One side of his mouth tilts up. "What do you mean?"

"Like in that old Jimmy Stuart movie, *It's a Wonderful Life*. The angel, Clarence, couldn't get his wings until he helped out George Bailey." I try to peer around past his shoulders, but they're pressed against the back of the booth. Surely if he had wings, I would have noticed them by now. "Is that it? Do you need to get your wings? Is that why you're helping me?"

His shoulders shake up and down. He's actually laughing. I've amused my angel. "No, I don't need any help in the wing department. But thanks for asking."

I'd like to know more about the wings. Does he really have them? Are they hidden? Do they only come out when he needs them? But I'm pretty sure he'll just dodge those questions. Better to move on. "So I'm not your project?"

"No. But you are my assignment. I'm here to take care of you, Allie."

Now I have to laugh. "No offense, Vinnie, but if that's your assignment, I think you need more training."

Rather than taking offense, he leans forward, clearly intrigued by my reasoning. "How so?"

"Hello! I was in an accident!" I start gesturing wildly, pointing behind me toward the front door. "I rolled my car in the middle of the desert. Remember the EMTs? They pulled my body out of the wreck. And now I'm nonresponsive and in some hospital."

"I remember," he says with a nod.

"So if you're supposed to take care of me, why did you let all that happen? Isn't your job as a guardian angel to keep me *out* of danger?"

"You would think so, wouldn't you?" He leans back with a sigh. "Most people think exactly like you do. But when you're in my line of work, there's only one rule: The Boss knows best." He jerks his thumb toward the ceiling. "See, we all get to glimpse different parts of the picture. You know your part, which is usually pretty small and exclusive to what directly affects you. We angels have a slightly bigger view of the picture. We see what's necessary to do our jobs. But The Boss, well, he sees the whole thing. What you'd call the big picture. And when he tells us to do something, we do it, even if we don't understand why."

Sounded like a thankless job. "What if you don't want to do it?"

A frown contorts his lips. "We have free will, just like you do. We can make a choice. There have been those who decided to do things their own way. But it didn't end well for them." He shakes his head and the corners of his mouth tip back up. "Personally, I've never considered disobeying orders, because I know The Boss's way is perfect. My way would just mess things up."

"So you're saying you weren't supposed to prevent the accident?"

He points his finger at me like he's aiming a gun. "Exactly. You assume the most important thing to worry about is your physical safety, but it's not."

141

"Then what is?"

"Your soul, Allie."

I swallow hard. "My soul?"

"Yes. Your body is temporal. It's going to die one day, no matter what I do. But your soul, that's eternal. My assignment is to be with you now and walk with you through this journey you're on."

So that's it. That's what all of this is about. A chuckle bubbles its way through my throat. Now that I know the truth, my ordeal must be coming to a close.

Vinnie drops his hand to the table and reaches out, like he's going to touch me, but then he pulls back. "I know you've been through a lot already, and I know you probably think it can't get any worse. But you're not done yet."

My joy is replaced by a choking sob. Figuring out who Vinnie is should have signaled the end of all this craziness. But now he's telling me there's more. And it sounds like it's not going to get any easier. What could be worse than what I've already gone through?

When I'm finally able to speak, my words come out in a pathetic whimper. "I don't want to do this anymore."

Now he does touch me. He takes the card from my fingers, sets it next to the chest, and wraps both his hands around mine. "You have to hold on, Allie. It may not make sense now, but this is something you've got to walk through. I'm here with you. And even though you can't see him, so is . . ." he hesitates, then grins, "Joe."

I glance at the front door, then turn back to Vinnie. "Joe. Is he an angel, too?"

Vinnie's grin twists, and he seems slightly appalled. "No. You're not thinking big enough."

I open my mouth, but before I can ask anymore questions, the door swings opens. My heart thuds once, twice. I really want it to be Joe, but the music that starts to play tells me it can't possibly be him. I've heard that guitar riff before. For a couple of months, four guys moved into the apartment next to Sandy and me. They were real metal heads, and we got used to hearing their music thumping through the paper-thin walls at obscene hours of the day and night. This particular song had been one of their favorites.

AC/DC. "Highway to Hell."

Panic constricts my chest. From the radio, an unfamiliar voice says, "Her heart rate's a little high."

I grab Vinnie's arm, clutching at the fabric of his shirt sleeve. "What do I do?"

His expression is calm, strong, exactly how he looked on the prayer card. "Face it. It's all you can do. You've got to face it eventually."

I look back to the front of the diner. The shape of a man, dark and shadowy, fills the doorway. I turn from him and look at the chest on the table. There's more stuff in there, I know it. There are things in my past we haven't gotten close to yet. I don't want to examine anything else, but it could be the lesser of two evils. It could buy me some time before I have to face whatever waits for me in the doorway.

I make my choice. Maybe Vinnie's right. Maybe I can't escape whatever's going to come at me next, but I can postpone it.

I plunge my hand into the chest, fishing around until my fingers close around something hard and round and cold. I don't have to look at it to know what it is. Memories slam into me, pushing me against the back of the booth seat, making me gasp for air. I squeeze my eyes shut. I feel myself hovering, swirling in midair, on my way to another memory. Another part of my life I don't want to revisit.

Maybe this wasn't such a good idea after all.

20

*B*ACK AT THE UNIVERSITY—*ONE MONTH EARLIER*

The swirling stops.

I open my eyes. I'm standing on the sidewalk in front of a pizza place. The door opens, and I watch myself—the me from just a month before—walk out.

"Seriously?" Jake asks the question as he holds the door open for me . . . for Allie.

"Yes." She walks past him, tip-toes around something questionable on the sidewalk, and heads in the direction of her apartment building. That's where Jake left his car. "Victor Garber played Jesus in the movie *Godspell.*"

Jake shakes his head. "It's hard to imagine Jack Bristow breaking out in song."

She laughs and so do I. Even now, I remember having the same reaction when Aunt Bobbie and I watched the *Godspell* DVD at her house. With his big seventies fro, red suspenders, striped pants and Superman t-shirt, Victor Garber as Jesus was a far cry from the deadly serious, emotionally withdrawn spy daddy I'd gotten to know watching DVDs of *Alias.* "Just goes to show," Aunt Bobbie had said, "you never can tell about people."

"You never can tell about people," Allie says to Jake. "Did you know he was the only guest at Jennifer Garner and Ben Affleck's wedding?"

"Really?"

"Yep," She says with a nod. "And he officiated."

Jake's eyes get a little bigger. "Is that legal?"

She shrugs. "Sure. He got a license through the internet, and they were good to go."

"Amazing."

"Not really. Lots of people do it."

He laughs. "That's not what I meant."

"What then?"

"You. You're amazing."

A weird, snorting kind of laugh bursts out of Allie. It's a noise I try never to make in front of people. But at this point in our relationship I was comfortable enough to let him see that much of the real me. "Yes, it's amazing all the worthless information I've crammed into my head." I sometimes have trouble with the sevens and the nines on the multiplication table, but I can tell you who won the 1950 Oscar for best picture—*All About Eve*—without blinking an eye.

"It's not worthless. Hey, you're an award winner. Don't forget that."

That's the thing about Jake. He is unusually positive and always goes out of his way to build me up. Sure he's human and must have faults, but I have yet to discover any. Sometimes, he seems too good to be true.

He's certainly too good for me.

I had so wanted to ask Jake to come on the Vegas trip with me, but there was no way I could. Early into our relationship, Jake told me he was a Christian and asked if I was. Of course, I told him yes. I liked hanging out with Jake, and something told me he wouldn't date a girl who didn't share his beliefs. I wasn't lying to him, not really. I'd been baptized as a child, although

I think that was less for spiritual reasons and more for the ceremony. My mother must have loved posing for pictures as she held her chubby little baby who was being swallowed up by the heirloom christening dress. As for God, I believed there was one out there somewhere. He just hadn't done me any favors.

So I played the part, even going to church with Jake on the Sundays when I couldn't think fast enough to come up with an excuse to stay home. As far as he was concerned, I was the model Christian girlfriend. Inviting him to share a room with me in Sin City would have blown my cover for sure.

Allie sighs. "It's so weird, having everything end at the same time. In three weeks, there'll be no more Shakespeare, no more trivia, no more late night pizza, no more . . ." Her words trail off, but I finish the sentence for her. *No more you.*

"That sounds pretty final. I hope you're not saying good-bye to everything you discovered in college." Jake puts his arm around her shoulder, hugging her to him as they walk. The gesture pulls her slightly off balance and she does a funny little foot-crossover step to right herself.

She puts her arm around his waist in response, sliding her thumb lazily into the belt loop of his jeans. "No, not everything." She pauses dramatically, then adds, "I just broke in my LBU sweatshirt. You know I'll be hanging on to that."

He laughs and kisses the top of her head.

Walking along behind them, I almost melt through the pavement. The feelings from that night wrap around me, as strong as the first time I experienced them. All I'd wanted to do was live the rest of my life in that moment, on that street, feeling as safe as I did right then. But I knew, like everything else that had ever been good in my life, it wasn't going to last. The only reason Jake and I stayed together as long as we did was because I knew there was a clear end in sight. In a few weeks, he'd go back to Kansas to spend the summer on the farm with his parents before heading to med school in the fall.

I'd either move on to my dream job or to some boring corporate gig. And we'd never see each other again.

At the corner, Allie and Jake go in two different directions, pulling apart from each other. She gives him a questioning look. He smiles and holds his hand out. "Want to take a walk in the park?"

She hesitates, starts to frown, but then smiles and takes his hand. "Sure."

They walk down a footpath, then around a corner, passing a few other people. One man makes an incongruous picture, his beefy hand wrapped around the skinny pink leash of the minute Pekinese prancing around his feet. Allie bites her lip as they walk by, not wanting to burst out laughing and embarrass the fellow.

"That little guy would make a great midnight snack for Grimm," Jake says.

Allie bumps her shoulder against his. "Grimm wouldn't lay paw on him. He's a lover, not a fighter."

Jake laughs. "For a non-fighter, he sure has a lot of scars."

"That just proves he had a tough life before I found him. Grimm's a survivor."

"That he is." Jake pulls Allie tighter against his side.

They don't say anything else until they get to an empty bench. Jake sits, pulling her down with him. She snuggles in against his shoulder, ignoring everything and everyone around them.

"My parents are coming out for graduation." Her fingers splay out on his chest. I know she's not really paying attention to what he's saying. She just likes being so close to him.

"That's nice," she mumbles into the soft cotton of his t-shirt.

"I want them to meet you."

She jerks away, pushing against his chest, eyebrows raised and mouth slightly open.

When he said that, warning sirens had gone off in my head. Why did he want me to meet them? You didn't introduce a temporary fling to your parents. I certainly had no intention of introducing him to my mother, even if she did show up for the graduation ceremony.

Now, Jake looks at the woman sitting next to him, his face full of hope and excitement and something else. Something that makes my stomach take a free fall.

"Your parents? I thought they couldn't get off the farm."

"That's why I was alone at Christmas, remember? So they could afford to come here for graduation."

"Oh, yeah. Well, that's great."

The skin between his eyebrows wrinkles, and he takes both her hands in his. "Allie, I hope you know by now how important you are to me. The last few months have been pretty incredible."

She looks down, swallows, then looks back up at him. "I feel the same way."

It was the right thing to say, the expected answer. But as I hear myself speak the words aloud, I know they are true. Jake wasn't just a fling. He wasn't just someone to have fun with. We'd connected, and I was happy with him, at a deeper level than I had ever thought I could be.

"But meeting your parents . . . that's a little scary."

He laughs. "I have the least scary parents in the world. Besides, they're going to love you."

"Oh yeah? How can you be so sure?"

"Because I love you."

Even though I've lived this before, that phrase still robs my lungs of breath. I've had guys tell me they love me, but only as a precursor to getting me into bed. After that, they rarely stuck around for more than a week. But it was okay, because we were playing the game, saying the words to pave the way for a physical release. I never expected, or wanted, anything more from them.

But Jake was different. Jake and I had kissed—a lot—but he had never pushed for anything else. It had been five months of wonderful, no pressure friendship. There had been times when

I thought about loving him, how it would be so easy to fall into that place. But every time I pulled myself back, because I knew deep down how wrong we were for each other. So to hear him say it, knowing that he meant it, and knowing how much I wished I could say it back . . . well, it was new territory for me.

Jake looks into Allie's eyes and smiles. "You're the answer to my prayers."

Whoa. No guy had used that line on me before.

Allie blinks hard, sending tears oozing out between her eyelids. "What?"

Chuckling to himself, Jake nods his head. "It sounds crazy, I know. But when I was a kid, my mom used to tell me that God had big plans for me, including the woman I would marry. She encouraged me to pray for my wife, even though I hadn't met her yet. So I did. I prayed that God would protect her, keep her safe, and that I'd know her when I saw her."

Allie tilts her head, and a tear skitters across the bridge of her nose.

Watching them, I shake my head furiously. He couldn't mean that. It was all wrong.

Jake cups her cheek in one hand and wipes the tear away with the pad of his thumb. "The day I saw you in the library, I knew. Before we even started talking, I knew it was you."

I feel myself being sucked into the scene, being drawn closer to the couple on the bench. I pull back, refusing to relive this moment. But it's already taking me over. A geyser of emotions erupts within me at the same time. Joy, excitement, uncertainty, anger, euphoria, fear . . . they press on me from the inside out, trying to escape from my pores, making every cell pulsate with the effort. They soak up the liquid in my body, leaving my mouth dry and parched. My eyes, once overflowing, are now dry as the California desert and burn as if I've been staring into the sun.

And now I'm there, sitting on the bench, feeling the warmth of his hand on my face. I press my cheek into his palm, begging for things to stay this way. Willing him not to say anything else that will move the moment forward. But I'm mute, unable to utter a single syllable. I just stare at him.

He pulls his hand from my face, leaving my cheek cold and exposed. He dips his head, reaches into his pocket, and pulls out something. It glints under the glare of the street lamp.

"Will you be my answer to prayer? Will you marry me?"

He holds out a ring. A small, simple ring. But that's not what I see. Instead, I see a gold cross hanging from a thin, broken chain. I see Ethan's face pressed too close to mine. Smell Ethan's sour breath, feel the stubble of his cheek scraping against me. I hear Ethan's voice in my ear, "I've been waiting for this since the first day I saw you." Had I been Ethan's answer to prayer, too?

I can't breath.

"Allie, are you okay?"

I shake my head. Jake is close enough to touch, but far away, too. Everything has gotten so dark. The colors are saturated, almost inky in their density. Something catches my eye. A movement off to the side, near a tree. I turn my head, but it's so hard, as if I'm up to my ears in quick-drying cement. I try to focus, but everything's blurry. Finally, I make out the figure of a man. He's wearing a long, black coat like someone straight out of *The Matrix*. His hair hangs in dirty blond strings to his shoulders. His face is dominated by sharp angles and sunken cheeks. His lips are pulled back in some kind of a grotesque smile. Everything about him makes me think of a carnivore ready to pounce.

I turn back to Jake, extending my hand, stretching my fingers as far as I can. "Help me." I try to scream, but only a whisper escapes.

What little light that manages to leak from the street lamps throws odd shadows all around us. Jake reaches for me, but he's moving away, getting smaller and smaller as though he's being pulled into a vortex until he finally disappears altogether.

The park begins to melt. The trees droop, dissolving slowly and dripping like rain to the ground. The grass pools forest-green and slick around my feet. The bench gives way beneath me and I fall on my back, sinking into a torrent of green-brown goo. The stranger stands over me now, looking down, his hair hanging like a curtain around his face.

From somewhere far in the distance, I hear the sound of scratchy voices coming through the radio speakers.

"Help! We need help, here!"

"We're losing her."

"Hang on, Allie!"

The last voice is familiar. Who is it? Jake? Vinnie? I can't tell. The stranger jerks his head at the sound, then looks back at me. He holds out his hand. "I can help you."

His voice doesn't match his face. It's sweet and beautifully rich. He almost sings the words as he speaks. Maybe I misjudged him. How can I be scared of someone with a voice like that? Maybe he really does want to help me.

Then he leans forward and something in his eyes snaps and glows, like a fire bursting to life, and I see Ethan all over again.

I need help. I try to shout but my mouth won't work. All I can do is call out in my head. *No!*

A sound like a trumpet rips through the night. At the same time something hurtles at the stranger, and the air around me echoes with a screamed proclamation. "You can't have her!"

Vinnie.

The stranger snaps up to his full height, eyes to the sky. Another body swoops in, moving so fast it's little more than a blur. I can't make out his features, but I know it's Vinnie.

The two collide with a deafening crash and a blinding flash of white light.

An unearthly scream pierces my ears.

Relief and fear clutch me simultaneously. The stranger is gone, but I can't feel anything. Not even the beating of my heart.

21

Sounds.

The steady *blip* . . . *blip* . . . of a heart monitor.

The familiar squeak of rubber soled shoes.

Is all of me actually in the hospital now?

No. Wait. The crackling of the speakers.

Someone is calling my name.

"Allie. Allie."

My back is cold. My hands, palms down with fingers spread out, are cold. The surface I'm laying on is hard and cold. I'm on the floor, not in a hospital bed. I open one eye, then the other. The shape of a man leans over me, silhouetted against the overhead lights.

"Welcome back."

I gasp in relief. It's Vinnie.

He hunkers down beside me and helps me maneuver into a sitting position. "Do you want to try standing up?"

I shake my head, a little too hard. Sparkles of light dance in front of my eyes like luminescent dust motes. I scoot back until my spine makes contact with the side of the booth and I let myself slump wearily against it. I wrap my arms around my upraised knees, hugging them tight to my chest. Even that effort is almost more than I can handle and my breath comes in shallow, short bursts.

I blink a few times. My vision clears, and I'm able to focus on my surroundings. The diner has been reduced to one small room. There's the booth I'm leaning against, the radio, the front door, one stool and one end of the counter. Everything and everyone else is gone.

"Where are the others?"

Vinnie lowers himself all the way down and sits cross-legged on the floor opposite me. "You don't have enough strength to have them around anymore." He reaches out and pats me on the arm. "Even if you did, they can't go where you're going."

I let my forehead drop against my knees. Maybe I don't need them, but I want them. I want Elvis to bring me some disgusting sandwich and twitch his eyebrow at me. I want Norma Jeane to wiggle into the booth, lean forward with her elbows on the table and her chin in her hands, and beg me to tell her more about the boy I sent away. I want to talk to them and ignore the strange nightmare place I've just come from.

"Are you ready to talk about it?"

My head jerks up, and I glare at Vinnie. Am I ready? How could anybody ever be ready for *this*? As a matter of fact, no, I'm far from ready, but I get the feeling my time is running out. It's taking all the strength I have to sit upright, to hold up my head. The realization hits me like a fist to the gut: I may die here. So I nod and hope Vinnie's going to lead me to the end of this insane maze.

"Good." He rests his elbows on his thighs, steepling his fingers together. "Why are you so afraid to love Jake?"

You've got to be kidding. "Jake? Why do you care about Jake? I want to know who that creepy guy was, and why the park turned to soup. And did I just almost die?"

"None of that matters until you deal with this first."

I pound the heels of my hands into my forehead, fighting the urge to scream. Why is my love life so important? Dropping my hands, I brace my palms on the floor and lean toward Vinnie. "I'm not afraid to love Jake, I just don't want to marry the guy. Okay? Case closed. Can we move on now?"

"No."

"Why not?"

"Because you're lying."

I swear, then clamp my mouth shut and bite down on my lower lip. It's probably not a good idea to swear around an angel. But instead of calling down some kind of punishment, Vinnie just laughs. This should make me feel better, but it only succeeds in stirring up a new wave of frustration. "Oh, so angels think swearing is funny?"

He shrugs, still grinning. "Not all angels, but I do. If you people could hear yourselves. You don't even understand what some of the things you're saying mean. Which brings me back to you." All signs of amusement are now gone from his face. He's my serious guardian angel again, intent on doing his job. "There's more to this situation with Jake than you want to admit. You've run from it, hidden it, even lied about it, and it hasn't done you any good. It's still eating away at you. If you don't bring it out into the light and face it, you can't move past it."

Panic rises up, threatening to choke me. For a moment, the lights in the diner become even dimmer. They flicker, the bulbs threatening to burn out and leave me in the dark, but then they stabilize, coming back on with a steady glow.

I can't. I can't do what he's asking me. I can't go to that place. It's bad enough that I have to live with the memories, but what will Vinnie think when he finds out? Right now, he sees me as the innocent girl, the victim in a life full of hard knocks and not very nice people. But he doesn't really know me.

Or does he?

I venture a look into his eyes. They are strong, kind, patient. There's nothing there to make me think he'll be shocked by anything I tell him. Is this just another of those times when he already knows exactly what I'm going to say, but he makes me say it anyway? I have the urge to swear again, but I rein it in this time. Vinnie can be exasperating, but if he really is an angel—and it's as good as any explanation I can come up with—then I should be able to trust him.

"Do you have any idea how it feels to be told you're the answer to someone's prayer?"

Vinnie's head tilts to the side, and I know what he's thinking. *You must be kidding.*

"Stupid question. You're an angel. That's your job, right?" I take in a breath, but it catches in my chest and I have to start over again: breath out, breath in, breath out. Like that old shampoo commercial: lather, rinse, repeat.

I shake my head and remind myself to stay on track. "But I'm different. I can't possibly be the answer to Jake's prayer."

"Why not?"

"Because I've done things . . . things no good Christian girl would do. At least not any girl Jake would fall in love with."

"Sounds like he fell in love with you," Vinnie says, his voice soft and low.

"That's only because he doesn't know. He wouldn't love me if he knew everything about me. And then he'd understand that this whole thing about me being an answer to his prayer is just a big mistake." I put my hand to my forehead, pinching the skin hard.

Vinnie leans forward. "But what if you are the answer to his prayer? What if God does mean for you two to be together?"

I drop my hand. Let my head fall back against the side of the booth. "That's even worse. Don't you see? He prayed that God would protect his future wife. He asked God to keep her safe. But if I'm the answer to his prayer, then God fell down on the job. He didn't protect me." The volume of my voice escalates until it reaches a shrill pitch that sounds almost manic. "God didn't keep Shooter from hitting me. He didn't keep Ethan from manhandling me. He didn't keep my mother from hating me. He didn't stop me from—"

The thought dies there, caught halfway between my brain and my lips. I can't make myself say it. So I do what I always do. What I've done my whole life as a way of surviving, living through the pain. I pretend it doesn't exist. "Don't you see, Vinnie? Either way, Jake gets hurt."

"So do you."

My throat feels like there's a fist lodged inside and I can barley swallow past it. "That's okay. I'm used to it."

Vinnie reaches out, takes one of my hands in his. "What did you do that was so terrible? What could make you think you don't deserve to be loved?"

I look up at the table. The chest still sits there, its top gaping open. There's probably some memento inside, some token to start me down this road. But I don't need it. I've revisited it so many times on my own that I know the way by heart. It's a place I go in my dreams, in my nightmares. A place I've never really been able to leave.

I pull my hand away from Vinnie.

"I killed my daughter."

22

SOUTHERN CALIFORNIA—SIX YEARS EARLIER

I'm staring down into a toilet bowl.

What in the . . . I look around, and my stomach lurches. I'm on the bathroom floor of my mother's house. No. I don't want to live this day over. A wave of nausea surges through me in a cold rush, and I swing my head back around.

Here I go.

"Allie, are you all right? What's going on in there?"

I hug the toilet seat, heaving up the rest of my breakfast while my mother alternates between yelling and pounding on the door. My heart is thudding a beat of its own, hard and deep, like the rhythm of a funeral dirge. Or a death march.

"I'll be out in a minute. I—" My sentence is cut off prematurely by another rush of nausea, and I hang my head over the disgusting contents of the porcelain bowl. This can't be happening. It can't. Not again.

But it is.

I reach blindly behind me, waving my fingers about until I feel the edge of a bath towel. Pulling it down, I bury my face in the soft terry cloth, but the smell of fabric softener makes me retch again, so I toss the towel in the bathtub. I stand up and flush the toilet. Then I close the lid and sit on top of it, taking a moment to calm down, to breathe more steadily.

The incessant pounding on the door makes it impossible to relax. So does my mother's screaming. "Open this door right now, young lady. I want to know what's going on!"

I wish I had the guts to scream back at her, to tell her "No, you really don't want to know!" But instead I call out, "Just a second." After quickly washing my hands and brushing my teeth, I unlock the door and slowly pull it open.

My mother is standing so close to the door that she's practically inside with me before I can get out of her way. She looks wildly around the room, as if she might find my secret hiding in a corner. Then she looks at me, looks at my stomach, looks back up at my face. I keep waiting for her to say something, but now that no door stands between us, she is weirdly quiet. When she finally does speak, her voice is flat and cold.

"You got yourself pregnant, didn't you?"

It's a rhetorical question, of course. She obviously doesn't need an answer. But I give her one anyway. "Yes."

Even though it's the answer she'd been expecting, I see her crumble a little. Her eyes slam shut, she turns her head, puts her hand to her mouth, sucks in a deep breath. I expect her to make that sound of hers, the shrieking wail signaling some terrible tragedy that's fallen in her lap. But she doesn't. Instead, she blows the breath out in a sharp gust, and when she looks back at me, she's her usual collected, hard as stone, self again.

"How could you let this happen?"

How could I let it happen? I want to say it wasn't all my fault, that there was another person involved, but that would just make it worse. Bad enough I'm in this situation, there's no point in reminding her how I got this way. It's useless to tell her that I've seen her with so many men and heard her talk for so long about women using their bodies to get what they want, that sex seemed like the natural next step when I got into a serious relationship. And I don't dare bring up the fact that not once over all those years did she talk to me about birth control or what happened after the sex was over. Nope, all that stuff is off limits. So I say the only safe thing I can think of.

"I'm sorry."

"You're sorry? You're *sorry?*" Her brittle laugh ricochets around the room, bouncing off the bathroom walls, colliding with the mirror, slapping me in the face. "Do you think that makes it all better? Do you have any idea how badly you've screwed up this time?"

A month ago, when I realized I might be pregnant, my first thought was to go to my mother. On the heels of that thought was one that made a lot more sense: *Are you nuts?* So I'd kept it a secret, praying for a period that didn't come, hoping the nausea was just a flu bug that wouldn't go away. But it got to the point where I couldn't ignore it anymore. So this morning at breakfast, I tried to tell her. I started to, but I had to break off in midsentence and run for the bathroom. Apparently I'd told her enough, because when the puking started, she put it all together.

Now she stands in front of me, hands on her hips, eyebrows, pulled down, her lips in a hard, thin line. She's an Amazon warrior ready to do battle. This is exactly why I was afraid to say anything to her. Yes, I messed up, but I'm scared. All I want right now is a little sympathy. A hug, a smile . . . anything. But I'm not going to get it from her.

"Yeah, Mom, I'm nothing but a big screw up." Hurt and anger propel me from the bathroom, and I manage to push past her. I'm heading for my room when fingers wrap around my arm just above my elbow. She pulls me to a stop and jerks me back around to face her.

"We're not done yet."

"Yes we are." I snap at her, getting right in her face. She wants to talk about this? Fine. Then she's going to have to listen to what I have to say, too. "I'm pregnant. I took a page out of your book and used my body to get what I wanted, only I ended up with a little something extra. It's not the way I planned it, but it's done and now I've got to figure out a way to live with it."

She doesn't respond to the insults I just tossed her way. Instead, she inclines her head in my direction, looking at me like I'm mentally challenged. "No, you don't."

I take a step back, pulling as far away as I can with her still holding on to me. "What do you mean?"

"Just what I said." She squeezes my arm tighter. "You made a stupid mistake, but at least it's early enough to take care of it."

The implication of what she's saying inundates me. Like I've been pushed into a swimming pool full of ice water, I'm sinking, going in over my head. "You mean have an . . . an . . ." I can't bring myself to say the word. Because I've thought about this. A lot. Heck, it's been impossible to think of much else since I realized I was pregnant. And I realized that this is my shot. This is my chance to have someone in my life to love and to love me back, unconditionally. I've played out a thousand scenarios in my mind, and I've already bonded with this child. To think of terminating it . . . I just can't.

But she can. "An abortion. Yes."

An odd, strangled cry comes out of me before I can stop it. It's the kind of thing that would elicit sympathy from most mothers, but it just gets mine more riled up.

"Oh, don't go getting all self-righteous with me." She rolls her eyes to the ceiling and lets go of my arm, flinging her hands up in the air. "It's a perfectly legal, sensible solution."

Maybe for her it is, but not for me. It's not what I want. In a defensive gesture that's pure reflex, I wrap my arms over my stomach. "I'm keeping her."

She wrinkles her nose. "Her?"

I nod. "The baby's a girl. I know she is."

My mother shakes her head, her expression close to disgust. "You're making a big mistake, thinking of it as a baby. This whole thing will be a lot easier if you accept the fact that it's not alive yet."

It seems odd that she's thought this through so thoroughly, especially since she just found out about what's going on with me. Then a thought comes to my mind, and I'm hit full force with another wave from the ice water pool. "You've had one, haven't you?"

A muscle in her jaw twitches. She swallows. "We're not talking about me."

No, but in her nonanswer, I discover the truth. My heart aches. She's had one. For all I know, she's had more than one. How many brothers or sisters might I have now if she hadn't taken advantage of this perfectly legal, sensible solution?

Lifting my chin, ever so slightly, I repeat myself. "I'm keeping her."

"Is that so? Well if you do, you can kiss college goodbye. And where are you going to live? How are you going to support yourself? You're going to need a job, and don't think I'm going to help you with . . . with . . . that." She points at my stomach like I'm holding a sewer rat in my hands.

I don't have a good answer for all her questions, but there's one thing I do know. I don't want her anywhere near my baby. "I don't need your help. Cody and I will be fine on our own."

Her eyes narrow. "Cody. Does he already know about your condition?"

My condition. Like I have a terminal disease. "I told him yesterday."

It had been terrible. When I showed up at his house the day before, he thought I was there to talk about the prom. It goes without saying he was more than a little shocked when he found out what I really had to say had nothing to do with fancy gowns, corsages, or whether or not to rent a limo.

"Did Cody tell you he's willing to drop his college plans and get a full-time job so he can support you and junior?"

We hadn't talked about details. We hadn't talked much at all. After the initial panic in his eyes faded, he'd said, "Baby, we're going to work this out. Don't worry." Then he'd taken me in his arms. Kissed me. And we ended up in his bed, back in the same spot where our little problem had been created in the first place. So no, I can't say for sure what Cody's plans are, but I know that he loves me, loves our baby, and that he's going to take care of us.

"We're going to do whatever it takes." I'm surprised how cool my voice sounds. It bolsters me with a newfound confidence.

Mom nods her head, slowly, assimilating the facts. "I see. Well, let me fill you in on how life really works. When a man says he'll do whatever it takes, he means he'll do whatever it takes to make his life easier. Your prince of a boyfriend is probably going to offer you the same solution I just did."

I take another step away. My resolve begins to crumble as tears push and burn against the back of my eyes. "No. He wouldn't do that."

Once more, she ignores me. "And even if you do manage to snag him and get him to marry you, it won't do you any good in the long run. One day, he'll wake up and realize that his life isn't what he wants it to be and he'll run out and leave you. And while he's creating a great new life for himself, you'll be tied down at home with nothing but a screaming baby, a broken heart, and a miserable future. Is that what you want?"

Tears cascade from my eyes, rolling down my cheeks. Some flow, hot and salty, onto my lips. Some barrel down my chin and drip onto the floor. I've always accepted that I don't have the kind of close relationship with her that some girls have with their moms, but I've never been able to figure out why. It certainly wasn't because I didn't try. No matter what I did there was always a wall between us. But now, standing there, hearing her predictions for my life, I really see my mother for the first time. And everything becomes achingly clear.

I was her stupid mistake. The thing that changed her life from the promise of what it could be to the reality it had become.

Of course she doesn't love me. She never wanted me in the first place.

23

I'm walking up the front steps to Cody's porch, but I'm not quite sure how I got here. The time since I ran away from my mother and out of the house is a blur. But now, as I push my finger against the illuminated plastic doorbell button, a sense of calm settles over me. I'm finally able to breathe without feeling like a rope is wrapped around my neck. This is a safe place. A place where I'm loved. I'll show my mother. I don't need any help from her. Cody and I will get through this, together.

I'm about to push the button again when Cody pulls the door open. When he sees me, his face is blank at first, but then he smiles. Not the full out, sexy smile that makes me want to throw my arms around him, but the polite, reserved smile he uses on teachers and other kids' parents. His eyes dart back and forth before he speaks. "Hey, Allie. What's up?"

What's up? That has to be the worst choice of words ever. Does he not remember what I told him yesterday? "I need to talk to you. About the—"

"Sure, yeah."

Okay, so he does remember. I expect him to step aside so I can pass by, but he just stands there, one hand on the doorknob,

167

the other on the opposite side of the doorframe, turning himself into a human barricade. "Can I come in?"

He looks around again, glances behind him, then gives his head a sharp shake. "You'd better not. My parents aren't home. Let's sit out here."

Like a yellow light flashing at a school crossing, a warning goes off in my head. He's never cared before if I was inside when his parents weren't home. In fact, he always preferred it that way. My legs wobble beneath me as I move to one of the white wicker chairs on the far side of the porch. Cody sits next to me, his hands clasped in a tight fist in front of him. I've seen Cody look a lot of different ways: sexy, angry, self-assured, sensitive . . . but never like this. He looks nervous. I put my hand on his balled up fingers and he jumps.

"Are you okay?" It's something he really should be asking me. Are you okay? What can I do for you? Is there anything you need? But instead, I'm the one checking on him. I try to cut him some slack. After all, I've been agonizing over this for two weeks. He's only known about it for a day.

"Yeah," he answers. "I'm just a little freaked out about the, well, you know . . ." He waggles his head in my direction.

"Yeah, I know. I'm freaked out, too. At least you didn't have to endure the wrath of my mother."

His eyes grow wide, looking twice their normal size. "You told her?"

"This morning."

"What did she say?" His voice is tentative. He's just as afraid of her reaction as I was.

"That I'm a screw up. Of course, I already knew that." I give a harsh laugh and wait for Cody to put his arm around me, to offer me some kind of comfort. But he doesn't. He just keeps looking at me with that scared, wide-eyed stare. So I just keep talking. "You're not going to believe what she suggested."

I didn't think it was humanly possible for eyes to get any wider, but his do. "What?"

"She wants to take me for an abortion."

"Thank God!" A huge burst of air rushes from Cody and his whole body seems to deflate. His eyes become slits, his shoulders sag, his head drops into his hands. He rubs his palms over his face, saying something I can't understand. When he pulls himself together and sits up, his old smile is back. Only I don't find anything sexy about it anymore.

"Cody?" It's all I can say. I can't even put into words what I'm thinking: that I don't know the person sitting next to me now, sitting back in his chair, ankle crossed over one knee, acting so relaxed it looks like he's getting ready to watch a football game.

He shakes his head and lets out a low whistle. "Boy, that was close, huh?"

Close. Like he dodged a bullet. "What do you mean? I thought . . ."

He looks confused. "You thought what?"

I feel small and stupid. "I thought we were going to keep the baby." I thought you were someone else.

His foot slides off his knee and hits the floor with a hard thud. Now he looks horrified. "Whoa, hold on. I never said I wanted to keep it."

It. He doesn't want to think about her as a person, either. "You said we'd work it out."

"Sure, and your mother just offered you the perfect solution." He takes my hand and pats it. It's an awkward gesture, like he's forgotten how to touch me. Or he's afraid to touch me. "Look, if you kept it, it would mess up both our lives. Why should we have to pay forever because of one stupid little mistake?"

What part of it was stupid, I wonder? Making love to me? His insistence that we'd be okay without a condom *just this once*? Or my being careless enough to get pregnant?

I can't look at him. Instead, I stare straight ahead, past the lawn his father obsesses over, past the flower bed his mother's so proud of. It's a beautiful day. There are kids out in their yards, playing with balls, running in circles for no other reason than the joy of falling on the grass in a dizzy heap. In front of one house, a young man blows soap bubbles through a tiny plastic wand. Beside him, his wife claps and their chubby toddler swats at them, shrieking in delight each time one bursts. Everything around me blurs except for that little family. They stand out, crisp and brilliant, vivid in their happiness. That was supposed to be us: Cody, the baby, and me. We were supposed to work this out by becoming a family.

"You—" The words stick in my throat. I swallow, blink hard, and start over. "You said you loved me."

"I do, babe. You know I do. But I'm too young to be tied down. There's a big old world out there, and I don't know what I want yet." He's got both my hands now. He stands up and pulls me to my feet with him. "Listen to your mom. It's the perfect solution. You know, you're lucky to have someone like her to take care of things."

Yeah, I'm the luckiest girl alive. A tear leaks out of the corner of my eye, igniting a burst of anger in my chest. I'm so tired of crying. I swat the tear away.

Cody tries to smile. "Hey, we knew we'd be going in different directions once college started. But we had fun while it lasted, huh?"

He moves closer, pulls me up against his chest, and even though I'm furious with him, even though he's essentially just told me that we're not a couple anymore, I let him kiss me. Because even though I hate him, I still love him. And there's a small part of me that expects him to realize he's made a mistake and to be the man I thought he was.

But when we pull apart, the relief radiating from his face is all I need to see. It's finished.

I remember every step of the walk home. Not my surroundings so much, but the journey I went on in my mind. I would have this baby. I couldn't count on my mother, but maybe Aunt Bobbie would help. And if she didn't, it wouldn't matter. I would raise her by myself. It would be hard, but we would persevere. It would be the two of us against the world. I even gave her a name: Penelope. I would call her Penny, for short, and use her first and middle names—Penelope Roberta—when I needed to be firm. Which wouldn't be often, because Penny would be such a good little girl. My spirits started to lift. I imagined us playing together, going to the zoo, to the beach, Disneyland. I pictured her first day of kindergarten and how proud I'd be when she graduated from high school. For about a mile, I talked myself into believing that I could be a successful, happy, single mother.

Then I turned onto my street. I walked up to the house. The same house I'd lived in with my mother ever since she married Ethan. The house she'd gotten from him in the divorce based on her promise to keep her mouth shut about his lecherous ways. I thought of my mother. How she hated me because I'd messed up her life. How much she would hate Penelope for adding to her grief. I really would be totally on my own.

The happy thoughts I'd had before changed, morphing into a more realistic image of the future. There would be sleepless nights. Times when she was sick. Times when there wasn't enough money to pay the bills. And I would continue to be alone, because no man wanted to take on the responsibility of a ready-made family. I'd had enough proof of that in my lifetime.

I thought I could raise this baby on my own, but how could I know? How could I know I wouldn't end up exactly like my mother? How could I know I wouldn't resent my daughter for keeping me from living the life I wished I could have had?

How could I know that I wouldn't end up hating my baby?

The weight of my situation pushed down on me, bending my will, as I trudged up the front steps.

In the end, I couldn't take the chance.

24

Vinnie's Diner

I stare down between my knees at the black and white checked tile floor. There was tile like this in the clinic. At the time, I thought it was weird. It was the kind of thing that belonged in a restaurant or a beauty salon, not a medical facility. There were also paintings of huge flowers on the walls, as if some interior designer thought the overly brilliant buds would distract everyone and make them forget why they were there. But the colors where so bright and glaring, they almost hurt your eyes. I couldn't look at them for long. So I looked down.

"I counted the number of tiles on the floor."

Vinnie scoots closer. "What floor?"

I drop one hand and run my thumb nail along the seam between two squares. "In the clinic. While my mother checked me in and filled out the papers, I counted the tiles. There were thirty black ones and thirty-one white ones." I look up at Vinnie, but I don't see him. I look right through him. "That's a strange thing to remember, isn't it?"

"I don't know," he says. "Sounds like it was the only way you had of removing yourself from a situation you didn't want to face."

173

"Maybe." I couldn't tell you what any of the people looked like in that office, but I'll never forget the floor. Or those darn ugly pictures.

My shoulders sag and I drop my forehead on one of my raised knees. I don't want to talk anymore. I want to close my eyes and sleep, forget any of this ever happened. I want to wake up in my own bed, back in a black and white reality like Dorothy in *The Wizard of Oz*, and realize this multi-colored circus was all a crazy dream.

But Vinnie keeps telling me I'm here for a reason, so I know he won't let me run away from this newest revelation.

"You had the abortion, then?"

I roll my head back and forth, letting the coarse denim fabric of my jeans grind into my skin. "Procedure," I mutter to the floor.

"What?"

I lift my head, but I still don't look at Vinnie. Instead, I stare over his shoulder across the room at a poster for *Gone with the Wind*. What I wouldn't give to be Scarlett O'Hara right now. She'd just say, "fiddle-dee-dee, I'll think about it tomorrow," and move on to something else. But I've been doing that most of my life, and it hasn't done me any good.

"They called it a procedure," I answer him. "No one ever used the word abortion."

The whole thing had been very neat and quick. The staff was friendly in a detached kind of way. I could tell they'd said the same things to any number of women, too many times to count. Like telemarketers with memorized scripts, they tried to put some feeling behind their words, but the spiel still came out flat and empty. When the doctor said "You'll just feel a little pinch," it reminded me of the time I had a tetanus shot and another time when I had blood taken. The lab techs always said the same thing—you'll just feel a pinch—and it always hurt worse than that. So I knew better than to believe this doctor.

It wasn't horrifically painful, but he still lied. I felt more than a little pinch.

After it was over, they put me in a recovery room. Only it didn't look like a room you'd recover in. It looked more like a little lounge. Instead of a bed there was a brown leather chaise. There was an overstuffed chair next to that and a television on a table at the end of the room. A counselor—her word, not mine—got me settled, gave me orange juice, turned on the TV, and left. In a few minutes, my mother walked in. She stood in front of me, looked from my head down to my toes and back again. Then she nodded and sat in the chair beside me. Not a word passed between us. We just stared at the figures flashing on the TV screen. I have no idea what was playing.

"How did you feel afterward?" Vinnie's voice breaks into my thoughts, pulling me out of that room and back into the diner.

"Fine. I spent the day in bed. Mom treated me a little nicer than usual. She brought me soup." She brought me ice cream, too. The way she was acting, you'd have thought I had my tonsils removed. It was just the beginning of the denial. I sigh. "The next day it was like nothing had happened. She went to work. I went to school. Everything went back to normal."

"I don't think that's true."

My eyes burn. "Are you calling me a liar again?"

Vinnie shakes his head. "No. I just think you're denying how deeply affected you were by the situation."

I suck in a breath, try to steady myself. He nailed that one. I had thought the hardest part was making the decision, having the procedure—no, the abortion. Might as well call it what it was. I owe my daughter that much.

But in reality, the hardest part didn't come until days later. That's when I took a good hard look at the situation and realized what I'd done.

"I knew it was wrong. In my gut, I knew. And it wasn't something I really wanted to do. But Cody had abandoned me.

My aunt had just been diagnosed with Parkinson's, so I didn't want to dump anything else on her. My mother was so insistent, and I . . . I was scared. Scared and totally alone."

A deep sadness shadows Vinnie's face. He reaches for my hand, squeezes it. "Child, you were never alone. How I wish you'd known that."

Being that he's an angel, I figure he means God was with me. If that's true, I never felt it. And I'm certain God didn't walk into that clinic with me.

Vinnie looks up and to the side. When he turns back to me, there's a smile on his lips. "Even in the dark times and in the places you'd never expect, you've never been alone. Just like you're not alone now."

I want to believe him. I want to believe there's someone in the world who loves me, even when I'm at my most unlovable. I want to believe there's something or someone who can fill this awful, empty void at my core. But I can't.

My mother and I didn't stop going to church after she threw Ethan out. We stopped going a month later when the rumors Ethan started about me began to spread. The gossip and finger pointing was finally so bad, we couldn't stand up under it anymore. I've seen firsthand how church people judge and turn on each other. How can the God they represent be any different?

How could Jake be any different?

"I've been let down by so many people, Vinnie. But this was something I did to myself. I made the choice to sleep with Cody. I let fear get the best of me, and I went to the clinic and asked them to kill my child. This was my own fault." I'm pounding on my chest now with the flat of my hand. My heart aches, as if someone's slowly tearing a Band-Aid from it, fraction by tiny, painful fraction. "I haven't been able to make peace with what I did. How could I expect Jake to accept me if he knew?"

Vinnie points at the radio. "Listen."

A buzzing whine comes from the speakers. Then a voice.

"I know why she pushed you away."

I shut my eyes against what I'm hearing. How can Aunt Bobbie do this?

"You do?" Jake sounds surprised and relieved at the same time. "Why?"

There's a sad sigh before she continues. "She didn't want to tell you about her past. She was afraid if you knew, you'd hate her."

"Hate her? Why? What did she do that was so terrible?"

"I can't tell you."

"But—"

"No. That's up to her. If . . . when she wakes up, she can tell you herself. I just thought you should know, it's not because she doesn't love you. If anything, she loves you too much."

The only sound I hear for a while is the blipping of the medical equipment. What are they doing in there?

"She's a new creature." Jake's voice is low. Certain.

"What?" Aunt Bobbie's voice is barely a whisper.

"I don't care what she did. It's over. It's passed away. I've got some pretty unpleasant stuff in my past, too. But none of it matters. What matters is who we are today."

I feel something warm against my ear, then hear Jake's whispered voice. "Why didn't you know that?"

The radio hums again and the volume lowers until it's little more than a buzz in the background.

"It sounds like Jake can handle the truth."

"He thinks he can. But he still doesn't know *me*. You heard him." My finger trembles as I point it at the radio. "He still believes I'm a sweet Christian girl. What's he going to think when he finds out I've been pretending all this time?"

Vinnie lets out a sigh so deep it could have come from his toes. "The truth is, I don't know how Jake will react. To any of it. And neither do you. But you need to give him a chance."

I move my head in a tired, dejected shake. "And what if he turns out to be like all the others?"

"Which others?"

"The church folks who talk about forgiveness, but don't know what it really means. Or worse."

Vinnie cocks his head to the side. "What could be worse?"

I turn away, dropping my gaze to the floor. There, under the table, I see the photos that I discarded earlier. Stretching out one arm, I anchor them with my fingertips and push them across the tile to Vinnie. "What if I tell him everything and he says he still loves me, but then it turns out he's just like these guys?"

He picks up the pictures, fans them out, nods. "The stepfathers and boyfriends."

"I never knew my real father so I can't say about him, but the rest of them . . . not one of them liked me. And they sure didn't love me." There had been so many times I had tried, in my simple, childish way, to win them over: smiles, hugs, being overly polite, staying out of their way. I even risked losing a finger feeding food off my own plate to Shooter's evil dog. But none of it had worked. They all walked away. My mother cried because they left her. But what nobody seemed to realize was every time one walked away from my mother, he walked away from me, too.

I clamp my teeth together, locking my jaws against a wave of emotion. I force myself to inhale deeply, hold on to my composure. I will not cry over any of them.

"You had a difficult time with these men, that's for sure." Vinnie holds up the two halves of the picture of Ethan. "But this one was the worst of all, wasn't he?"

I nod, not trusting myself to speak.

By the time Ethan came around, I'd convinced myself that I'd only get hurt if I trusted another man. So I held back. I didn't want to like Ethan, or to give him a chance. But Ethan wouldn't give up. He was sweet and funny. He paid attention to me. Slowly, he wormed his way into my affections until he became my great hope. By the time they got married, I truly believed he loved my mother and me in an honest, pure way. This one, I convinced myself, was real. This one would last forever. I loved him with my whole heart, and I trusted him. But everything he pretended to be was a lie.

"I trusted Ethan. And when he . . . when he tried to . . ." I can't say the words, but Vinnie nods, encouraging me to go on. "When that happened, he destroyed that trust."

My teeth sink into the inside of my bottom lip. It's getting harder to breath, to talk. Vinnie reaches out to me again, puts his hand on my arm. Warmth radiates through my body, and a sense of relief floods over me. Finally, he's going to lead me through this. Maybe I'm not as alone as I thought I was.

"You didn't just lose your trust in him," Vinnie says softly.

"No."

"You were determined never to trust another man again."

"Yes. But then Cody . . ." My composure cracks. A sob slips out, but I swallow it back. "I was so stupid. I knew better, but I thought he loved me." After Cody, I never let myself trust, never let myself love. I used men, just like they used me. Period.

"But Jake's not Ethan. He's not Cody. He's not any of those men."

"I know. I didn't mean for it to happen, but I fell in love with Jake. I really love him. And if I were to trust him and then find out that he was no different than the others . . ."

It would kill me.

"So you rejected him before he could betray you. Just like you've done with every other man since Cody."

Vinnie's sad words break me. I let the sobs come. They roll out, convulsing through the space between us. He reaches out, gathers me in his arms, and holds me while I cry.

I don't know how long we stay like this. Seconds? Minutes? In this unorthodox place, it could be days. But rather than sap more strength from me, each sob energizes me. Each tear builds me up. And when no more tears will come, I edge away and sit back. He hands me a square white handkerchief with a fancy "V" embroidered in one corner. I wipe at my eyes and nose. Then I look past him, blink, and take in the room.

"The diner got bigger." There are two stools at the counter now, and the lights seem a little brighter.

Vinnie pats my arm. "You've faced the thing you fear the most. You're stronger now."

I glance up at the table. The chest is gone. I settle my head back against the booth and take in a strong, clear breath. We did it. I have no secrets left, nothing more to hide. The journey is over. Each one of my muscles begins to loosen, and I slump into a wonderfully relaxed state.

BAM!

The front door bursts open with such force that I jump where I'm sitting, muscles once more tightly clenched, on the alert for what's coming next. There's no music this time. There's just a tall man with long, pale hair and a long, black coat, standing in the open doorway. His face is not as gaunt as before, but I recognize him right away.

It's the stranger from the park.

He claps his hands together in a slow, staccato beat. The sound reverberates through the diner like a twenty-one gun salute. "What a touching, sickeningly sweet scene this is."

Vinnie is instantly on his feet, turning himself into a barrier between me and the man. "You are not welcome here." My affable guardian angel bristles, growling like a wolf protecting his territory.

The man puts one hand to his chest, his long fingers splaying out over his heart. "Vincent, you hurt me. You really do. I know better than to break the rules." He folds his fingers into a fist and raps it against the door frame. "Behold, I stand at your door and knock."

The tone of his voice is as sweet and enticing as it was in the park, but the cadence, the rhythm, is mocking. I lean around Vinnie's leg to get a better look at him. He keeps knocking his knuckles on the wood, but it's me he's paying attention to. His eyes lock onto mine and his lips curl.

Vinnie reaches down and puts his hand on top of my head. "What do you want, Ba'al?"

A shiver convulses through me. I've heard that name before. And not just in the Bible story about the showdown between the prophet Elijah and the priests of Ba'al. This is the kind of obscure fact that can trip up your average trivia buff, which is why I've made it a point to study the worship practices of ancient cultures.

The facts I've accumulated about him flip through my mind like flash cards. Seen by some as a god, Ba'al worship included ritual sex acts meant to arouse him into bringing rain to the land. The early Christians called him a false god, and therefore a demon. And there were those who believed he held a place of power in Hell, a kind of duke with legions of demons under his command. Of course, I'd always considered the stories to be myths, holding no greater weight than Mother Goose rhymes or fairy tales. But now, here he is. And I'm almost in the same room with him.

He doesn't answer Vinnie's question. He just keeps knocking, the same monotonous beat, and staring at me.

Vinnie repeats himself, louder this time. "What do you want?"

Ba'al's fist stalls against the door frame. His eyes burrow into mine, cutting through me like a flame thrower cutting through ice. Finally, he unfolds a bony finger and points it straight at my chest.

"I want her."

25

He wants me?

There's a demon in the doorway, and he wants me?

I look up at Vinnie, my guardian angel, my protector. I wait for him to hurl a lightning bolt at Ba'al, or make the ground open up and swallow him, or turn him into a pig.

Something.

Anything.

But Vinnie does nothing.

Ba'al squats down, and his coat pools around him in a big, black circle. Even though he's still across the room, we're at eye level now and I feel like he's right in front of me. He shoots a quick glance at Vinnie, then looks back at me. "I bet you're wondering why angel-boy isn't doing anything to stop me."

Yes, I am. But I'm not comfortable nearly being in the same room with a demon. I certainly don't want to speak to one. So I nod instead.

Ba'al sneers. "He's not trying to stop me because he can't."

He's got to be lying. I look up at Vinnie. "Is that true?"

Vinnie frowns, but doesn't take his eyes off Ba'al. "Right now, yes. It's true."

183

I take hold of the corner of the seat and pull myself to my feet. Ba'al rises, too. I grab Vinnie's arm. "But you're my guardian angel. You're supposed to protect me. Can't you just smite him or something?"

Vinnie turns slightly, still keeping his body between me and Ba'al. "There are rules, Allie. He can't come in here, but I can't keep him from talking to you."

"And he can't stop you from leaving with me, either."

Ba'al's statement shocks me out of my fear of talking to him. "Why would I go anywhere with you?"

He levels a finger at Vinnie. "Because there are things going on right now, outside of this diner, that your protector hasn't told you about. Things you deserve to know."

"You're lying," I bark at him. Vinnie wouldn't betray me. I know he wouldn't.

Ba'al shrugs. "That's always a possibility. There's only one way you can know for sure." He looks confident as he turns his eyes to Vinnie. "Why don't you ask him?"

I almost don't. I'm more afraid of asking this question than just about anything else I've done since I walked away from my rolled car. Because if Ba'al is telling me the truth, Vinnie's answer could change everything. But I can't leave it alone. I have to know.

"Is what he's saying true?" I ask Vinnie. "Is there something you haven't told me?"

Without even a second of hesitation, he answers me. "Yes."

A hiss escapes from between Ba'al's clenched teeth. "Ooo, that's gotta hurt. Here you are, thinking you finally found someone you can trust, an angel no less, and he turns out to be just like all those other lying sacks of . . ." The words trail off, and he smiles smugly. He puts a hand on either side of the door frame and hangs his body as far in as he can without actually stepping over the threshold. "Turns out the angel is just like the rest of the men you've known."

His words attack me like a terrible poisonous snake wrapping itself around my heart and squeezing, squeezing, squeezing it tight. After all the time I've spent here with Vinnie, everything I've gone through with him beside me, I had been sure that I could trust him. But now . . .

Vinnie lays his hand on my shoulder. "Don't listen to him, Allie. He's a master at manipulating the truth to suit his own purposes."

Ba'al shakes his head, making his hair sway listlessly, resembling dry stalks of wheat in a parched field. "There you go again, Vincent, casting aspersions on my character. She doesn't have to take my word for it." He zeroes in on me again. "Listen for yourself, and make your own decision."

He jerks his head toward the radio and the volume blares.

"What are you saying?" I recognize my mother's voice. It's tight with strain and frustration. I know how she feels.

"The situation isn't good." A female voice. I don't recognize this one. Probably a nurse or a doctor. She continues speaking, her words peppered with complicated medical jargon. From that and her authoritative tone, I decide she's definitely a doctor. "She's gone into cardiac arrest once already. If it happens again, we might not be able to bring her back."

I hear a gasp and a whimper. Mom's not the whimpering type, which means Aunt Bobbie's in the room, too.

The doctor clears her throat. "Then there's the spinal injury."

Spinal injury?

"We won't be sure how severe that is until she comes out of the coma."

Coma? "Just how far did I roll my car?" I shout into the speakers, hoping again that somehow, someone will hear me. Of course, nobody does. I don't even manage to garner a comment on my heart rate.

Ba'al jerks his head again and the volume becomes a whisper, an indistinguishable background noise like the whining of a mosquito. "Amazing what a difference a shoulder belt makes."

I back away from the radio, squeezing my eyes tight. I'd been able to afford my car because it was old, and therefore cheap. I also bought it from a private party, not a dealer, so it was somewhat lacking in safety features. It only had lap belts. Jake told me more than once that I should get new belts put in, but I never wanted to spend the extra money.

"So now you know," Ba'al says in his sing-song way. "You may never walk again, and you could have brain damage. Seems like your good friend *Vinnie* should have shared all that with you." He spits out Vinnie's name like it's something dirty that he can't wait to get out of his mouth.

I feel a little dirty myself. Vinnie should have told me. I should have heard news like that from him, not from someone like Ba'al. Even though Ba'al looks better than he did in the park, I know he is sleazy, slimy . . . evil. I know it. But he's telling me what I want to hear. He's sharing information with me, which is more than my angel did.

Ba'al pushes himself away from the door frame and rubs his hands together. "I'm done waiting here. Alexandra, your future is bleak. But I can help you. I can tell you what you want to know. And I can make your earthly pain go away." He pauses, giving that time to sink in. "When you're ready to talk, come outside. I'll be waiting for you."

He leaves. The door swings shut behind him. The diner is once more quiet, peaceful. Vinnie turns around, giving me his full attention. His shoulders are pulled back, and his lips are set in a thin, straight line. This is the most serious he's been since we met.

I look past him to the closed door. Now that Ba'al's gone and I don't have to look him in the face, it's a little easier to think. Maybe talking to him isn't such a bad idea. It's not like I'm going to give my soul to the guy. I just have to get the information I need.

I look from the door, to Vinnie, to the door, and back to Vinnie again. So. I have a choice to make. I can stay here in the diner with my angel and hope that everything works out.

Or I can go outside and maybe learn everything I want to know. From a demon.

26

"I never lied to you."

At Vinnie's earnest words I give him my full attention again. Sadness and resolve are reflected on his face. I get the feeling he disagrees with what I'm going to do, yet he's not going to try and stop me. Some friend he is.

I cross my arms hard over my chest and blow out a sharp breath. "You may not have lied outright, but you've been keeping things from me. Why didn't you tell me about the injuries? Why didn't you tell me how bad it is? Why did I have to hear it from . . . from . . . him?" I can't bring myself to say his name, so I just point at the closed door.

Vinnie takes a step closer, holding his hands out palms up. He inclines his head toward me, his forehead pinched in a frown. "Did you really listen to what he said?"

"Of course, I did." I frown back at him. "He said I might have brain damage and I might never walk again."

"That's right, Allie. *Might.* He doesn't know about any of those things. Not really. He's making up worst-case scenarios and using them to scare you. He doesn't know the truth, and neither do you."

"And that's what's scaring me. I don't know!" I scream at him, even though we're practically nose to nose. "Why can't you understand that? Why won't you tell me what's really happening to me?"

"Because I don't know, either!"

I take a step backward, shocked both by the volume of his comeback and the force of this new revelation. "You don't know? You're an angel. How can you not know?"

His shoulders droop slightly. I can tell he's sorry he yelled at me. "Because angels aren't omniscient. We don't know everything."

I push my hair back from my face, totally confused by what he's telling me. "What do you mean you don't know everything? You've been practically reading my mind since you pulled me out of the car."

"That's because I needed to know those things in order to help you. I only know what I'm told. And I haven't been told what's going to happen to your physical body."

Great. He works on a need-to-know basis. He's like some sort of one-man *Mission: Impossible* unit. I look up at the ceiling, rolling my head from one shoulder to the other. "So you get your info from higher up on the food chain. Tell me, does the tape automatically self-destruct, too?"

He lets my sarcasm slide by. "There's a reason for everything that happens, including the things you don't know about yet." His voice has returned to its regular soft, modulated tone.

"And the things that don't make sense," I add.

He nods. "And the things we don't like."

Vinnie's face freezes. He stuffs his hands in his pockets and takes a step back. His chin almost touches his chest and his lips are pursed tight. I think he realizes he's told me too much and wishes he could take it back.

I squint at him and take a step toward him, once again closing the distance between us. He's not talking about me now. He's talking about himself.

"You don't want me to go out there, do you?"

He hesitates, then says, "No."

If I'm not supposed to go outside, there's no reason for him not to stop me. In fact, it would be his duty. The only reason for him to be unhappy about me going out there is . . .

He's following orders.

"I have to go out there, don't I?"

Vinnie nods.

I look over at the door. It's just an innocent rectangle of glass with a shiny silver handle. But it's the only thing standing between me and something evil. Something I know I have to face, whether I want to or not.

I was thinking about going out there when I thought I had a choice. But now that I know I have to do it, I'm not so sure. Because that means there's something else I have to walk through, and I really don't want to do it with a demon.

"Why?" I end up sounding like a spoiled little girl, but I don't care. I put my hand up and rush on before Vinnie can offer me any platitudes. "Please don't tell me it doesn't matter. Because it does. It matters to me. I need to know why your God would send me out there with a demon."

Vinnie lifts his head. He pulls his hands out of his pockets. The defensive posture has vanished. "Did you hear what you just said? *Your God.*"

The pain in his eyes is so sharp it cuts to my core.

"You've never made a choice, Allie. You've been introduced to the Lord, you've been told about His love and His goodness. And you've experienced it, whether you want to admit it or not. But you've pushed Him away time and again. That distance you feel isn't because He's left you, but because you've built a wall around yourself to keep Him out."

I am hollow inside, empty. The dull ache of my denial has turned into an acute pain. Justifications and excuses fight to get out, but I keep my lips shut tight against them. Now isn't the time to argue. For once in my life, I need to shut up and listen.

"God isn't sending you out there," Vinnie continues, pointing toward the door. "The actions and choices you've made during your life have brought you to this place. You're at a crossroads, Allie, and you can't hide anymore. Your life literally hangs in the balance, and you have to make a choice. You have to pick a side."

"Fine. I choose God." I cringe as soon as the words leave my mouth. Even to my own ears, my answer is too flippant.

Vinnie shakes his head. "It has to come from your heart. And your heart is still carrying so much grief that it's blinding you to the truth." He reaches into his pocket and pulls out a miniature version of the chest that used to be on the table. He places it in the middle of his flat palm and holds it out to me, but I recoil.

"I thought I was done with that. I went through everything in the chest."

"There's one thing left, but it's the biggest thing you have yet to face."

I want to knock the little box out of his hand and refuse to look in it. Instead, I reach for it, slowly, tentatively. I wrap my fingers around its sides and carefully lift off the top.

It's empty.

I look more closely, but don't see anything. I turn it upside down and shake it the way a kid looks for money inside a Christmas card, but nothing falls out.

"I don't understand. There's nothing in here."

"That's because it's in here." Vinnie puts two fingertips on the spot above my heart. "In here, you're still a little girl who was hurt and betrayed by every father figure in her life."

The box falls from my hand and bounces across the tile with a clatter. Vinnie ignores it. So do I.

As if I'm looking at the pictures again, my mind sees every "father" I've had over the years. Every one of them disappointed me. Some had devastated me. And the person that should have given me comfort never did. A thought coalesces, one that has poked at the corners of my mind in the past, but that I'd never dared acknowledge. "The men were awful. But you know the worst part? No matter how bad they were, my mother was always sad when they were gone. And she blamed me for driving them away."

Vinnie folds me in his arms again, but this time, my eyes are dry. There was a time, when I was younger and full of ridiculous optimism, when I would have cried over my mother and her disregard of me. But the more times I saw the same story played out again and again, the harder my heart became until it was finally encased in a solid shell. I won't let her hurt me anymore, and I've stopped feeling sorry for her.

"You and your mother aren't so different." Vinnie's breath is warm against the top of my head. "She was once a scared little girl, too, and she handled her pain in the only way she knew how."

It's hard to imagine my mother ever being scared of anything. But maybe that's part of what I have yet to discover.

Something stirs in my chest. And I know. It's time to go. I've heard of people saying they had to face their demons. I could never imagine that I'd be facing mine in such a literal way.

I push gently away from Vinnie. "I've got to go now."

Vinnie nods, but he holds onto my wrist with one hand. "You were right. I really don't want you to go out there. But I know it's something you need to do. Remember, you're not alone."

"I'll remember."

I walk to the door. My fingers are wrapped around the handle when Vinnie calls out to me. I look at him over my shoulder.

"Ba'al can't keep you from coming back in here. He'll lie to you, tell you he can, but he can't. He has no power over you except what you give him."

"Okay." I nod. Smile. "I'll remember. I promise. And I'll be back."

"It won't be easy," he says. "But when you need help, call on The Name."

My smile slips. I'm not sure what he's talking about. "You mean call you?"

Vinnie shakes his head. "Nope. You're still not thinking big enough."

27

OUT OF THE DINER

I blink my eyes, just once, but that's all it takes.

Vinnie's gone.

The diner's gone.

I'm standing in the middle of a run down drive-in theater. Rows and rows of evenly spaced poles, their white paint chipped and speakers hanging on either side, remind me of the rows of crosses at Arlington National Cemetery. Warm air gusts past me, sending an empty popcorn bucket scuttling across the cracked pavement. There's a squeaking sound in the distance, and I turn my attention to the old play area at the base of the giant screen. Several swings in the set are swaying. One is broken, the seat hanging uselessly by the end of a rusty chain.

A tall man stands off to the side, hands on his hips, staring intently at the playground. It has to be Ba'al, but he's changed his appearance again. He's wearing the same black duster, only it seems newer, crisper. His long hair, which now looks clean and silky, is pulled back from his face, giving me a clear view of his profile. The cheeks are filled out and the sharp planes and angles of his face have been replaced by classic, fine features. He looks almost pretty, like Orlando Bloom in *The Fellowship of the Ring*.

Prickles of electricity pierce my body, as though every limb, every piece of me had fallen asleep and the blood is now rushing back to my skin, trying to break through to the surface. I'm overcome with a strong desire to run away, but my legs are locked in place. There's nowhere for me to go anyway. This constantly changing being has information, information I need, and I can't leave until I get it. But he doesn't strike me as the kind who'll answer a direct question. I decide to make him think I'm starting to trust him, just for a while. Just to get what I want.

"Why do you look so different?"

He laughs but doesn't bother to look at me. "Vincent and his kind bring out the worst in me. But now that you and I are alone, I can be myself."

I've seen so many different versions of him, I have no idea which one is real. But before I can counter his claim, he starts shaking his head, still looking out at the sad playground.

"Such a shame, isn't it?"

"What's a shame?"

The corner of his mouth twitches slightly. "How people let things fall into disrepair. There was a time, not so long ago, when this place was full of life." He lifts his hand and I see the images of ghostly people, carrying ghostly snack trays, walking to ghostly vehicles. He drops his hand, and the images float away, wisps of fog weaving their way through the pole graveyard. "But this place outlived its purpose. And when something's not useful anymore, it's ignored."

He turns to me, his now icy blue eyes burrowing into mine. "It happens with people, too. The more trouble you are, the less convenient it becomes to be around you, then . . ." His voice trails off, and he shakes his head, giving me a smile that he probably intends to come across as sympathetic. But it doesn't quite get there. To me, it just looks condescending. "Well, I guess you'll find out all about that for yourself soon enough."

I take a step away from him, trying to pull my thoughts together, trying to hold on to what Vinnie had told me. "You don't know that," I spit out. "You don't know what's really going to happen to me."

He crooks a pale, perfectly shaped eyebrow, tilting his head to one side. "Oh, don't I? Do you have any idea how many people I've seen in your condition? People who fight and scrape to stay alive, determined to conquer the odds. And they try. Oh, they really try. At first, the excitement of the challenge is enough to carry them through. They see it as something they need to conquer, the mountain they need to climb. They've got their loved ones by their sides, you see, and they can feel all that love and support seeping into their bones. It's truly inspiring."

Why is he saying these things? The words he's using should be encouraging, but his tone turns them into something else. He sounds like someone who's about to say "I told you so." I don't think I'm prepared for where this conversation is going.

He puts a hand to his mouth. A high pitched, almost maniacal laugh leaks out from between his fingers. "I'll never forget this one young woman. She was about your age. If memory serves, and it usually does, she was in a car accident, too." He looks up and taps his lips with his fingers, as though searching for the memory of her.

"She fought so hard, and her husband was right there. He spent every night and every day in the hospital until the day she was discharged. He swore he'd always be there to support her, help her. He meant it, too. At first, he did everything. He helped her with her physical therapy. He fed her. He bathed her. He changed her catheter bag. When the bag leaked in bed one night and made a mess of both of them, he swore under his breath, but then he kissed her on the forehead and cleaned it up. And while he cleaned, he thought of a time when being woken in the middle of the night would have meant intimacy with the woman that used to be his wife. That night, he grieved her loss and blamed the tears on the fumes from the ammonia cleaner." The longer he speaks, the louder he gets, and the pace of the story intensifies. Now he's sporting a full blown smile. "Do you want to know how the story ends?"

I don't respond. I don't want to know. But he goes on anyway.

"It ends with him hiring someone to take care of his wife. It ends with him finding more and more reasons why he has to be away from the house. Away from her. It ends with him confiding in a special friend, someone he knows from work. Someone who understands him, who supports *him*, who makes him feel like a man again and who takes away his pain. It ends with him leaving his crippled wife for a very beautiful, very successful, very able-bodied woman."

In my mind, I see an image of myself lying in a bed, twisted and helpless. And I see Jake walking away from me and into the arms of a beautiful, strong, healthy woman. I know Ba'al's baiting me, trying to make me think the worst. I need to resist him, to ignore the poison that's seeping through my body. But I can't help myself. "What happened to the wife?"

"Poor thing." He makes an unconvincing *tsk tsk* sound and shakes his head. "She was devastated, of course. All she could do was lie there in that bed, tortured by thoughts of what her husband was doing with his new girlfriend . . . things she'd never be able to do again with anybody. Finally, she convinced the one friend that still came around every now and then to help her end it all."

"You mean . . ."

"She killed herself. Pills. It was quick and then her suffering was over." His black eyes soften to dark gray and take on a far off, almost wistful quality. "Looking back, it would have been better if she'd just died in the car, but this was the next best thing."

My legs tremble, threatening to dump me into a heap at Ba'al's feet. I've already heard Jake say that he's going to be with me to the end. He's the kind of man who would try to do the right thing. I can see him, leaning over me, taking care of me. Terrible images assault me: him spooning food into my mouth, struggling to dress me, bathe me, change me. What right do I have to tie him to that kind of life? And how can I bear to live that way?

Ba'al points at me. "So you see, I can tell you exactly what will happen if you go back."

My mind is a tornado of whirling feelings and emotions. There are too many thoughts in my head, and they're all pushing so hard to get out they've become trapped. There were questions I wanted answered but now they've become a blur. Something about my mother. Things I need to remember. Things Vinnie told me. I'm trying to grab hold of them, but something else makes its way through and snaps to the front of this jumbled mess. Something Ba'al just said.

If?

"If I go back? Are you saying I have a choice?"

He contorts his face into an overemphasized look of surprise. "Of course you have a choice. Didn't your angel tell you that, either? That's usually one of the first things he spouts off about. The one he answers to is big on people making their own choices." His lips pull back in a sneer, and for a second I get a glimpse of the face I saw back in the park. "Free will," he growls, "is yours."

I put before you life and death. Choose life.

The words, strong and sure, cut through the haze in my head. Where did that come from? I look around for the owner of the voice I just heard, but I don't see anyone else in the drive-in.

It's impossible for Ba'al to miss my searching looks. He frowns. "What are you looking for?"

He must not have heard it. What was it Vinnie said? Oh yeah, angels aren't omniscient. Apparently, neither are demons, which is good. I don't plan on giving this one any more information than he already has.

"Answers," I say, hoping to throw him off track. "I'm looking for answers." An image of my mother pops up in my memory, and I regain some level of clarity. She has something to do with this. "What do you know about my mother?"

His eyes narrow but he remains silent. I think he must be trying to decide whether or not to answer my question. "Georgia Burton," he finally says, letting the name fall lazily from his tongue. "She and I go way back."

My head jerks in an involuntary shudder. It can't be good that he's so familiar with her. But I need to know more. "Tell me what you know about my mother."

His eyes are almost dancing now. "Are you sure you want to hear this? It's not a pretty story, and you humans can be so squeamish."

Through clenched teeth, I make my demand. "Tell me."

He lowers his eyebrows, drawing his features together. "Oh, I can do better than that. Let me show you."

Angry, dark clouds roll in, obscuring the sun and turning the sky black. The drive-in screen begins to hum and glow, like an old tube television warming up. Lightning cracks through the air and now he's behind me, palms pressing on either side of my skull, squeezing, forcing me to look at the screen. I try to turn away, try to pull from his grasp, but he's too strong. He leans over my shoulder, his mouth close to my cheek. His breath, the same odor as burnt out matches, assaults my nostrils.

"Let's see whether or not the truth sets you free."

28

*T*HE *D*RIVE-*I*N

The living room of my grandmother's house fills the screen.

I'd been to that house once. My mother took me along with her and Aunt Bobbie after grandma died. Mom and her mother weren't close. In fact, I'd never met the woman. Mom didn't tell me why they didn't get along, but going into the house gave me a good idea.

Up on the screen, it's pretty much like I remember. Anything you can sit on is covered with plastic. A big pot in one corner holds a tall rubber plant with leaves such a dark, shiny green they almost look fake. I saw that pot when we were in the house for the clean up, but all it had in it then was dust-dry dirt and a broken off, shriveled stalk from the dead plant. What I'm seeing now must be how the room looked a whole lot of years ago.

There's a small bookcase in the other corner, filled with an odd mix of Bibles and metaphysical and religious self-help books. A book called *Let Go and Let God* shares shelf space with a large print King James Bible, *Discovering the Power of the Zodiac*, and *The Prophecies of Nostradamus*.

During the cleanout I had found a box of steamy romance novels shoved under the bed. Seeing the contents of the bookcase makes me wonder if those other books are already in my grandmother's room, hidden in the shadows, or if her reading habits changed later in life.

My eyes move to the walls. Representations of Jesus are everywhere. At least a dozen Jesus pictures cover the walls. Some show him before the crucifixion, some during, and some after. One's a creepy combination of all three: Jesus, a crown of thorns on his head, walking across the water while holding his nail-pierced hands out to a crowd, while a burning heart glows in his chest. I'm not sure what to make out of that one. The only thing all the pictures have in common is that Jesus doesn't look happy in any of them.

"Why are you showing me this?"

"You'll see." Ba'al whispers in my ear. At the same time, he turns my head toward the front door. "Here she comes."

The door swings open, and a girl walks into the room. She's a teenager, probably fifteen or sixteen. She's wearing a denim mini-skirt, high-top tennis shoes with slouchy white socks, and a baggy, cut off t-shirt that says RELAX in big, bold letters. A portable cassette player is clipped to her waistband, and she's bopping to the music that filters through the headphones. Then she starts singing.

"Wake me up, before you go go . . ."

Shock nearly knocks the air right out of me. Aunt Bobbie told me once that my mother used to love Wham, but I hadn't believed her. No way could I picture my mom being so loose and carefree. But here's the proof.

The girl who just danced through the door is my mother, and she's an eighties cliché. Even more astounding, she looks happy. I can't even begin to reconcile the teenager I see in front of me with the woman who raised me. There's no glimmer of the person I know in young Georgie Burton.

She hits a button on the cassette player, pushes back the headphones so they hang around her neck, and gives the room a good sweep with her eyes. Probably checking to make sure grandma won't find her listening to devil music.

Her attention is pulled to the hall, and she cocks her head to the side. She hears something. My eyes follow her gaze, my ears strain, listening closely. Now I can hear it, too. A low, muffled, wailing sound, like someone crying into a pillow.

"Bobbie?"

She heads down the hallway. I turn my head in the same direction, making the view on the big drive-in screen change, as if I were a camera man operating a steady-cam. There's a bathroom at the end of the hall. In either direction from that there are closed doors. She turns to the right, opens the door, and walks into a room with two twin beds. One is neatly made except for the clothes strewn across the foot of it. It looks like someone couldn't decide what to wear that morning. I ignore that bed and turn my attention to where Georgie is looking.

A girl lies curled in a tight ball on the other bed, her pillow clutched to her face. Her slight frame shakes as she cries, and her silky blond hair is tangled and pushed off to one side.

"Bobbie?"

I should have expected the other person in my mother's room to be her sister, but I still can't believe it. This little wisp of a girl is my Aunt Bobbie?

With a quick sweep, Georgie pulls the headphones from her neck and tosses them and the player on her bed. Then she sits next to Bobbie. She puts her hand on her sister's shoulder, shaking her gently.

"Bobbie, what's wrong?" When she gets no response, she tries to make a joke. "The Go-Go's didn't break up, did they?"

This just brings on a fresh round of wailing and head shaking. Georgie sits there, awkwardly rubbing Bobbie's shoulder, until finally the crying subsides and muffled words fight to be heard through the pillow.

Georgie leans forward. "What? I can't understand you."

Bobbie lifts her head, and I gasp. Her whole face is swollen. Her eyes, nose, cheeks are all red and puffy. She's already soaked from tears, but she can't stop crying. The pain and agony spilling out of her is worse than anything I've ever seen. Worse than that film clip of Marilyn Monroe. It scares me, and I suddenly don't want to know what could have done this to my aunt.

"I've had enough," I say. "I don't want to see anymore."

"Sure you do," Ba'al says in my ear. "How can you stand not knowing what caused all this? It's like turning off a soap opera before the big reveal."

I hate it, but what he said makes sense. Just like digging through the contents of that awful chest, this is something I have to do. There's no going back now.

Bobbie opens her mouth to speak. She stops. Gulps in a breath. Tries again. "I can't do it anymore."

Georgie's eyebrows pull into a confused V. "Can't do what?"

"I can't keep it a secret. What he—" Another gasp. Another gulp. "What he makes me do. I can't. I can't . . ."

Bobbie throws herself onto Georgie's lap, clutching at her legs, grabbing on as if her sister is a lifeboat in the middle of a stormy ocean. I go cold, and I can tell from Georgie's face that she feels the same way. She'd like nothing more than to leave the room, start the day over, never know the terrible secret she's about to find out. But there's no going back for her, either.

She lets Bobbie cry a bit longer, then grasps her by the shoulders, pushing her up, looking her in the eye. "I need you to stop crying. I need you to tell me what's going on."

Bobbie sniffs. She wipes the back of her hand across her nose and mouth, smearing tears and snot and saliva across her cheek. "It started three years ago. When I was ten."

I quickly do the math in my head. That means Bobbie's thirteen now, which makes Georgie sixteen. Not that it matters to the girls in the room. No matter how old they get, I have a feeling none of this will ever make any sense.

"What started?" Georgie prods gently.

Bobbie makes several false starts, opening her mouth to speak, but then snapping it shut and taking in several quick breaths. But when the words finally come, they spill out of her fast and sharp, like water barreling through a broken dam. "At first, he just touched me. He said it was our special secret, something just between him and me. Then he made me touch him. I didn't like it. I didn't like any of it, but I didn't want him to be angry with me. He said I couldn't tell anybody. He said people wouldn't understand. They'd think I was a bad girl, and I'd get in trouble. You have to believe me. He said no one would believe me."

The pressure on my head increased. The demon is enjoying all this. His breath comes harder and faster beside my ear as his fingertips dig into my scalp. My stomach churns. I think I'm going to be sick.

Bobbie looks up into her sister's eyes. "I was so scared. So I kept quiet. I didn't want to make him mad. And I didn't want anyone to think I was bad. But then last week . . ."

She trails off. Georgie keeps herself calm. I don't know how she's doing it. If I were in her position, I would have exploded by now. But when she speaks, the wobble in her voice gives her away. "Bobbie, who is *he*?"

I think she already knows. From the way she asks, I think she's figured it out, but she doesn't want to believe it. Bobbie bites her lip so hard I can see blood on the tip of her tooth when she opens her mouth to answer.

"Uncle . . . Uncle George."

Uncle George. Mom's namesake. The guillotine-sharp blade of the words fall, slicing the world into two parts: before she knew the truth, and after.

Georgie reels as though she took a punch. She stares at the wall on the other side of the room, focusing on a poster of George Michael and Andrew Ridgeley. She looks like she wants to tear it down, rip it to shreds. The background of the poster is a white and black checkerboard, just like the tiles on the clinic floor. Maybe she's counting the squares, too.

When she finally turns her head back to Bobbie, she's managed to bury her emotions again and her eyes are hard as glass marbles.

"Uncle George. Mom's had him picking you up every day from summer school."

Bobbie nods. "But he hasn't been bringing me straight home, he . . . last week, he—" She can't do it. She breaks into sobs, unable to put the monstrous thing into words. So her sister does it for her.

"Did he rape you?"

Bobbie's head jerks up and down.

"More than once?"

It jerks again.

I watch it play out in front of me, a terrible movie I wish I could walk out on, but I'm unable to look away. I've seen enough. I get the point. I don't need to see anymore. "Make it stop." I mean for it to be an order, but my voice is barely a whimper.

The laughter in my ear is mocking, menacing. "Oh, come on, you don't want to quit now. I'd offer you some popcorn but you look a little green. Besides, we're just getting to the good part."

My head snaps hard to one side. The screen goes blank. Everything's silent. For a moment, I wonder if I've finally died. But then another picture materializes in front of me.

Georgie is standing outside a house, pounding her fist on the front door. A man opens it and smiles as soon as he sees her.

But before he can say hello, she pokes him hard in the chest with her finger. "I need to talk to you."

A flash of anger crosses his face. Then just as quickly, his expression changes. It's so fast I wonder if I really saw the anger in the first place or if I imagined it. Now he looks somewhat amused. Stepping back, he ushers her into the house with a wave of his hand. "I'm glad you're here, Georgie. Because your mother and I need to talk to you, too."

Georgie is as shocked as I am to see her mother sitting on Uncle George's couch. The older woman's face is pinched, and she's wringing her hands in her lap. She looks at her daughter standing in the doorway, and her expression becomes even more dismayed. Either she doesn't like the way Georgie talked to her uncle or she disapproves with what the girl is wearing. Or both.

"Well come in," her mother says to her. "Maybe you can shed some light on this situation."

Georgie walks into the house, stands beside the couch, and looks from one adult to the other. My heart goes out to her. She probably had a speech all worked out on the way over. I'll bet she knew exactly what she was going to say to her uncle. But now that she sees her mother, I can tell she's been thrown completely off balance. "What situation?"

Uncle George walks around to the front of the couch, his hands stuffed in the pockets of his slacks, shoulders bent forward. "I'm worried about your sister."

"What?" The word bursts out of Georgie and me at the same time.

"She's been acting different lately, secretive." George shakes his head. He looks deeply saddened by what he's about to say. "You're mother and I have been discussing it, and we can come to only one conclusion." He pauses. "I'm afraid Bobbie may have become sexually active."

I can't believe the nerve of this guy. And the slickness. He must have realized Bobbie was getting ready to spill her guts and figured he'd beat her to the punch. Now that Georgie's come to confront him, he's doing the same thing with her.

For a second, the room is deadly still. No one moves, no one breathes. It's the eerie calm before the inevitable storm erupts.

Georgie glares at her uncle, her cheeks flaming red. "She's not sexually active, you pig. You raped her."

Ba'al begins to laugh as all hell breaks loose in the small living room. Georgie jumps at her uncle, fingers outstretched as if she's ready to claw him to bits, but she runs into the corner of the couch and stumbles. Her mother clutches her chest and starts calling out, "Oh dear! Oh dear!"

George catches Georgie as she falls, grabbing both of her wrists and holding her at arm's length. A shadow in the corner of the room moves and catches my eye. It's behind the rubber plant. I try to take a closer look, but Ba'al's palms squeeze harder against my head. He turns me forcefully so I'm once more looking at my mother and her uncle.

"Young lady, calm down right now," George growls and gives her a shake. "Is that what your sister told you?"

Georgie struggles against him. She's clearly disgusted to have those hands on her skin, but he's a strong man and she can't pull away. "Yes. She told me you've been molesting her for three years and now you've moved on to rape."

Still on the couch, rocking back and forth, Betty's cheeks are as red and shiny as a Roma tomato. "How could you?" She pushes herself up and staggers over to the other two.

Then she points her finger directly at her daughter.

"How could you accuse your uncle of something so vile?"

Georgie stops struggling. Stops moving. George lets go of her, and she drops her hands, stumbling backward. She stares at her mother in utter disbelief. "You're defending him?"

The older woman pulls herself up to her full five feet and puffs out her ample chest. "Of course I am. Your uncle is a good Christian man. He would never do what you're suggesting. He's a deacon, for goodness sake."

I cringe at the words. He's a deacon. As if that makes all the difference.

Georgie blinks. "But why would Bobbie say he did those things if he didn't?"

"It appears she's trying to deflect the guilt she's feeling by assigning it to someone else." George is speaking now, his voice low and mournful, as if he can't believe the depths young Bobbie has sunk to. He looks at his sister. "Don't be too hard on her, Betty. Bobbie's obviously a very confused child." He slides his arm around Georgie's shoulders, pulling her hard against his side. "And Georgie, here, is just being a good big sister."

Georgie jerks out from under his arm and turns on him. A loud crack echoes through the room as her palm makes contact with his face. "Keep your filthy paws off me."

Betty gasps, steps backward, and almost falls over the coffee table. Georgie is trembling.

George frowns and holds his cheek. He turns to the older woman, his movements slow and deliberate. "Would you give us a minute alone, Betty?"

I can feel what Georgie's thinking. *Don't leave me alone with this monster. Please, Mom. I need you here.* But her mother is oblivious. Shaking her head, she totters from the room. "Yes. I need to . . . to . . . splash some water on my face."

As soon as the bathroom door clicks shut, George drops his carefully maintained veneer of civility. He lunges at Georgie, grabs a handful of her hair and bends her backwards over the side of the couch.

"I could snap your neck if I wanted to, so keep your mouth shut." Not only is he strong, but he's quick. Somehow, he gets both of her hands behind her back and is able to hold them with one of his. Then he lets go of her hair and moves his hand to her neck, ringing his fingers around her throat as he talks.

"I told your sister nobody would believe her. She should have listened to me. Little idiot."

She came to this house to protect her sister, but now that she's in danger herself, Georgie has been reduced to a scared little girl. A mixture of terror, disillusionment, and anger contort her face as tears slide unchecked down her cheeks. "I don't understand."

"You don't understand what?"

"Why? How could you be like this?"

He swears, then he shakes his head, as if she ought to know better. "You girls just don't know how hard you make it for a man. You parade around in your revealing clothes, tempting us. Everything you do screams 'come and get me' but then you get all freaked out if we try to touch you." His gaze travels down her body, and his breath comes a little faster. "Just look at you. Not quite as pretty as your sister, but you'll do."

His hand leaves her neck, following the path his eyes had just taken. Down the front of her shirt. Her eyes grow wide as she realizes what he wants to do.

In that instant, everything changes. The fear leaves her. Her eyes flash. Her face is hard. She becomes a woman determined to do what she needs to do in order to survive.

Manipulating her lips into a brittle smile, she says, "If you want me so bad, then who's stopping you?" Her voice is breathy, inviting. Tempting.

George is thrown for a moment. He's wary of her sudden turn around, but his ego and carnal desires get the best of him. Even I can see the lust in his eyes, blooming, exploding. Just like Ethan.

She takes advantage of those few seconds of confusion. Her knee comes up hard, catching him in the groin. He grunts, doubles over, loses his grip on her. She rolls off the side of the couch and before he can straighten up she brings the toe of her Reebok crashing into his nose. Blood spurts out on the carpet. Betty walks out of the bathroom just in time to hear her brother spitting out a string of swearwords that no deacon should know, let alone say.

The woman screams, one hand clutching the door frame, the other balled in a fist against her stomach.

Georgie is breathing so hard her shoulders jerk up and down from the effort. She stands over her uncle, like a teenage version of Wonder Woman, hands on her hips, his blood spattered on her right shoe and sock. "Stay away from me and my sister. Or I will kill you. That's a promise."

She looks up, and it's as if we're staring at each other, eye to eye, nose to nose. My heart cries out to the sixteen-year-old girl in front of me. That morning, she was a carefree teenager with a world of possibilities spread out in front of her. Her biggest problems had been figuring out what to wear and what cassette to pop into her Walkman. But she's just become a different person.

I recognize her now.

She's just become my mother.

29

*T*HE *D*RIVE-*I*N

"Enough!"

I gather together all the strength I have left and inject it into the screamed demand, twisting my body hard at the same time. The images fizzle and disappear from the screen, leaving it a blank rectangle of dirty white. The clouds roll back, but instead of bright sunshine the drive-in is bathed in harsh, brown-orange light. Ba'al, who now stands across from me, seems to be losing his luster as well. His long black duster has faded to a dull, dark grey, and his hair, once again the color and texture of old straw, whips around his face on the hot wind blowing through.

It's like I've ended up on the set of a post-apocalyptic sci-fi movie. If only the director would yell "Cut!" Then the lights would come up, and I'd be able to join the actors as they walked off set.

But despite the location, this isn't a movie. And as much as I'd like to walk away from what I've just learned, I can't.

"So now you know," Ba'al says, rocking back and forth on the balls of his feet. "The good Christian uncle raped one niece and threatened the other." He throws his head back and laughs.

The noises he's making crawl up my spine like a sharp-nailed rodent. "I don't find it funny."

"I wouldn't expect you to." He dabs at an imaginary tear in the corner of his eye before he continues. "I was just relishing the irony. Weren't you molested by a good Christian man, too? It seems to run in your family."

I wince at his comment. I don't want to think about Ethan now. But how can I avoid it? "He didn't molest me. He tried to, but I stopped him."

Ba'al shrugs. "If that makes you feel better. But you have to admit, the church hasn't done you or your family any favors."

Vinnie had told me that Ba'al would lie, that he'd twist the truth and use it to his own advantage. But I can't argue with what he just said. The church hadn't helped me. In fact, Mom never would have met Ethan if we hadn't gone to church that day. And what about young Bobbie? Jesus stared down at her from every corner of that hypocritical house, yet she was still abused and betrayed by someone she should have been able to trust. Someone who worked in the church and claimed to love Jesus.

I have no part in him, and he has no part in me.

There it is again. This time, I don't look around for the owner of the voice. As before, Ba'al gives no indication that he's heard anything. A little seed of hope sprouts deep in the core of my being. Someone's trying to help me. But who? The most logical choice would be Vinnie, but it doesn't sound like him. It doesn't feel like him.

Look in the shadows.

The shadows. Throughout my life, there have been so many shadows.

I think back to what I saw moments ago. My mother attacking her uncle, her mother nearly having a nervous breakdown . . . and the shadow in the corner, behind the rubber plant. Like someone standing in the wings, watching the dysfunctional melodrama unfold. I'd tried to look at it, but Ba'al stopped me.

I remember Ethan, his disgusting hands, his vile breath. The shadows that seemed to consume me. The shadows that I threw the cross into, never wanting to see it again.

Finally, I remember the man in the park, standing in the deep, dark shadows of the trees at night. I remember the doubts that assailed me, the fear that Jake would be like all the others.

The truth hits me with the force of a semi-truck.

I look at Ba'al. "You were there."

His lips pull back across his now gaunt face, stretching into a horrible smile. His eyes, circled in dark shadow, grow wide and wild. I know that look. It's the same look I saw on George's face. The same look I saw on Ethan's.

"Every time, you were there."

Confusion and anger fill my chest like a water-soaked sponge, expanding, overwhelming me. "You've plagued my family for decades. You've stalked me, and when you couldn't hurt me physically, you filled my head with doubt and fear. Why? Why us?"

The expression on his face changes, becoming flat and bored. "Why not you?"

It makes no sense. But it has to. I can't believe it was all random. There has to be a reason. "And those men. George, Ethan . . . why would you make them do such hideous, repulsive things?"

He frowns and a growl-like rumble rises from his throat. "You still don't get it, do you? We can't *make* you do anything." He moves toward me, hands slicing through the air as he talks. "All we can do is present you with options, suggestions. We can make a situation available to you, entice you, tempt you." Now he's standing right in front of me, toes almost against mine. "We can show you the possibilities. Arouse your senses. Fill you with desire." He stops, and the next words shoot out of him like machine gun fire. "But we can't make you *do* anything."

I shake my head. "I don't understand."

"You people love to shift blame to someone else. I'm fat because of the fast food industry. I had an affair because that woman is just too sexy. I embezzled the money because the economy is so bad and it's the only way I could put my kids through college. But sometimes, you can't find anyone else to blame, and then what do you do?"

He waits for me to answer. When I don't he sneers and goes on. "When you've got no one else to blame, you say 'The devil made me do it.' As if that absolves you from any responsibility. All that free will is wasted on you. You have no idea what to do with it."

His eyes narrow into slits. Before I have time to react, he grabs my arm and pulls me against him so that my back is flush against his chest. His arm snakes around my neck and he grabs my chin with his hand, pointing me toward the screen again. "I think I'll show you something else."

Waves of heat envelope me. It's hard to breathe, and I think I might pass out. But then my head clears.

I'm looking at the inside of a garage. It's dark, but enough light comes in through three big windows at the top of the door that I can make out a car. It's a light blue, four door sedan with a huge chrome grill, sporting the Chevrolet logo. While I'm no car expert, I'd say this one is from the fifties.

"Why are you showing me this?"

"You'll see."

A squeal echoes through the room. A crack of sunlight squeezes through under the garage door and grows fatter as the door goes up. But it doesn't go up all the way. A long, flat box is pushed under it. Then a child rolls through. Then another. Then one more. After the last one is in, he jumps up and pushes the garage door closed with his foot.

They move around in the shadowy room.

The tallest child, a boy, waves to the others. "Set it up over here."

He sits cross-legged beside the car. The other two, a younger boy and girl, join him. The middle boy opens the box. He takes out a board and puts it in the center of their circle. The girl turns on a flashlight and shines it on the board. It's made of wood. The letters of the alphabet stand out fat and black in two curved rows. At the top is the word OUIJA.

The girl looks at the older boy and shines the light right in his face. "What do we do now, George?"

He screws up his face, swatting at her hand. "Dang it, Betty, watch where you point that thing."

My body begins to shake. George. Betty. That must make the little one . . .

"I want to go first!" The small boy grabs a triangular piece of wood with a round piece of glass in the middle. He holds it up to his eye like a monocle.

"No fair," Betty whines. "It should be ladies first."

"Yeah, well, you ain't no lady." George laughs and points at the other boy. "Let Robby go first."

Robert.

Betty.

George.

My knees start to give out and I almost fall, but Ba'al's arm tightens around me. "Oh no you don't," he hisses. "You're going to watch this."

The kids lean toward the board. Robby is about to put the piece of wood down when George stops him. "Don't you want to know the rules first?"

The other two nod. George goes on.

"We're about to consult with Ouija, god of the magical, mystical talking board." His voice has taken on a tone of overdone reverence. His siblings are a captive audience, which he clearly relishes. "We all get to ask it a question."

"How do we get an answer?" Robby sounds as if he's in awe of the whole process.

George points at the piece of wood in Robby's hand. "That's called a planchette. You put it on the board, and we all touch it with our fingertips. Then it will move around the board and spell out the answer."

Betty's eyes are round with amazement. "It moves all by itself?"

George nods. "Yep. But only if we do it right. First, we have to hold hands and welcome the spirit of Ouija."

He reaches out and takes first Robby's hand, then Betty's. She sets the flashlight on the ground so the beam points at the board, then she grabs Robby's hand. When they're all connected, George takes a deep breath.

"Oh spirit of Ouija," he intones. "We welcome you in the middle of us. Bring us your wisdom and tell us the future."

They look around as if expecting something to be different, but nothing has changed. They let go of each other's hands. George points at the board. "Okay, Robby. What do you want to know?"

Robby can't be more than five or six. He wrinkles up his nose. Then he sits up straight, smiling widely. "I know!" He gazes at the board. "Tell me what my future holds."

Betty wags her head. "That's no fair. You read it off the side of the box."

"Doesn't matter," Robby shoots back. "It's still a question, and I wanna know."

George raises his hands. "Pipe down you two. Do you want to drag Dad out here? Robby said what he wanted to know. Now let's get the answer."

The boy puts the piece of wood on the board. Six sets of fingertips rest gently on it.

Nothing happens.

"See, you did it wrong," Betty says.

George frowns at her. "Say it again, but this time, say it like a question."

Robby stares at the planchette, his eyebrows drawn together. "What does my future hold?"

The room is silent. The piece of wood starts to move. It stops over a letter.

D

It moves again.

E

The fear in the room grows until it's palpable. The children watch, terrified, as the planchette moves, hovering over three more letters, and the mystic board spells out the answer: DEATH.

The silent, shadowy room explodes in shouts and movements.

Robby bursts into tears.

Betty scrambles backward, kicking the board, and sending the planchette flying.

George jumps to his feet.

"Why did you do that?" Robby cries.

"I didn't do anything," Betty shouts. "It was the board."

Robby cries harder.

George steps to his brother. Puts an arm around him. "Calm down. It's just a stupid game. It didn't mean anything."

The door to the house opens. Someone flips the light switch, bathing the area in light.

"What's going on in here?"

A man walks into the garage. He's got a beer bottle in one hand.

"Sorry, Dad. We were just playing, and Robby got upset." George tries to kick the Ouija board under the car, but he's not fast enough.

"What's that?" His father stalks over. Looks down. Then he looks back at George. "You know better than to bring that kind of filth into this house. I'm going to beat the devil out of you, boy."

He grabs George by the collar and pushes him toward the door. Then he looks back at the other two children who are now both crying. He waves his beer bottle at them. "When I'm done with this one, I'll come back for you other two."

30

The movie is over.

Ba'al lets me go and I stagger, stepping away from him, turning back to look at him. He's getting uglier by the minute.

"You wanted to know why I've shown such an interest in your family," he says. "Now you know. They invited me."

My mouth tastes like metal. "No," I barely croak out the word. I swallow and try again. "No. They didn't invite you. They called for some made up spirit of Ouija. They were just kids. They thought they were playing a game."

He grins like an evil jack-o-lantern. "That's the crazy thing about calling on a demon. Sorry, a *spirit*. You never know which one you're going to get."

I still can't believe what I just saw. "They were only kids."

He snorts in exasperation. "Look, it's not my fault the little brat asked such a stupid question and then couldn't handle the answer. You all die eventually. The kid was going to die, and I told him. If he didn't want to know, he shouldn't have asked."

My mom's Uncle Robert died of pneumonia. When he was only six. "How long after that did he die?"

"About a month. Which proves that I'm honest and accurate."

George and Betty must have been terrified after their brother died. It explained Betty's obsession with Jesus pictures and self-help books. But what about George? Why did he turn out the way he did? His father said he was going to beat the devil out of him. Obviously it didn't work.

Which brings me back to Ba'al.

"You're a liar and a manipulator. If you'd just left those kids alone, everything would be different."

He purses his lips and looks down at me as if I am a slow-witted child. "I think you need another example. Let's use Ethan."

"No!"

"Yes." He snaps back at me. "What could have caused Ethan to do the things he did? It's possible that his father abused him so he grew up feeling weak and powerless. And it's possible I might have filled his head with thoughts about how sex is really all about being dominant and in control. And I might have whispered to him about how strong he'd feel if he bagged a babe like you. I might even have let him have you in his dreams."

He reaches out and runs the tip of his finger lightly down my arm. The touch burns like a soldering iron even though he barely makes contact. I jerk away, scramble backward, and he continues.

"It's possible that I put all those thoughts into Ethan's mind. But in the end, the choice was his."

With each sentence, the demon moves closer to me.

"*He* chose to fantasize about pretty young girls. *He* chose to put his hands on you. *He* is responsible for the choices he made, *not* me."

With every step he takes, I hear the crunch of his footsteps, like boots on sand. And now another memory comes to me. During the accident. I thought I saw a man. I swerved the car to avoid hitting him. That's why I'd gone into the ditch. And after, when I was lying injured in the car, before Vinnie came,

I heard the crunch of boots. I heard the voice, sweet and melodious, saying "Let me help you." And then the flash of white.

"It was you."

He doesn't answer, but I know I'm right. Ba'al is the one who put me in this position. He tried to take me when I was lying in that car. But Vinnie stopped him.

Ba'al takes another step. He's so close to me now, I can smell his breath. It's putrid, like rotten meat. My stomach roils, my head swims. The ground undulates beneath my feet and I fall, first to my knees, then my hands hit the pavement. Little pieces of rock and grit bite into my palms. I hold up my left hand and stare at it. Pain radiates from my fingertips and up through my arm. I try to stand, but fire shoots through my legs and I fall back down.

This is very bad.

I force myself to look up. From this perspective, Ba'al seems to tower over me. I'm like a bug at his feet, one he could easily crush. "What's happening?"

"You're very weak. I'm afraid our little chat has taken a lot out of you." He cocks his head, looking at me like a bird looks at a worm just before pecking it up. "And now, it's time to choose."

I let my head fall. That's why he's been so willing to share all this with me. He knew it would wear away at what strength I had left. Once more, I try to stand, but collapse in a heap by one of the speaker poles. I grab at it, trying to steady myself, but I only succeed in pulling the speakers off and sending them clanging to the ground. I grip the pole to hold myself up and look around, searching for the diner. Vinnie said I could go back any time I wanted. Where is it?

"I want to go back to the diner."

Ba'al just laughs at my request. "You're in no shape to go back there. But you don't need to. I can help you more than that angel can." He kneels down in front of me, and I see he's put on his beautiful face again. "Just let go, Alexandra. You don't need to suffer anymore."

The world turns sideways, and I clutch at the pole. Is the ground really moving? I'm light-headed, and my brain is muddled. Ba'al leans in closer.

"Think of all you've been through. Think of how much pain you've already endured in your life and how much more is to come."

A searing pain shoots through my arm, like someone's taken a chainsaw and hacked into the bone. I scream and sweat breaks out on my forehead. The inside of my body is burning up but chills dance across my flesh.

"What is there to go back to, anyway? Men who only want to use you. A mother who hates the sight of you. But it can all be over. I can take away your pain."

The tones in his voice lull me, tempt me. No more pain. How wonderful that would be. "How?"

"Just come with me, and your earthly pain will cease."

He holds his hand out. I stare at it. A spike of pain shoots through my head, in one temple and out the other. Oh, how I want this to all be over.

Choose life.

But I hurt so much.

Choose life.

But I don't want to go on like this.

Choose life.

Why? What have I got to live for, anyway?

I collapse, and my head hits one of the speakers on the ground. I close my eyes, ready to give up, ready to end it all, when I hear voices.

"I wasn't a good mother."

Mom?

"I wish I could have a second chance."

So do I.

"Bobbie, will you pray with me?"

Two voices, the ones I've heard my entire life, blend together. "Our Father . . ."

Choose life. Choose me.

Who are you?

I am the way, the truth, and the life.

A burst of color explodes inside my head. Words I heard at church, songs I sung standing beside Jake, words spoken in prayer by my mother and Aunt Bobbie calling out from the speaker . . . *deliver us from evil* . . . they crowd inside me, pushing away the fog, pushing away the doubt.

Images, like a well executed movie preview, unspool inside my head. I see Joe standing far away. In his hands is the chest which contains all the hurt and pain and confusion I'd collected over the years. "I carried it for you," he says. He walks toward me. The chest grows, becoming bigger and bigger, until it's twice the size of the man. He shifts it to his back and now he's dragging it along behind him, bent over from the weight of it.

The image becomes wavy as though I'm looking through curtains of heat in the desert, then it morphs into something else. A man, covered in dirt, dripping sweat and blood, trudges across the sand. He stumbles under the weight of the huge piece of wood on his back. The cross that he carries. He stops in front of me, looks up at me with eyes full of love and pain, and says, "I carried it for you."

My head clears. One limb at a time, I feel the pain subsiding and the strength returning to my body. Vinnie's voice echoes in my head, "Call on the Name." I hadn't understood who that was.

I hadn't been thinking big enough. But I am now.

I take a deep breath and look up at Ba'al. The beauty of his face is melting away, leaving him as grotesque and contorted as the souls he's manipulated. Now, for the first time, I see him as he really is.

There's no doubt in my mind anymore. No confusion. I know exactly what I have to do. Through dry, cracked lips I rasp, "You lose."

An unearthly shriek bursts out of him. He shoots upright, grabbing the lapels of his coat and ripping it in half, exposing leathery skin stretched across a skeletal chest. Despite my resolve, fear grips me. I try to stand, try to get away, but my heel catches on something and I fall backward. I scream as the speaker wires begin growing like possessed kudzu vines, wrapping around my arms and legs, holding me down.

Ba'al points at me. "We will have you. You belong to us!" There's no music left in his voice, just ugliness and discord, like a hundred angry voices all clamoring at once. He drops to one knee and lets out a growl as he hits the pavement hard with his fists. Great cracks emanate around him in every direction, shaking the ground. All around me, the white posts fly from their moorings and black, ghost-like figures emerge, rising into the air in a swirling frenzy.

The air grows cold and echoes with sounds no human ear should hear. He's calling in reinforcements. I know I can't do this on my own.

"You can't fight us." He snarls at me and saliva drips from one corner of his mouth.

I struggle against the wires that encircle my neck, against the fear that clutches at my heart. "Not me," I choke out.

The ground shakes again, but this time it takes him by surprise, almost knocking him from his feet. He jerks, regains his balance. "What are you doing?"

"You can beat me. But you can't beat him."

He recoils, and for the first time, I see fear reflected in him. "I've got a name."

Thunder cracks.

He puts his hands over his ears. "No!"

The speaker wires loosen, and I'm able to free myself, pull myself into a standing position. "The only name that matters."

He grabs handfuls of his hair and rips it out by the roots. "No!" His scream is nearly drowned out as the wind picks up speed. All around me are ear-splitting wails and shrieks. But they can't stop me. Nothing can stop me. Not now.

With my hands and face lifted to heaven, the name comes up from the depths of my gut, loud and clear and pure.

"*Jesus!*"

Wind like a hurricane rushes through the drive-in, blowing away everything until I'm left standing alone in the middle of the maelstrom.

A blinding flash of golden light encompasses me, fills me. It blocks out thoughts of anything else but the name I just uttered.

I feel myself falling, floating. I let myself go, but the name still pours from my lips.

Jesus.

31

AFTER THE DRIVE-IN

I'm sitting on grass.

The drive-in is gone. Ba'al is gone. But I'm not alone. There's a man sitting beside me, wearing slightly wrinkled, beige Dockers and a long sleeved, blue shirt. His feet are bare and his arms are wrapped around his raised knees. He's smiling at me. It's Joe. Only now I know who he really is.

"Jesus?"

He nods. "I knew you'd get my name right eventually."

And not a minute too soon. "What just happened?"

"That was a battle for your soul, Allie. You had to choose."

I can still hear the voice in my head, feeding me the answers, prodding me in the right direction. "Choose life. That was you, wasn't it?"

"Yes," he says slowly. "You chose wisely."

I cock my head to the side, looking at him closely. Am I imagining it, or did the Son of God just make a very sly Indiana Jones reference right out of *The Last Crusade*?

He puts his hand on my shoulder, and I forget all about the possible joke. The sensation that fills me is unlike anything I've experienced in my life. It's more than peace, more than love or contentment. It's all those things and a million more. I close my eyes and dig my fingers into the ground, feeling the damp earth underneath my nails, relishing the fresh, green scent that rises to fill my nostrils. I want to stay like this forever, sitting on the grass with Jesus.

Wait a minute—I'm sitting on the grass, out in an open field, with Jesus. How can I be doing this? "Am I in heaven?"

"No. I'm just letting you regain your strength before I send you back to the diner." He motions off to the side with his thumb.

I look in the direction he's pointing, to the left of us, past a row of leafy elm trees . . . Ah, now I can see it. The pink walls are brighter than before and the neon sign glows bright, flashing the full cup, empty cup, full cup, empty cup. My heart skips in my chest, both from the joy of seeing something familiar, and the disappointment that I'm going to have to leave the peaceful place I've settled in.

"Why do I have to go back?"

"You're not quite finished there. There's still some work to do, choices for you to make." He chuckles a bit under his breath. "Besides, Vinnie's worried about you."

"Really? You mean he doesn't know what happened?"

He shakes his head. "Not yet. Angels aren't omniscient, you know."

"So I hear."

I breath deeply, desperate to absorb as much of the moment as possible. I feel stronger now than I have since the accident, and somehow I understand that my time here with Jesus is almost over. I wish I could simply relax and bask in the tranquility of the moment, but I can't. There's something I need to know before I leave. "Can I ask you a question?"

"Always," he says without hesitation.

"The things that happened to me . . . to my mother . . . why didn't you stop them?"

The pounding in my ears equals the thudding in my chest. I want him to tell me it was a mistake. Just some slip-up in the great celestial scheme of things, and now that I've called on him, now that I believe in him, nothing bad will happen to me again.

But he doesn't say that. In fact, he doesn't say anything right away. Instead, he pulls a dandelion that has gone to seed up out of the ground. Holding it in front of his lips, he blows on it, sending the white shoots flying. We watch as they bob and weave, like tiny white umbrellas turned inside out, carried along by the breeze until there's not a trace of them left.

He turns his face toward me. "Do you have any idea where all those seeds will end up?"

"No."

"Of course not. How could you? There are so many unknown factors determining their paths: wind patterns, obstacles that might get in their way, predators." He drops the bald stem on the ground beside him, then turns his whole body toward me, legs crossed. "You don't know, but I do. I know what will happen to each one of them. And if I know about something as small as where a dandelion seed will end up, don't you think I know everything there is to know about you, my precious child?"

Tears burn the rims of my eyes. "But if you know, if you knew, then why . . ."

"Why did I allow you to be hurt? I could explain it all to you, but it wouldn't make sense. The simple version is this: The Father never intended the world to be the way it is. He knew what was going to happen, but it wasn't his perfect plan."

I crinkle my forehead and he smiles. "See, you're already confused. Let me give you the *Reader's Digest* version. The first humans were created in our image. They were given free will. And they chose poorly." He pops open the button on one shirt cuff and starts rolling up the sleeve. "That's why you live in a sinful world full of people who have the ability to make their own choices, to choose between right and wrong. Sometimes, they do very well, especially if they're seeking the will of the Father. But other times they do a terrible job at it, and that affects everyone around them."

That part makes sense to me. After seeing my mother, I know she would have grown up to be a different person if not for the evil done to her and to her sister. George didn't know it, but the sins he committed spiraled down, through the generations, leaving a legacy of guilt, shame, and pain. It affected how my mother raised me and how she approached every relationship she ever had with men, which also spilled over onto me. So really, my own relationship issues can be traced back to George. Maybe even further.

"What a mess," I mutter.

He nods, moving on to the other shirt sleeve. "Indeed. And not only in this world, but in the next. The cycle of sin never stops, and the price it demands is very high. Which is why you need a Savior."

My eyes drop to his arms. Now that his sleeves are pushed up, I can see the scars. They're not neat little holes in his hands like you see in paintings. These are jagged, angry red and white welts weaving a pattern across his hands, his fingers, around his wrists and up past his elbows where they disappear beneath the blue cotton of the shirt. My mind fumbles through all the random Bible stories and verses I've heard over the years, stories of Jesus's sacrifice and his amazing love. Now, they finally begin to make sense. It all clicks into place. I may not understand everything about my life, but I understand the price Jesus has paid for me.

I reach out, then pull back, not sure if I'm allowed to touch him.

He smiles and moves one arm so it's closer to me and easier to reach. "Go ahead."

I extend my hand slowly. My fingertips barely make contact with the scars before I have to pull away again. I can't do it. I'm not worthy to look at them, let alone touch them.

"What's wrong?" His voice is a soft, gentle whisper, like the breeze that makes the wild flowers around us bend and bow.

I close my eyes and drop my head, shaking it from side to side. "I don't deserve it."

"Of course you don't. Nobody does." He has every right to sound harsh and resentful, but he doesn't. There's nothing but love in his voice, and it breaks me down even more.

I open my eyes, but turn away and look in the direction of the diner. So many memories were stirred up in there, things I've been carrying around with me. Baggage that's weighed me down, shaped the person I've become, no matter how hard I tried to ignore it. Is it possible I can finally let it all go? I want to. I want so much to put the past behind me, once and for all, but I don't know how. "I've done things . . . things I'm not proud of. Really terrible things." I turn my head and look into the eyes of Jesus. "I can't figure out how to forgive myself. How can you ever forgive me?"

"All you have to do is ask."

He makes it sound so easy.

"It is easy," he says with a smile, holding up his scar ravaged arms. "I did the hard part, remember?"

A sob jumps up from deep inside me, but I hold it back and force out the words I should have said a long time ago. "I'm so sorry. Forgive me. Please forgive me."

"Done."

He opens his arms wider, and I fall into them. Every other time I've been held by a man, I've wondered if there was an ulterior motive behind his touch. But this is different. There is nothing strange or uncomfortable about being in these arms, no purpose other than to love and comfort me. He pulls me onto his lap, cradling me, like a father holding a child. And there on the grass, in the arms of my savior, the broken pieces of my heart begin to heal.

A moment later, he speaks, his breath soft and sweet against the top of my head. "Penelope says hello."

A new wave of tears comes as emotions bubble up from deep inside my spirit. It surges through me, needing to burst out. And on its way, it pushes out all the guilt and grief that's clawed at my soul. These tears aren't the bitter, pain-filled tears I've cried for so long. These tears are pure joy. He knows my daughter. She's with him. And one day, I'll be with her, too.

He hugs me tightly and then moves me from his lap so we're sitting side by side again. "And now, someone needs to say goodbye."

He blows out a sharp whistle. Barking sounds from far off, and then a dog bounds through the tall grass. I don't recognize the animal until he knocks me flat on my back and licks my face like crazy.

"Grimm?"

I push him back enough so that I can sit up. His eyes are the same, his body shape is the same, but gone are the scars that used to reshape his features and make him look like something that stepped out of a nightmare.

"Grimm, you're beautiful." I look at Jesus. "You fixed him."

He smiles. "This is how Grimm was always meant to look. Did you ever wonder how he got all those scars?"

I shrug while scratching Grimm between his shoulder blades. "I always assumed that he got into a lot of street fights."

"There were a lot of fights, but not because he wanted to participate. He was raised to be a fighting dog. But when his owner put him in the ring, he'd only fight enough to protect himself. He wouldn't go for the jugular and finish the other dog off like he was expected to do."

My heart breaks at the thought of what his life had been like, always struggling, always protecting himself, and never knowing if the next fight would be the one that finished him off. I wrap my arms around his neck and hug him to me, laying my cheek on the top of his head. "No wonder I was drawn to him at the shelter."

"You saw Grimm's heart. Just like Jake sees yours."

My head jerks up. "Jake. Are you saying . . . ?"

"I'm saying that Jake sees you. The real you that you were always meant to be. That's all. You have to take it from there." He stands and dusts off the knees of his khakis. "And now, it's time for Grimm and me to be going."

My arms tighten around Grimm. "Both of you? I don't understand."

His smile is gentle. "I'm taking Grimm home."

That can only mean one thing. My mind goes back to the accident. Grimm jumping into my lap, wedged between me and the steering wheel. His wet fur. What had the fireman said? *The dog probably saved her life.*

Grimm died in the accident. He died saving me. And now he's going home with Jesus. Part of me wants to cry, but instead, laughter tumbles from my lips as I give Grimm's neck one last squeeze. "We'll see each other again one day."

When I turn him loose, Jesus reaches his hand down to help me up. "Are you ready to go back now?"

I sigh. "Do I really have to?"

"Yes, you really do. Remember, you've got more work ahead of you."

I don't want to leave him. Of course, he knows this because, unlike angels, he *does* know everything. He rests his hand on my shoulder and gives it a firm but gentle squeeze. "I am always with you, even when you can't see me as you do now. I will never leave you, even in the midst of trouble and despair."

And there it is. He isn't promising me a perfect life, but he's not asking me to walk alone, either. How could I ask for anything more? "I think I'm ready."

The diner is closer than I thought it was. It only takes a few steps, and I'm at the front door. I reach for the handle, then turn and call, "Thank you!"

All that's behind me now is an empty meadow, the wild flowers and tall grass dancing gently with the breeze. Jesus is gone from view, but a familiar warmth fills my chest. I can still feel him.

I know he heard me.

32

"Surprise!"

Excited cheers, frantic clapping, and the shrill call of noise-makers pour out the door of the diner. The wave of noises rushes to meet me as I step inside. The diner is back to being the size it was the first time I walked in, but there are some noticeable changes. A colorful banner proclaiming "WELCOME BACK ALLIE!" stretches across the back wall above the kitchen pass through. Music blares from a flashy red and chrome trimmed jukebox which stands where the radio used to be. Twinkling white lights, the kind you'd find on a Christmas tree, line the perimeter of the ceiling.

I stand in the doorway, shocked into immobility. It's a lot to take in all at once.

A hand reaches out and grabs me. Fred Astaire waltzes me into the room, gives me a dip, then passes me off to Gene Kelly. Gene twirls me around, then passes me off to someone else. Trying to catch my breath through the laughter and dancing, I look up into the face of my new partner.

Vinnie.

He does a move with each of our arms over and behind the other's neck that's straight out of a disco movie, then takes me by one hand and pulls me further into the room, deeper into the throng of people. I have to do a double-time step to keep up with him. "What's all this?"

His smile is so big, it just might split his face in two. "What does it look like? This is a celebration."

"I knew you could do it. I just knew it!" I hear Norma Jeane's voice and strain to see her, rising up on my tip toes. But when she finally makes her way through the crowd, I see she's changed, too. Her now platinum hair frames her face in short, stylish waves and she's wearing a shimmering, white halter dress and silver high heeled shoes. While I was gone, she morphed into Marilyn.

Looking around, I see the same kind of transformation has taken place with all the others. A very young and trim Elvis saunters through the kitchen door. His jet black hair is slicked back in a neat pompadour, his sideburns are trimmed, and he's abandoned his fry cook get up. Now he's wearing a white suit and blue shoes which I have no doubt are suede.

Beside the jukebox, a young Judy Garland stands fresh faced and happy, clapping her hands. Her dark hair is pulled back in two low, thick ponytails and she's wearing a sweet white dress and red sequined shoes. Sitting on the floor next to her, Lassie looks the same as always, except for the big white satin bow tied loosely around his neck.

I look sideways at Vinnie, who still has one arm draped over my shoulders. He's decked out in a vintage white three-piece suit with an ice blue silk dress shirt underneath. Without the suspenders and the paper hat, he reminds me a little of John Travolta in his *Saturday Night Fever* days.

"What's with all the white, Vinnie?"

"It's symbolic. To commemorate the next step of your journey."

I look around again. They all look like a bunch of celebrity angels. No, it couldn't be . . . I step out from under his arm and scrunch up my nose. "*This* isn't heaven, is it?"

Vinnie roars with laughter. "No. Not even close. And before you ask, it's not what some people call limbo, either. This is simply the place where you decide what your next step will be."

At that, the mood in the room comes down a bit. Everyone's still smiling, but they're more subdued now that they realize the celebration's almost over. They move away from me, going to booths and stools on the outer edges of the diner, until it's just Vinnie and I standing together in the middle of the room.

"Way to kill a party, Vinnie."

He gives his head a slow shake. "There's that sarcasm, again."

He's right. It's time I got serious. Whatever's coming next, I'm ready. "What do I have to decide?"

"If you live or if you die."

I forgot, he still doesn't know about that part. "I already did that," I answer seriously. "I chose life."

Vinnie is beaming. Literally. The light filling the room seems to come from all directions, and it bounces off him like he's a disco ball. "Yes. You chose eternal life. So now, your soul is safe, no matter what your next choice is."

"*Now* I'm safe. Meaning . . ."

"Meaning that now, you're a child of the King. Eternal life in heaven is yours, whether you die today or sixty years from today."

The gravity of what I've been through settles on me. That time in the drive-in was more important than I'd known. "You mean, if I had died before all this, before the showdown with Ba'al, there would have been no eternal life?"

He doesn't speak, just nods gravely.

"I would have gone to hell?"

Another nod.

So when Ba'al offered me a way out, he hadn't been trying to help me at all. Of course he hadn't. He's a demon, and demons aren't in the business of helping people. But I hadn't realized until now just how high the stakes were. It had been his last desperate attempt to secure my soul. And he almost succeeded.

"In the drive-in, with Ba'al, I was so tired," I tell Vinnie, "and I was in so much pain. I just wanted it all to stop. I almost listened to him. I almost let go."

Vinnie reaches out and squeezes my shoulder. "But the important thing is, you didn't let go. You knew what to do. You cried out to God for help, and he heard you."

I cross my arms in front of me and narrow my eyes. "How do you know that? I thought you were worried about me because you didn't know what happened."

"I was." He points at the ceiling. "But I got an update right before you got back."

I should've figured as much. "That's some grapevine you have." A wave of exhaustion hits me, and for a brief second, my vision grows fuzzy. I may be stronger now, but I'm still not functioning at full capacity. "Can we sit down?"

Vinnie extends his hand to the booth we were in before. I fall onto the seat with a sigh, relishing the give and squeak of the cushion beneath me. "What a day. Or I guess it's been several days in the real world, huh?"

"A little over a week, actually." He sits across from me and clasps his hands together on the table. "You're still in a coma. Your family and friends have been taking turns staying with you. And no one knows exactly how severe your brain and spinal injuries are. They won't know until you wake up."

I gape at Vinnie. After all this time of trying to pry information out of him, did he just volunteer some? He can be very succinct when he wants to be. "So what should I do?"

"That I can't tell you. But I can make a suggestion, if it's all right with you."

Now he starts asking my permission? I have to laugh. "I wish you would."

"When you make your choice, don't just think about yourself. Think about how it will affect the people who care about you."

I look down at my hands and consider Vinnie's words. I chew on my lip. Wiggle my foot under the table. He's right, I should consider my family, but I can't help but think about myself first. I remember the pain I started to feel in the drive-in. No doubt it was only a shadow of what I'll experience if I decide to go back to my physical body. It would be so nice to leave that behind, to say goodbye to trauma and discomfort. How I wish I could spend more time in that peaceful, pain-free field, sitting on the grass with Jesus and blowing dandelion seeds to the wind.

But what if I do choose to give up? I think of Freud, who in his life had hung on until the pain was so great that he couldn't bear it anymore. Would letting go now make me like him? Of course, what happened to me was an accident. I hadn't planned on flipping my car. But he hadn't planned on having cancer, either.

This isn't just about me, though. Like Vinnie said, if I die, it will affect the people who love me.

I lift my head and search Vinnie's face for an answer. "If I decide I'm done, if I choose to..." I can't bring myself to say the word.

"Die," he fills in for me bluntly.

"Yes, die, thank you. If I choose that, I don't know what it would do to my Aunt Bobbie. We're very close. And she's gone through so much already."

Vinnie nods. "Yes, she has. But she's stronger than you think. She gave her life to the Lord years ago. Still . . ." He hesitates, looks away, then looks back. "It's hard to know how a person will react when they lose someone they love. It could shake her faith to the point that she walks away from it. Or, she could find strength in her faith, cling to it, and come out even stronger."

I look over Vinnie's shoulder. Elvis stands loose and relaxed, leaning one hip against the counter. Our eyes meet and one side of his mouth curls up in his slow, lopsided grin. Aunt Bobbie would pass out if she could see him. Not to mention Marilyn. To have both of them right there in front of her, standing side by side . . . I think of all the hours Aunt Bobbie and I have spent watching old movies, playing Trivial Pursuit, watching *Jeopardy* and racing to see which one could shout out the answers first. It was Aunt Bobbie who got me interested in trivia in the first place. She was the one who encouraged me to enter my first tournament. She quizzed me to help me get ready. She made me those study-aid cassette tapes for the championship. If it hadn't been for her—

I jerk my head back toward Vinnie. "If it hadn't been for my aunt, I never would have been on that road going to a trivia championship. And if I hadn't been on the road, I wouldn't have been in the accident. If I die, she's going to blame herself. Especially since she figured out why I was so determined to win the thing."

"She might," Vinnie agrees with me.

"That would be terrible." I plunk my elbow on the table and rest my chin against my fist. But what if I go back and my physical condition is so bad that it's a constant reminder of the accident? What if she can't stand to be around me? "The alternative might not be any better."

"That's true. But she and Jake know what kind of condition you're in. They've been told the possible prognosis. And they're still praying for you to come back."

Jake.

"If I don't come back, it will hurt Jake, but he'll be okay." He's young and incredible. He'll find someone else. Not that I want him to. Right now, the thought of him moving on without me hurts more than I expected. Ironic how it's taken a choice between life and death to make me realize how much I want to be with him again.

"What about your mother? How do you think she'll feel if you die?"

"Relieved." The word comes out of me with no thought. It's just there at the front of my brain. The truth of it is like a steel-toed boot to the gut.

I sit back, putting distance between Vinnie and I, but he just leans farther forward, invading my personal space. "Why do you say that?"

"My mother can't stand me."

"Are you sure? From what I've been told, she's pretty upset right now."

I think back to what I heard through the drive-in speakers. She admitted to not doing a great job at mothering. She'd said she wanted another chance. But that's now, when emotions are running high and the situation is dire. People say a lot of things they don't mean in times of high stress.

"I'm sure she's upset that I've been hurt," I say slowly. "But if I go back, it's still not going to change the reality of how she sees me."

"And how's that?"

My breath catches in my chest. It's not like I haven't thought about this before. There was a time when it was all I thought about. And then, I got to the point where I refused to think about it. But speaking it out loud . . . that's new territory for me. "I've never been what she wanted me to be." I hold up my hand and pull back one finger at time, ticking off the ways I've been a disappointment. "First, I was an accident. She never wanted to have kids. If she hadn't been married when she got pregnant, I'm sure she would have gotten rid of me." My mind jumps back to our conversation about the abortion when she all but admitted it. I blow out a short breath and continue. "Then, after she was forced into having me, I had the nerve to be a girl. She always said my dad would have stayed if he'd had a son."

"Do you think that's true?"

I shake my head. "I used to think so, but not anymore. After remembering the day he left, seeing my mother and father together . . . it wouldn't have mattered if I was twin boys. He left because of what was going on between the two of them, not because of me."

"You're right," Vinnie says, his voice soft. "What happened between your mother and any man was between the two of them. None of it was your fault."

"I know, but she thinks it was. She blames me for every breakup she ever had. And she blames me that she never made anything great out of her life. How could she, being strapped down with a kid like me?" I had felt the responsibility of my mom's failures every time a man left her. It rained down on me in her bitter tears, flailed me in her wail of despair, cut through me like buzz saw blades in the angry looks she threw my way.

Vinnie's palms are flat on the table, his thumbs rapping out a beat as he digests what I've just told him. "Did it ever occur to you," he says slowly, "that the way she treats you might really be her response to the way she was treated and the way she sees herself?"

"What do you mean?"

"Think of how she felt when she discovered what her uncle was doing do her sister. The anger, the betrayal, the guilt. She has never let go of it."

Even after seeing what happened with my own eyes, I hadn't really considered the long term effects that day might have had on my mother. But now, it's starting to make sense. She must have loved her uncle. To find out he was violating her sister like that, and to have her mother not believe anything she said . . . it changed her life. I had seen it happen. Right there in that living room, her shoes covered with her uncle's blood, she decided to use men before they could use her. It had colored every choice she made from that day on. And when she ended up with me, another person—another girl—to take care of, she panicked.

"She wasn't able to protect Aunt Bobbie," I say, thinking it through out loud. "So maybe she was afraid that she couldn't protect me, either."

"It's possible. And maybe putting emotional distance between herself and you was the only way she knew of coping with it."

"And when Ethan attacked me—" I gasp. I can see my mother's face clearly, as if it's happening right now. So many emotions play across her features. Her despair, her pain, and something else, something I never noticed before . . . resignation. As though she'd known all along that something like this was going to happen and there was nothing she could do to stop it.

Vinnie shakes his head sadly. "Her worst fear came true."

"But there's something else I don't understand." I reach my fingers out toward Vinnie, as though begging him to put the answer in my hands. "If she's so distrusting of men, why does she keep marrying them? Why didn't she end up more like Aunt Bobbie?"

"How can we measure the damage done by a broken heart?" He weighs his words carefully. "Your aunt endured not only emotional, but physical abuse. She also has a different kind of personality, more pliable, less adept at confrontations. It's why the uncle went after her and not your mother."

I cringe at the thought. "Because he could get away with it. My mother would have fought back." My mother probably would have killed him.

Vinnie nods. "Yes. And it's why she's so angry now. But remember," he holds up one finger, waving it slightly, "only someone who cares deeply can feel so much rage. I think the reason your mother keeps dating and getting married is because she desperately wants to believe that love exists for her. It does, of course. She's just looking in the wrong places."

My heart breaks, but this time, it's not for me or for how hard my life has been. For the first time ever, my heart breaks for my mother. It breaks for the happy teenager who watched her world tilt on its axis and split in half at her feet. It breaks for the bitter woman she became. And mostly, it breaks for all the time she and I have wasted over the years.

I lean forward, hands gripping the edge of the table. "But Vinnie, my mother is who she is. I can't go back and change her past. She's always going to look at me and see everything that went wrong in her life."

Vinnie's lips turn up in a slow smile. "It might surprise you to know that your mother has been at your bedside more than anyone else."

My heart lurches at this new revelation. "Really?"

"Really. She hardly ever leaves. She even made the nurses put a cot in there for her. I think the accident may have given your mother a new perspective on her relationship with you. I can't say how that will pan out if you decide to go back, but it's a start."

Had my father been right? Does my mother really need me after all? And could almost losing me in this accident make her see that? It's wild to think my mother and I could ever be anything but antagonistic toward each other. But then, I never thought I could be forgiven for some of my life choices. I've been given a second chance . . . maybe it's time I gave her one, too.

"If I go back, what can I do for her? Is there any way I can help her?"

"You can pray for her. Love her. Show her that you're not like everyone else. Let her know she can trust you. That you'll be there for her even if she's awful to you. That's really all you can do." Vinnie levels his gaze at me. "But you can't do any of that if you're dead."

True. So I need to go back for my mom, and for Aunt Bobbie. Which brings me back around to Jake. What about him? "You really don't know how bad my physical condition is?"

Vinnie raises his hands in surrender. "I really don't."

"What if I've got brain damage? Or I'm partially paralyzed?" I start chewing on the end of my thumb nail.

Vinnie reaches across the table and nonchalantly pulls my hand away from my mouth. "What if you are?"

"Jake will want to stay with me. He'll want to help me. What if that happens, and he gets tired of being responsible for an invalid? What if he starts to resent me and has an affair with a hot blond at the office and then he leaves me?"

Vinnie shakes his head in confusion. "Where did the blond come from?"

I wave my hand. "It's something . . . someone told me."

"Someone. Someone like Ba'al?"

I don't answer him right away, but finally I admit it. "Yes."

He wags his finger at me. "Allie, I told you he would twist the truth and lie to your face. Let's take this one piece at a time. First off, you don't know how bad things are. There may be nothing major wrong with you, or you might just need a little therapy. Or you could be paralyzed from the neck down and have severe brain damage. The point is, we don't know. We also don't know what's going to happen with Jake. But there's one thing we do know with absolute certainty." He pauses to make his point and looks me straight in the eye. "You can't base any decision on something you heard from a demon."

His statement is such a bald face truth it lifts the huge weight that's been sitting on my chest and pressing the air out of my lungs. I take a deep breath, reveling in this new sense of freedom. "How can I argue with you when you put it that way?"

"You can't." The smile comes back to Vinnie's face. "So, have you made your decision?"

I look around the diner, at the young, eager faces of the people standing against the wall and sitting at the counter and in the booths, and I nod. "Yes, I have. But there's one more thing I need to do first."

33

Vinnie leans across the table. "What do you need to do?"

"I've got to know how much of this is real." I stand up and face the others, waving my arms to get their attention. Then I cup my hands around my mouth and shout out to the crowd. "Everyone who's not an angel, it's okay for you to leave now."

The whole diner changes. The posters and movie props vanish, leaving the walls a clean, sparkling white. The "WELCOME BACK ALLIE!" banner is gone, as is the juke box. The stools are gone, the kitchen pass through is gone, and the only booth left is the one Vinnie's sitting in. The people disappear, gone all at once as if they'd never been there. This leaves Vinnie and me alone in a big, white, empty room.

Except for one couple.

They stand across from us where the pass-through window used to be. Elvis puts two fingers to his forehead and gives me a cocky salute. With one last crooked smile he says, "Take care, little darling."

Beside him, Marilyn holds her hand palm up in front of her lips and blows a kiss in my direction. "Bye bye, honey." She threads her arm through the crook of Elvis's elbow and then they're gone, too, disappearing in a slow fade.

Now it's just Vinnie and me.

"Disappointed?" he asks.

I turn back to him, feeling slightly sheepish. "A little," I say with a shrug. "Out of everybody, I was really hoping those two were angels."

"It doesn't work that way, you know."

One corner of his mouth quirks up, and I wait for him to explain what he means. But he doesn't. Oh great, we're back to me pulling information out of him.

I sigh. "What doesn't work what way?"

"Angels. They're not people who died and went to heaven. People are people and angels are angels, and never the twain shall meet."

He is inordinately pleased with himself. There's no telling how many times he's had to explain this to others over the past hundreds of years, but apparently it never gets old.

"Okay. So the people I met here weren't angels. Then what were they?"

"Does it really matter?"

Maybe it's time to take a different approach. I put one hand on my hip and lean the other against the table. "So why did you bring all of them here?"

"What do you mean?"

"Don't get me wrong. I appreciate everything you did, even if it was a little over the top. But being an angel, I'm sure you could have done the job by yourself."

"Yes, I could have." He stands up and looks down at me. "That's why I didn't bring any of them here."

I squint at him. "You didn't?"

"No."

"You mean . . ." I point upward.

He shakes his head. "Nope."

"So if it wasn't you, and it wasn't him, then . . ." I smack my palm flat against my chest. "Me? You mean I brought them here?"

Vinnie nods, looking pleased. "Like I told you, you have more control than you realize."

This new information is difficult to digest. I think back over everything: Elvis's fried peanut butter and banana sandwich, Norma Jeane's fascination with jewelry, Mark Twain's speech patterns, Einstein's theory of time being relative . . . that was all information I already had. I try to pinpoint something, anything that I heard from those people that I hadn't known before. But I can't.

"You mean it was all a figment of my imagination?"

Vinnie crosses his arms over his chest and frowns. "I never said that."

"But you said I brought them here. And they didn't give me any new information. In fact, I told them things about themselves they didn't know." Now I'm frowning. "So I took all the trivia I've learned over the years, all the facts I've soaked up in preparation for the championship, and let it come to life."

"No," he shakes his head. "You're going in the wrong direction."

Good grief. A terrible thought knocks on the inside of my skull. "Was any of it real?"

"Of course it was. Every thought and every feeling you've had since you got here is real."

"But . . . was Ba'al real?"

He wrinkles his nose as if he can still smell the sulfur. "Yes."

"Was Jesus real?"

"Absolutely." His reply is emphatic. "Was and is."

Okay. Good. "And you? Are you real?"

His expression becomes soft, warm. "What do you think?"

I look him up and down. This is Vinnie, who's been with me from the beginning. Who guided me through the convoluted

JENNIFER ALLEE

labyrinth of my own fears and pain and baggage. Vinnie, who
is more real to me now than some of the flesh and blood people
who have strolled through my life. Of course he's real. He has
to be real.

"Yes, I think you're real. But . . ."

"But what?"

Lips pressed together, I take a moment to work up my cour-
age. I don't want to imagine it, let alone say it. "What if you're
just a drug- and coma-induced dream? How can I know for
sure that any of this was real?"

He holds his hands out in front of him, palms up. "Faith,
Allie. Most of the best things in life are a matter of faith."

"So I'm supposed to blindly believe that you, Jesus, and Ba'al
are all real?" There's nothing funny about this, but a snort of
disbelieving laughter bursts out of me. "It's like the beginning
of a bad joke . . . an angel, a demon, and the Son of God walk
into a bar . . ."

The look Vinnie gives me stops me cold. "Faith is never
blind. But you can't reason it out, and you won't see it if you
look with your eyes. What does your heart tell you?"

I close my eyes and let Vinnie's words sink in, through my
pores and into the core of my being. And I know. Deep in
my spirit I feel the rightness of it, the absolute certainty that
what he tells me is true. I've experienced a miraculous event.
It's unexplainable and impossible to believe, except to take it
on faith.

I look around the empty diner, and something else becomes
unavoidably clear. It's time.

"I have to go." My voice catches in my throat. "I have a life
to get back to."

"Yes, you do."

"Am I going to remember anything that happened? Am I
going to remember you?"

"Yes and no. Don't worry, your salvation will stick. And the choices you made here will remain. You'll feel differently, look at your life differently. But most of the details will stay behind. As it should be." He reaches out, cradling my chin in one hand, smiling at me with fond consideration. Then he puts both his palms on top of my head, his touch light and energizing. "Never forget that you are a child of God. Go with him and live your life to the fullest, no matter what it holds."

I don't know if it's proper etiquette to initiate a hug with your guardian angel, but I do it anyway, throwing my arms around his waist. He squeezes me in return.

"Easy now," he says in my ear. "Watch the wings."

My fingers brush against something soft and I pull away with a gasp. I see Vinnie's clothes have changed again. He seems much more the stereotypical angel now in a beige linen tunic that reaches to his sandaled feet. Peeping over his shoulders are the arcs of snowy white feathers. I give him a questioning look, and he shrugs.

"That polyester suit was getting hot. And I don't think I'll ever get used to how binding those waistbands are. How do you people stand it?"

I roll my eyes toward the ceiling and shake my head. "You've got your wings!"

"I've always had them," he says proudly. "I just thought you might like to see them before you go." He flexes his shoulders and they fan out behind him, making him resemble a big albino peacock about to strut his stuff.

I laugh. It's just as well I won't remember most of this. If I did, I'd want to tell people, and no one would ever believe me if I did.

I take a step backward and lift my hand in farewell. "Bye, Vinnie. Thanks."

As I walk to the door, the walls of the diner become misty. When I reach for the silver handle, it's almost gone. I'm ready to walk outside, but stop when a voice calls out to me.

"Allie."

I turn. Vinnie's gone. The diner's gone. All that's left is a bright, clear light all around me. But I hear Vinnie's last message loud and strong as he sends me off. "You know that piece of tire rubber that hit your car? Truckers call them road gators."

I smile, and my heart feels as though it might burst with happiness.

I never knew that.

34

"Allie?"

I blink. At least, I try to blink, but my eyelids have been cemented shut. I try to speak, but my throat is full of sand and no sound comes out. I try to move, but my arms and legs are strapped down. I can't move, can't speak, can't see. Yet, I must have managed to make some kind of contact because the voices are going crazy.

"She opened her eyes! I saw it!"

"Nurse! Nurse, help!"

"We need help in here!"

I want them all to be quiet. There's something I need to remember, something important. No, not something. Someone . . . *Vinnie.* I can just barely remember him, but it's enough to know I don't want to lose him. If everybody would only shut up, maybe I could hold on to the wisp of memories. Could hold on to the place I just came from.

"Allie! Allie, can you hear me?"

Jake. I hear Jake. His voice is anxious, deep, familiar. It touches a place deep in my heart, sending a zing through my brain, and I don't mind the shouting quite as much anymore.

Choose life.

255

A sense of calm settles over me, despite the frenzied atmosphere.

I choose life.

It takes a concentrated effort, but I force one eye open, then the other. The light is so bright that I immediately want to squeeze my eyes shut again, but I resist the temptation. As I try to focus I can see the shape of a head leaning over me. I expect it to be Jake, but instead I finally make out the round face of a woman, her hair caught up in a ponytail. She looks very serious and before I realize what's going on, she pulls back one of my eyelids and shines an even brighter light back and forth in front of it, then repeats the process with the other eye. Only when she's done does she finally crack a smile. "Welcome back."

She looks over her shoulder, speaks to someone, then steps away. Another woman moves in to take her place, leaning over the bed and smiling. "Alexandra, I'm Dr. Frasier. Can you hear me?"

I open my mouth to speak, but my throat is so dry and tight it seems to be collapsing in on itself. Rather than speaking, I end up gagging.

The doctor puts a gentle hand on my shoulder. "Easy now. Breathe through your nose. You had a tube down your throat for a few days. It's gone now, but it might be hard to talk for a while. Just give me a little nod, or a blink, okay?"

I look at her. Blink. Nod.

You'd have thought I just gave her the cure for cancer, her smile is so big. "Ah, I see we have an overachiever. Wonderful. Now I'm just going to check a few things and see how you're doing."

She fiddles around, poking different parts of my body and making affirmative noises. More people have moved in, nurses who check the IV needle in my arm, change out bags of fluid, note readouts on machines. Finally, the doctor comes back up to my head where I can see her.

"Alexandra, you were in a car accident. You're in the hospital now. We've got a neck brace on you, just to be on the safe side, so you won't be able to move your head very far. You've been unconscious for a little over a week, but it looks like you're doing very well."

I want to say thank you. I try, but only manage to grunt instead.

The doctor looks over her shoulder then back at me. "Your family has been worried about you. Do you feel up to seeing them?"

I try to nod my head, but something pokes me in the chin. Oh yeah, I forgot about the brace. I open my mouth and squeeze out my first intelligible syllable. "Yaz."

I've impressed her again. She's like a proud parent whose child has just delivered the valedictorian address. "Wonderful. I'll send them right in."

She gives my shoulder a quick rub, then talks to the nurses in the room, giving them instructions about fluids, ice chips, keep an eye on her . . . I want to look at them, but I can't turn my head that far. Why does it feel like it's locked in place? Oh yeah, the brace. Why can't I remember that? My head hurts. I don't know if that's good or not, but at least I can feel it. What about the rest of me?

I try to move my hands. They don't go far, but I can flex my fingers. Now, my legs. When I try to move them, it's as if someone has set fire to my lower body. Tears well up in my eyes. I've never felt such pain before. It's awful, but it's wonderful, too. Because even though I can't make them do what I want them to, at least I can feel my legs.

"Oh, Allie. Praise Jesus!"

I hear Aunt Bobbie before I see her. Her footsteps lumber across the floor. Then she's hanging over the bed, about to fling herself on top of me when someone stops her.

"We need to be gentle with her for awhile, don't you think?"

Jake.

Aunt Bobbie nods enthusiastically, then stands calmly beside the bed, a Cheshire cat grin taking over her face. Her made-up face. I squint, making sure this is my aunt I'm looking at. Yep, it's her. Not only is she wearing makeup, but I think she's had her hair done. I'll have to talk to her about that later.

Jake stands next to her, looking almost like I remember. Handsome. Solid. Eyes sparkling behind his black rimmed, Clark Kent specs. But he's got one goofy grin on his face.

Next to Jake, standing the farthest away from my head, is my mother. I don't think I've ever seen her out in public in such bad shape. Her eyes are bloodshot and sunken, she's wearing no makeup, and her hair looks like it hasn't been washed in a day or two. But besides the obvious physical difference, there's a different quality about her. A vulnerability I'm not used to seeing in my mother.

There's something I need to remember about her. Something important. I try to pull it up to the front of my head, but it won't come. What I do know is that I'm happy to see her, which is surprising in itself.

"Mom." My throat is raw and ragged from the exertion of forcing out that one word, but I have more to say. I can't remember why, but I know it's important. "Love . . . you."

She bites her lip, blinks hard. She nods and takes my hand in hers, squeezing it twice before letting it go. Somehow I know that's all she can do right now. It's enough. As she pulls her hand from me, her fingers brush my skin, and I feel the edges of her nails. They're sharp and ragged.

She's been biting them. If I had the strength to laugh, I would. For now, all I can manage is a twitch of my lips.

Aunt Bobbie is stroking my forehead, pushing aside clumps of my oily hair, which I can tell is quite in need of a wash. Despite that, Jake continues grinning down at me as if I'm the most beautiful thing he's ever seen. My heart constricts. I hurt him, but he's still here, still by my side. I focus on his eyes, and push out one more excruciating word.

"Sorry."

He closes his eyes, and when he opens them, they really are the windows to his soul, just like the old saying says. "It's okay. When you've gotten your strength back, I'll let you make me dinner." He smiles. "Or something."

I twitch my lips again, hoping I look better than I feel.

"We've been praying for you, sweetheart," Aunt Bobbie says. "All three of us have." She leans a little closer to my ear and adds quietly, "Even your mother."

My eyes shift to the end of the bed. Mom nods. Her cheeks are marked with the tracks of the tears she hasn't bothered to wipe away.

"Wha . . . what . . . happened?"

I want to know what happened to these three while I was otherwise occupied. Why has Aunt Bobbie spent any attention to the way she looks for the first time in years? And why is my mother so emotionally raw that she doesn't care what she looks like? And after the way I treated Jake, why is he still so attentive?

But he doesn't know that's what I mean. He answers the more obvious question. "The EMTs said the truck ahead of you had a blowout and it threw off a piece of tire rubber. It slammed into the windshield of your car and made you lose control. It was a freak accident."

"We're just so happy you're back with us, safe and sound," Aunt Bobbie says. Then she claps her hands together. "Oh, and I learned a nifty new bit of trivia. Do you know what the truckers call those pieces of tire rubber that are all over the highway? They call them road gators. Isn't that great?"

Road gators.

Striped suspenders.

Red bow tie.

Paper banana boat hat.

Vinnie.

I smile. Try to nod my head but can't and then remember the brace again, so I make an affirmative noise instead.

Yes, now I know.

Group Discussion Guide

1. Allie describes her dog, Grimm, as "the ugliest beast in all of California, and most likely the entire West Coast." What does it tell you about Allie's character that she would adopt a dog that everybody else looked past?

2. Allie has driven Interstate 15 often enough to be familiar with the roadside sights. Is there a daytrip you've taken so many times you know exactly what to expect? What would you think if a strange building popped up out of nowhere?

3. When Allie and Aunt Bobbie talk about Marilyn Monroe, Allie says that Marilyn had it made because of her looks. Aunt Bobbie calls her beauty a curse, and we find out that Allie's mother thinks a woman needs to use her body to get what she wants. Is beauty a blessing, a curse, or something else entirely?

4. When the EMTs pull Allie's body from her car, there's no doubt that Vinnie's Diner is not your normal food joint. What do you think the diner represents?

5. When Joe brings in the chest, Allie says it's not hers. His response is, "Oh, it's yours all right. You've been lugging this stuff around with you for years." What does he mean by that?

6. Allie, her mother, and her aunt have all experienced a lot of pain and disappointment when it comes to men. How was each woman affected? Why do you think they all had such different responses to their past experiences?

7. The discovery that Jake has been praying for his future wife even before he met Allie scares her into running from him. Why would she have such a severe reaction?

8. During the showdown with Ba'al, he tells Allie that the devil can't make a person do anything. Do you think that's true?

9. Allie didn't believe she was worthy of being loved because of the mistakes she made in her past. Is there something in your past that holds you back? Do you believe Jesus is big enough to erase that and give you a clean start?

10. In the end, Vinnie reveals that he's Allie's guardian angel. Do you believe such angels exist? Have you felt the presence of one in your life?

Want to learn more about Jennifer Allee
and check out other great fiction from
Abingdon Press?

Check out our website at
www.AbingdonFiction.com
to read interviews with your favorite authors,
find tips for starting a reading group,
and stay posted on what new titles are on the horizon.

Be sure to visit Jennifer online!

www.jenniferalleesite.blogspot.com

1

Your daughter's on television."

"What?" I just about drop the spoon I'm using to stir my custard mixture. Is this a joke? A wrong number? I pull my cell phone away from my ear and read the ID on the screen. Nope. That's Jules's name, right under the picture of her wearing a red, white, and blue stovepipe hat at last year's July Fourth picnic.

"Monica? Are you there?"

Her voice calls through the speaker, and I slowly put the phone back to my ear. "Yeah. I'm here."

"Did you hear what I said?"

I close my eyes and shake my head, as if that will bring some clarity to my mind. It doesn't work. "I heard, but . . . are you sure?"

"Absolutely. I recorded it to the DVR so you can see for yourself."

Leave it to Jules to think of the practical answer to my questions. "I'll be right there."

"I'll leave the porch light on."

As we end the call, I look down at the spoon I'm still holding, motionless in the sauce pan. Instead of creamy custard, I now have something more akin to runny scrambled eggs. It's ruined. Being a chef, I don't usually make such stupid mistakes, but I'm more than a little shell-shocked from the bomb that just fell on me. I turn off the flame, pour the contents down the disposal, then drop the pot and spoon into the sink with a clatter.

Running upstairs to grab my shoes, scenes from the past flash through my memory.

The hospital. All those white walls. The antiseptic smell. The rhythmic *squeak-click-click-squeak* of the gurney. The turtle-shaped water spot on the delivery room ceiling. The sharp cry of lungs being filled with oxygen for the first time. When I turned my head away, one nurse said to the other, "She's not keeping it. We're supposed to give the baby right to the adoptive parents."

That had been my idea. Don't give the baby to me. Why should I hold something that's not mine to keep? I thought it would be easier that way.

I was wrong.

Still, twenty-five years later, I do believe I made the right decision for my daughter. As I stuff my feet into my sneakers, I still think it was the right thing to do. For everyone. Even so, my knees feel slightly wobbly as I trot back down the stairs. My hand shakes as I grab my house keys. And when I call to my dog, Ranger, my voice shakes.

"I've got to go out."

He lifts his shaggy brown head from the couch and looks my way, no doubt thinking he can stop me with a longing look from his big, soulful eyes. But I dash right past him.

"Sorry, buddy. No walk tonight."

As I pull the front door closed behind me, a velvety breeze rubs across my cheeks, my bare arms, and my shorts-clad legs. I've lived in the Las Vegas valley long enough to know that 100-degree weather during the day often results in the most wonderful nighttime conditions. Everyone else on the block knows it, too, and it looks like most of them are taking advantage of it tonight.

Mr. Williams raises his hand in greeting as he approaches, and I wave back. His dog, a black-and-white Great Dane named Caesar, tugs him along, straining at the leash. It's obvious who's walking whom.

"Where's Ranger?" Mr. Williams asks.

I motion behind me. "Hanging out at home. I'm heading over to see Jules."

The wind picks up, and a gust lifts his silver comb-over and drops it on the other side of his head. Smoothing it back in place with one hand, he nods. "Have fun, then. See you—" The rest of his words are blown away as Caesar propels him down the block.

I'm thankful for the wind. It provides an excuse to keep my head down. Hands stuffed in my pockets, shoulders curled forward, ponytail swinging wildly, I speed walk the three-house distance to Jules's without having to interact with anyone else.

Just as she promised, the porch light is on and I open the front door without knocking. Inside the foyer, I kick off my shoes and call out, "It's me!" I'm immediately swarmed by tweenager John and eight-year-old twins Jerrod and Justin.

"Hey Aunt Monica!"

"Did you bring something yummy?"

"Where's Ranger?"

Opening my arms wide, I try to hug them all at once. "Sorry, boys. Only me tonight." It's pretty rare for me to come over here without some kind of food offering for the rug rats.

"Guys, give Aunt Monica some breathing room." Jules leans her five-foot-nine-inch frame over the boys, bracing one hand on Jerrod's head, and plants a kiss on my cheek. Then she looks back down at her sons. "Head upstairs. Now."

The three grumble in unison, but they don't argue. It makes me wonder what Jules said to them before I got here. Did she tell them we needed to have a big-person talk? Or did she warn them there might be crying? The threat of experiencing female emotion would be enough to scare them away for at least the rest of the night. Possibly till puberty.

Jules links her arm through mine and pulls me through the house. We pass the room they use as an office, and a voice calls out. "Hey, Monica."

"Hey, Jackson," I call back to her husband. Apparently, he's also been warned about the high likelihood of hysterics.

"You want a drink?" she asks as we walk through the kitchen.

"What have you got?"

"Everything we need for killer root beer floats."

"Ooh, the hard stuff." I shake my head. "Maybe later."

When we get to the family room, my eyes immediately fly to the flat screen TV mounted on the wall, but it's not even on.

"In a second." Jules pats my back. "First, you need some details. Let's sit down."

We settle on the worn, chocolate brown sectional. I was with her when she picked it out. Chocolate was my suggestion, because I thought it would hide stains. She angles toward me and puts one hand flat on the seat cushion, right next to a big, dark spot of something. As it turns out, the antics of three young boys can't be hidden, no matter how hard you try.

We look at each other, and I realize that for once my strong, take-charge friend is at a loss for words. So I get us started. "What was she doing on TV?"

Jules tucks a piece of blond hair behind her ear, but her hairstyle is so short, it just looks like she's stroking the top of her ear. "You know that reality show I watch? *Last Family Standing?*"

I nod. "Yeah. It's the one with the hot-but-snarky host."

She sighs, but her mouth quirks up into a grin. "Why is that the only thing you remember about the show?"

Because I only watched it once, just to please her. And since I didn't know who any of the contestants were or what was going on, all I had to concentrate on was the host. Who was pretty memorable.

"The basics are simple," Jules says. "The season starts out with eight teams made up of two family members. All the teams are dumped in a remote location and have to rough it while they compete against each other until only two family teams are left. Then the audience votes to decide the winner."

I hold my palm out to her. "Forgive me if I'm not fascinated, but what difference does it make? What does this have to do with my daughter?"

"Tonight was the season finale, and at the end, they introduce some of the contestants for the next season. She was on the show tonight." Jules looks down for a second, rubbing her finger along the edge of the cushion stain.

Now that I've had some time to process the news, questions begin to bubble up in my brain. "How do you know it's her? You don't even know what she looks like. Heck, I don't even know what she looks like."

"She looks a lot like you."

I immediately picture a younger version of myself: dark auburn hair, blue eyes, and an upper lip that I've always thought was a bit too thin. Does she feel the same way? Does she ever look into the mirror and give it a pouty smile, making her lips as prominent as possible?

What am I doing? I shake my head, banishing the daydream and pulling my focus back to reality.

"But that could be a coincidence. I have one of those faces, you know? People are always asking if they know me from somewhere." I sigh. That's it. That has to be it. "It's just a mistake. She must be someone else's—"

"She has your picture."

The blood in my veins immediately converts to ice water. "My picture? Are you sure?"

Jules offers up a gentle smile. "Yes. It's your graduation photo. And it has your first name and the date written on the back."

My spine seems to have lost the ability to hold me upright. My shoulders slump, and I plop back against the cushions. I don't understand any of this. I chose the birth parents from a book full of hopefuls, and we even met once. But I never gave them my name or a photo or anything that would tie us together.

"Hey," Jules grabs my hand and squeezes it between both of hers. "Are you okay?"

"No." Only a handful of people know about this chapter of my life. Looking into the concerned eyes of my best friend, I'm glad she's one of them. "I'm about as un-okay as you can get."

She understands. The consummate nurturer, Jules also understands the importance of what we want to do versus what we need to do. She leans over and snatches the remote from the coffee table. "You ready?"

Can I ever be ready for this? Half an hour ago I was living a happy, uncomplicated life. My biggest worries were wondering if I should take Ranger to the vet for a teeth cleaning, and keeping the eggs from curdling in my custard. Now, I'm a woman with a past. A past that's about to come to life before my eyes.

God help me. Please help me. I'm so not ready.

Without waiting for me to answer, Jules pushes a few buttons, bringing the TV screen to life.

Ready or not, here she comes.

2

Seeing my daughter is simultaneously the most amazing and heartbreaking experience of my life. Jules was right; she does look like me. From the nose up, at least. Her eyes are blue, and her hair is auburn, although it's much brighter than mine. But the jawline, the chin, the lips . . . those are reminiscent of Duncan. I sure hope that's all she inherited from her father.

The young woman—who, if I've done my mental math correctly is twenty-five years, three months, and thirteen days old—smiles down at me from the wall-mounted flat screen. It's a sedate smile. A Mona Lisa smile that could mean any number of things.

I'm content.

I'm bored.

I secretly want to slap my birth mother silly, but I'm keeping that to myself until the opportune moment.

An off-screen voice blares out. "Twenty-five-year-old fashion designer Jessica Beckett comes to us from—"

The buzzing in my ears drowns out the rest of that sentence. Jessica. My daughter's name is Jessica.

I shake my head, and the male voice registers again. ". . . has a special reason for being on *Last Family Standing.*"

My daughter—Jessica—opens her mouth to speak. I lean forward, desperate to finally hear her, to know how her adult voice has transformed from the newborn cries imprinted on the auditory center of my brain. But she freezes, and I almost tumble off the edge of the couch cushion.

I swing my head in Jules's direction. "Why did you do that?"

"Just checking on you."

"I'm fine."

"You're whiter than an Alaskan albino."

I'm not sure why Alaskan albinos would be whiter than any others in the world, but I get her point. "I never knew her name."

"Your choice?"

"Yes." My fingernails press into the bare skin on my thighs. "I figured the less I knew, the easier it would be to let her go."

I don't know if that line of reasoning was correct or not. What I do know is that I can't imagine the whole experience being any harder than it was.

I look at Jessica's frozen face. "Where did the announcer say she lives?"

"Irvine. California."

So close. You can drive from here to there in about five hours. Did she grow up there? Has she always been just a car drive away?

"He's not the announcer."

"What?"

Jules motions at the TV. "The man talking is Rick Wolff, the host of the show."

My head cocks to the left. "Does that matter?"

She ignores the question. "Are you ready for me to hit play?"

I nod. Jules aims the remote like a gun, and my daughter begins to speak.

"I was adopted as a baby. Don't get me wrong," she waves her hands wildly, palms out, "I had a very happy childhood. No problems there."

She laughs. It sounds a bit forced, but then I don't know her well enough to judge. That could just be the way she laughs.

"My parents and I are very, very close."

Heat floods my cheeks and I swallow back something vile that tries to creep up my throat. She's close to her parents. That's good. That's what I always wanted: for all of them to be happy. There's no reason to feel like I've been kicked in the gut.

Jessica's lashes dip, as though she's taking time to compose her thoughts. When she looks at the camera, that shadow of a smile is back.

"Even though I'm happy, I think it's time I met my birth mother."

Ice replaces heat as all the blood drains from my face. "She wants to find me?"

"Keep listening," Jules says.

Jessica's face is replaced by a montage of still photos from her childhood as Rick Wolff's voice once again takes command of the program. "Jessica may want to find her birth mother, but does the mother want to be found? Jessica has located no information about the woman who gave her up twenty-five years ago. Her only clue is an old graduation photo with the name Monica written on the back."

There I am. My senior picture fills the screen. I was barely eighteen, excited to leave high school behind and head off to culinary school. Jessica hadn't been born yet. She wasn't even a glimmer in my eye. It wouldn't be until two years later that I'd meet her bad-boy father and lose all grip on common sense.

"Where did they get that?" I ask aloud. "I never gave her parents anything."

"They didn't get it," Jules answers. "Jessica had it when she got in touch with the show."

A moment later, I hear the exact same thing recounted by Jessica herself. The host asks her how she got the photo, and she shrugs. "It's always been on the mantel with all the other family photos. When I was old enough to understand, my parents told me it was my birth mother. They got the picture the day I was born, but they never did tell me from whom."

The mystery of how Jessica got the picture is replaced by another, far more important question. "Pause it."

Jules hits the button and looks at me.

"So she's trying to find me?"

"Yes."

"But why is she talking about it on this show?" It's a physical competition based on endurance and mind games. It's not a show that reunites families.

The corner of Jules's mouth quirks up. "Why do you think?"

I don't want to say what I think. It would be better to hear it from someone else. Maybe then it won't be real. Elbows to knees, I hang my head and wave blindly toward the TV. "Restart it."

"I can't think of anything better," Jessica's voice says, "than competing on *Last Family Standing* with my birth mother."

I raise my head slowly, just in time to see Jessica look directly into the camera, tilt her head, and grin. Good grief, it's exactly what Duncan used to do. And I never could say no to him.

Jessica's image is replaced by Rick Wolff. Wearing a khaki shirt and shark tooth necklace, he has a quasi-rugged look, like a model from a safari-wear catalog. "Will Jessica find her mother? That's yet to be seen." He crosses to a tiki torch and wraps his hand around the pole. "If she doesn't, her flame will be snuffed out before she has a chance to begin." With something resembling a coconut shell on the end of a stick, he covers the top of the torch, extinguishing it. Then he looks straight at the camera, as if he knows I'm sitting on my best friend's couch and holding my breath. "If you're out there, Monica, or if you know Monica, please call or text us at the number on the screen."

Jules aims the remote again, and the TV goes blank. "That's it. He moves on to someone else now."

Silence settles between us. I don't know what to say. A thousand thoughts are crowding my mind.

My daughter wants to meet me.

She's beautiful.

She wants me to be on a reality show.

All I have to do is call that number.

Who gave her my picture?

A reality show? Me?

Jules leans over and squeezes my knee. "Talk to me. What are you going to do?"

What am I going to do? No way I'm going on a reality show, especially this one. Jules has told me all about it. I've heard about the harsh conditions, the lack of food that drives contestants to insect consumption, the duplicity that's required in order to win. How can I willingly subject myself to that?

But how can I not? My daughter wants to meet me. My daughter. Jessica. For years, I've put her out of my mind. Not because I wanted to, but because I had to. It was the only way I could survive the heart-wrenching decision to let her go. And letting her go was the only way I could ensure she had a good, happy life. I never expected to see her again. But now, I can.

My daughter wants to meet me. And I will do whatever it takes to meet her.

I look at Jules, blinking hard. "Can I use your phone?"

3

What did you do?"

When Jules gave me her phone, I had every intention of calling the number on the TV screen. But halfway through dialing, a thought occurred to me. How did Jessica's family get that photo of me? She said her parents had it since she was a baby, but there was only one other person outside our little group who knew what I was doing.

"What do you mean, dear?" My mother's voice is smooth, innocent. She's obviously not a fan of *Last Family Standing* because she has no clue what I'm talking about.

"You gave a copy of my high school graduation picture to the Becketts, didn't you?"

Thick silence is followed by a long, deep sigh. That's admission enough for me.

"Mom, how could you? You know I wanted to stay out of their life."

"If you wanted that, you never should have given them your baby." She sighs again, but this time it's short and final, more like a snort. "I'm sorry. That didn't come out the way I wanted it to."

Maybe not, but it came out exactly the way she meant it. Mom has never understood how I could give up my baby for adoption, and she never agreed with my decision to cut all ties with the Becketts. If she'd had her way, we would have been one big, extended family, exchanging letters and pictures, getting together on holidays. It had almost killed me to walk away from my child when all I knew of her was the glimpse of her tiny, newborn body. How could I stand to get to know her, watch her grow, and have to leave her again and again and again? Mom's philosophy was "better something than nothing." But I knew better. It was like the one time in high school that I took a drag off a friend's cigarette. There had been something seductive about it, how it warmed my whole body. In that second, I knew I had two choices: keep smoking and become addicted, or never, ever smoke again. I chose the latter, just like I did with my daughter. If I stayed in contact, spent any time with her, I would have become addicted. I would have needed more and more of her, until I'd want her back, all for myself. The only choice, the one that would result in the least amount of broken hearts, was to go cold turkey. But Mom never got how I could quit my daughter.

"When did you even see the Becketts?"

"At the hospital, the day after she was born. I was looking at her through the nursery window, and there was a young couple next to me. It didn't take long for us to realize we were looking at the same baby." More sighing blows through the phone.

I'm not an insensitive fool. I know this whole thing has been difficult for her, too. But right now, I need information. "What did you tell them?"

"That I was your mother. That you were a good person who just lost her way. And I showed them your picture, the one I kept in my wallet."

They already knew what I looked like, and Mom knew it. But I guess she wanted them to see what I looked like before I fell into a life of sin and questionable choices. "And you gave it to them."

"Because they asked if they could keep it." Her voice has a hard edge. "And I'm glad they did. At least someone realized that sweet baby needed a connection to her real mother."

"Susan Beckett has been her mother for twenty-five years. She deserves that title way more than I do. I'm more like an after-the-fact surrogate."

"Be that as it may." Mom's dismissive tone is more than a little insulting. "Why are you asking me about this now? How did you even find out?" She gasps, sucking back in all that previously sighed-out air. "She contacted you, didn't she?"

"Not exactly."

"Have you seen her?"

"In a manner of speaking."

"Either you've seen her or you haven't. It's a simple question."

This situation is many things: bizarre, uncomfortable, thrilling, confusing. The list goes on and on. The one thing it's not is simple.

So, I tell Mom about the TV show, which I was right, is not on her list of shows-she-never-misses. In fact, she's never even heard about it, so I have to take a side trip and tell her not only what it's about but also what time it's on and which network.

"Well, that explains why I've never seen it," she says. "It's on at the same time as my cooking program. The one where they have to make a three-course meal out of whatever leftovers they find in the fridge. I never miss that show."

"Mom, focus. We're talking about Jessica."

"Who's Jessica?"

I fall back on the couch, my head lolling against the cushions. "She's my daughter." Before Mom can run off on another tangent, I tell her about Jessica looking for me to be on the show with her, and how she showed my photo on air.

"Thank the good Lord. You see, I knew I was right. I knew she'd want to find you one day."

"You still should have told me. Then at least I would have been prepared."

"Monica, your attitude is baffling. You should be thanking me for helping your daughter find you, not haranguing me for doing the right thing."

Jules comes back in the room, and through a series of exaggerated facial features, we share a silent conversation.

How's it going?

Exactly how I expected.

Oh man, I'm sorry.

There's only one way to end this phone call. "I'm sorry if I upset you, Mom. I know you only want what's best for me."

"I always have." She sniffs for effect. "When are you going to see her?"

"I have no idea. I still need to call the show."

"You haven't called them yet? What are you waiting for, an engraved invitation?"

We've gotten to the point in the conversation where Mom pulls out the clichés and platitudes. My instant response is sarcasm. "Yes, that's exactly what I'm waiting for."

She laughs, because we've done this dance enough times that she finds my dry wit, as she calls it, endearing. "Well, you got something better. You got an invitation in front of a national audience. You'd best stop chewing the fat with me and give them a call."

"Yes, Mom. I will."

We exchange the usual I love you and I love you too, and I end it.

Jules plunks herself down next to me. She's holding two bowls of ice cream. One is plain strawberry, the other is vanilla surrounded with sliced bananas, covered in chocolate fudge and whipped cream, and crowned with three maraschino cherries.

I point at the big, decadent bowl. "Please tell me that's for me."

"Of course. We've passed the point of root beer floats. Now, it's sundae time."

"God bless you." I take the bowl and dig in.

"I figured if you needed to avoid the issue for a bit, at least this is a tasty way to do it."

"I'm not avoiding anything." I give her a stern look, but there's no conviction behind it.

She laughs, and a little bit of ice cream flies out of her mouth and lands on her leg. "Of course you are. Why else would you call your mother?"

"Good point."

She swipes the ice cream from her jeans, considers her fingertip for a moment, then shrugs and licks it off. With three boys who are forever dropping food, Jules is a firm believer in the five-second rule.

The ice cream is having the desired effect. With each sweet, silky mouthful, I relax a little more, until finally, my bowl is empty, and I'm slouched down on the couch, staring at the now-blank TV screen.

"Why do you think she did it?"

Jules takes the bowl and sets it inside her own. "Because she wants to meet you."

"I get that, but why this way?" I waggle an accusing finger at the big, black rectangle. "Why on national TV? She could have hired a private investigator, kept it all hush-hush."

"Hush-hush?"

"On the down low. Nice and quiet." I press my finger to my lips. "Sh!"

"Uh oh." Jules grins. "Someone's sugar-drunk."

"Am not." But as I draw my brows down into a scowl of consternation, the buzzing in my brain grows louder. "Okay, maybe a little."

"Why don't you stay here tonight and sleep it off?"

I shake my head. "I'm fine."

"Friends don't let friends walk home while on a sugar buzz." She stands and heads for the kitchen. "But if you insist, I'll force-feed you some coffee first."

The family room is much too quiet and empty, so I follow her. While she fires up the Keurig, I grab two mugs from the cupboard, set them on the counter beside her, and then drop down on one of the barstools surrounding the island.

Jules puts one of the mugs beneath the spout and presses a button. "To answer your question, I have no idea why Jessica is looking for you on television. It could be that she's a fan of the show, and she figured her unique twist would get her on as a contestant."

"It worked."

"Or, she could be trying to shock and embarrass you."

"That worked, too." I brace my chin on my fist and sigh.

"But the only way to know for sure is to ask her."

"And the only way to ask her is to go on the show."

The coffee stops dripping, and Jules brings the mug to me. I wrap my hands around it, breathing in the rich aroma of French vanilla. As the steam rises, I blink and look up at the woman I trust more than anyone in the world. "Will you help me?"

Without hesitation, she sits on the stool opposite me and squeezes my knee. "Every way I can."

"If I do this, I'm going to need you to coach me so I don't kill myself on that show. Or worse, look like an idiot."

Jules laughs and gets up to make her own coffee. "Your priorities are seriously messed up."

"So I've been told."

She frowns at me. "You know I was kidding."

"I know." But she's also right. What kind of a person gives away her own flesh and blood? Sure, I've always said I did it so my daughter would have a better life, but is that the total truth? How much of my decision was based on what would be easier for me?

My nose starts to tingle, and I sniff it away. "Did I do the right thing, Jules?"

"You did what you felt was best at the time. At this point, it doesn't matter if it was right or wrong. What matters is that you have a daughter who wants to meet you. What are you going to do about her now?"

If I meet her, it may be the most painful, excruciating experience of my life. Or it could be the best. But if I don't meet her, then it will be like I've abandoned her all over again. There's only one thing I can do.

"I'm going to sleep on it."

4

By the time I get home, I've convinced myself that a good night's sleep is essential to the decision-making process. The fact that I'll probably toss and turn and be unable to shut off my brain is immaterial. At the very least I need to be in my bed, curled into the fetal position with my covers pulled tightly around me.

I can barely open the front door because Ranger is right there, bouncing and circling and whining.

"Back up, buddy." Sucking in my stomach, I slide through the cracked door, and shut it behind me. "You missed me, huh?"

Then the phone rings, and his actions make sense. I might have the only dog in the world who freaks out at the sound of a telephone. Ranger isn't excited I'm home; he's having the equivalent of a doggie panic attack.

"Come on." He stays so close to me he presses against the side of my leg as I walk to the phone. I'm about to answer when I notice the digital display. The phone number isn't familiar. And I have twenty-six missed calls. It's a miracle poor Ranger didn't chew his way through the door.

After the ringing stops, I dial into voicemail. The robotic female reports, "You have twenty-six new messages."

That can't be good. I sink to the floor and wrap my arms around Ranger. We both need the emotional support. He climbs over my legs until he's sitting half in my lap and half on the floor. There's a comfort to the weight and heat of another living being, because it means I don't have to go through this alone. Sure, Ranger's just a dog, but he loves me in that unconditional way only animals can. Right now, I need all the love I can get.

My back is against the wall, in every sense of the phrase. A deep breath, a few buttons punched, and the messages begin to play.

"Monica, I think I just saw you on TV! Call me. It's Wendy."

"Saw you on *Last Family.* Are you going to call them?"

"Monica. Wow, it's been a long time. Do you remember me? Tom. We had freshman biology together. Uh . . . I'll try again later."

It's a weird combination of people. Some I know now, like my pastor, who is concerned about me and makes a point of mentioning that his wife is a fan of the show, not him. Some are people who knew me in high school or culinary school. And some I haven't heard from in over twenty years. But now, thanks to the marvels of modern technology, they've all found me. It's a slightly disturbing thought. "Maybe I'm overreacting." My fingers thread through Ranger's thick, shaggy fur. "Why would anybody care about me, anyway?"

Sure. This is just a momentary blip of excitement for a few people who have nothing better to do than sit glued to their TV screens every Tuesday night, watching a bunch of emotionally vulnerable people live out an exaggerated month of their lives. Tomorrow, no one will give me a second thought.

The phone rings again and Ranger's head jerks up. If this keeps up, neither one of us will get any sleep. I turn off the ringer, then gently push him off my legs so I can stand.

"Time to hit the hay."

Ranger bounds upstairs and I follow, turning lights off as I go. Things will look different in the morning.

I'm sure of it.

Things look different in the morning, all right. They look worse. They sound worse, too, thanks to the incessant trilling of the door chimes at the obscene hour of 7:00 a.m.

I'm able to extricate myself from the bedsheets without disturbing Ranger, who's spread out on the end of the mattress. Crazy mutt. A phone call sends him into fits, but the doorbell doesn't faze him.

Slipping into my bathrobe, I shake my head. "If a thief ever broke in, you would be less than useless."

The doorbell sounds again. I hurry down the stairs, grumbling to myself that whoever's out there better have a darn good reason for being so irritating. On my way to the door, I pass the phone table. Thank goodness I decided to turn off the ringer because not only have more calls come in but also for the first time ever there's a light blinking to inform me that my voice mailbox is full.

Go figure. Your photo gets flashed on one TV show, and suddenly you're the most popular girl in school.

I yank the front door open. "Yes?"

The man on my front porch is much too chipper for this hour of the morning. His smile—which reveals blindingly white, yet not perfectly straight, teeth—rearranges the features of his face, crinkling the skin around his eyes and exposing perfect twin dimples. "Good morning, Monica."

He acts like we know each other. Even though there is something familiar about this man, I know we've never met. None of my friends have smiles like that. And none of them come with a cameraman pointing the big, black eye of a camera straight at me.

The floor is suddenly very shaky beneath my feet. "You're him."

"That's what they tell me." His laugh rumbles as he extends his hand. "Rick Wolff."

I take a step backward, as if the mere act of not shaking his hand will fix everything. "How did you find me so fast?"

An easy shrug lifts one shoulder. "Several people called in during the show last night, including a couple of your friends who provided your full name and your address."

"Some friends," I mutter.

He lets it slide. "By the end of last night's show, we were already prepping the plane to come out here."

I cross my arms over my chest, feeling more vulnerable than usual. "I was going to call in. You didn't have to fetch me."

His eyes remind me of a big jug of fresh-brewed sun tea, especially when he opens them wide. "Then you watch the show?"

"No. My friend does. She's obsessed with you. With the show." His smile shifts into a lazy grin, and I know exactly what he must be thinking. "She's married," I stammer.

He steps forward. "That's okay. She's not the one I'm interested in."

Not only is this wildly inappropriate, it's being documented on film. I've got to put an end to it. "Please, this isn't a good time. I'll call you later. When I can talk." When I'm wearing clothes.

He's about to say something, probably something smooth and charming to coerce his way into my house, when a vehicle pulls up at the sidewalk. The white van has all kinds of weird equipment on its roof, including what looks like a satellite dish. If that doesn't tell me enough, the words My News 3 painted on the side give it away.

The man on my porch doesn't look surprised. "You should probably let me in now."

"Look, Mr. Wolff, I—"

"Rick."

"Fine. Rick. I can't do this now."

Something close to sympathy changes those facial features again. "Take my word for it, Monica. It will be much better if you let me in now. That news crew isn't going anywhere until they get a story."

"And how will talking to you take care of them?"

"Because after you and I talk and come to an agreement, I'll come back out here and give them a statement."

There's no denying I want to avoid speaking to the press. But there's something even more important at stake. "Will you tell me about my daughter?"

He takes another step closer. "You can ask me anything you want."

"And you'll answer me?"

"You can ask me anything you want," he repeats, with a grin that says he may or may not answer.

But there's only one way to find out.

"Okay. You can come in." I point at the cameraman, whose face I still haven't seen. "But he stays outside."

Rick shakes his head. "Sorry. Where I go, he goes. If you don't sign a release, we can't use the footage, but for now, he shoots everything."

I'd like to shoot something. Over his shoulder, I see the news van doors open and people start to pour out. Considering the postage-stamp-size of my front yard—aka, rock garden—there's no time to argue. "All right."

Once Rick and the bearer of the one-eyed monster are inside, I shut the door and lock the deadbolt with a forceful twist. Toenails click on the tile behind me, and Ranger lopes in, tongue lolling out one side of his mouth, greeting our visitors with the closest thing a dog has to a smile.

The camera is trained on Rick as he hunkers down and becomes my dog's new best friend. This is as good a time as any to make myself decent.

"I'm going upstairs to get dressed. The living room is that way." I point. "Make yourself comfortable."

Halfway up the stairs I stop, turn, and head back down, leaning over the rail to yell at them. "But not too comfortable. Don't dig around in my medicine cabinet or anything like that."

Back up I go, then stop, come back down again. "Not that there's anything I don't want you to see in there."

I give it one more try: up, stop, come back down. "Or anything you shouldn't see. It's just rude."

By this time, Rick is looking at me like I've lost my mind, and the camera is bouncing up and down on the other guy's shoulder, which reminds me he's recording every asinine thing I say. Clamping my lips together, I trudge up the stairs in silence. I haven't even agreed to be on their silly show yet, and already my life is a circus.

Once in my room, I go straight to my dresser, not daring to look in the mirror hanging above it to see how truly hideous I look. Instead, I open the top drawer, rummage underneath my underwear, and pull out a grainy, black and white sonogram photo. For all these years, it's been the only memento I have of my child. That and my stretch marks are the only proof I have that I gave birth to another human being.

Running my fingertips lightly across the surface, I take a deep breath. She is the reason I'm doing this. If I want to meet my daughter, I have to play along.

And I want to meet her more than anything else in the world.

5

"I'm tellin' ya, Rick, we should have done it. If nothing else, it'd be hilarious."

I can hear the two men talking as I make my way down from my room. It sounds like they accepted my invitation to wait in the living room. Since you can't see the staircase from there, I stop. It's not eavesdropping, not really. More like fact-gathering. And from what I understand, I'm going to have to get used to this kind of low-class, underhanded behavior if I want to survive on that TV show of theirs.

"I've never gone through anyone's medicine cabinet, and I'm not about to start now." Rick's voice is amused, but there's an undertone of seriousness. "The woman's spooked enough. I don't want to give her any extra reasons to back out."

"You really think she'll do it?"

Silence. Is Rick whispering his response? Or is he thinking about it? Without moving my feet, I lean forward, ears straining to hear.

"I think she's too curious not to." His voice is much closer now. If I hadn't been white-knuckling the banister, the boom of it would have sent me tumbling down the stairs. He appears at the landing and grins up at me. "What do you think?"

I think this man knows how to handle people. If I'm not careful, he'll have me agreeing to all manner of ridiculous things, and then thanking him for the opportunity. Summoning the bits and pieces of my shredded dignity, I walk calmly past him. "Would either of you like coffee?"

His companion is behind him, back to being the strong, silent, camera-bearing type. Not knowing his name is driving me nuts. "What's your name?"

"Bruce." Rick answers for him.

I turn to Rick. "Is Bruce mute?"

From behind the camera comes a muttered "Hardly."

Rick laughs. "No, Bruce has quite a vocabulary. It just works better if I do the talking. And no."

"No?"

"No. To the coffee. But thank you." He motions toward the living room then leads the way in, as if he's the homeowner and I'm the visitor. Before I turn around to follow, I catch the hint of a smirk from Bruce.

Narrowing my eyes, I wag an accusing finger at him. "Careful. I'm watching you." His smirk evolves into a grin, but he remains mum.

In the living room, Rick indicates that I should sit on the couch. Then, instead of sitting in the adjacent chair, he sits beside me, angling in my direction so our knees almost touch. His proximity is a little unsettling, until Bruce squats down across from us and I realize the positioning is just so we're both in frame.

"I'm sure you've got a lot of questions," Rick says.

"When do I meet my daughter?"

"That depends on you. Are you ready to be on the show?"

"No."

"No?"

I take great pleasure in the fact that he didn't expect that answer. "I'm far from ready. But if I don't go on the show, I don't meet Jessica, do I?"

His expression softens. I'm pretty sure he feels sorry for the spot I'm in, even though he's the master puppeteer manipulating the strings.

"No, you don't. At least, not now. That isn't to say you two won't connect later some other way." When I don't answer right away, he keeps talking. "I'm sure this isn't the way you'd hoped to meet her, but if you think about it, it's really a great thing. Jessica wants to meet you."

"But why? What if the only reason is so she can be on television?"

"That's a possibility. And after thirty days on the island, you'll either hate each other or create a bond like you've never imagined. *Last Family* changes you."

The weight of his words presses down on my already hunched shoulders. "For better or worse?"

"That's up to you."

Up to me. Once again, I will make a decision that affects not only me, but my daughter, and any number of people who are now touched by the familial fingers that connect us. It's too much.

I look down at the floor, focusing on the variegated pattern of greens and browns in the Berber carpet. If I stare long and hard enough, I can block out everything: Bruce, Rick, the news van outside, the daughter I'm only barely acquainted with, the fact that I still haven't had my morning coffee. . . . Maybe, if I focus on the simple, normal, ever-present carpet, I can make it all disappear.

"Monica? Are you okay?"

Rick's voice is far off and muffled, as if he's talking through a scarf wrapped around his mouth. I try to answer, but when I open my mouth, a sob escapes. A wave of reality crashes down, pulling me out to sea in a riptide of regret and fear. Body shaking, I curl into myself, arms crossed, hands clutching my own arms, desperate to hold my head above water.

"Turn it off." Rick cuts through the torrent of emotions. A moment later, he slides closer, puts one arm around my shoulder, and offers a consoling hug.

With a sigh, Bruce rises to his full height. "I told you we should have called first."

"Just give us a minute."

Bruce leaves the room. Rather than talking, Rick rubs his hand up and down my arm. It's the kind of contact you'd expect from a brother or a platonic friend, not from the ruggedly handsome host of a popular reality series. I wonder how many other hysterical females he's had to comfort over the years.

As the sobs subside, my body starts to relax. A tissue appears beneath my nose, and I take it with a mumbled thank-you. I wipe my eyes, thankful there's no mascara to run, and look up. Bruce is rummaging around in my kitchen.

"What's he doing?"

"I'm trying to make coffee," Bruce rumbles.

"God bless you." Now I look at Rick, surprised at how unfreaked out he is by my mini-breakdown. "Thank you."

"No problem." One more squeeze, then he removes his arm from my shoulder. "You're on a pretty intense journey. I doubt that will be your last crying jag."

Oh great. "Well, before I dissolve again, let's talk about the details."

He grins. "Then you will do the show?"

"Of course. I don't really have a choice."

Rick pats my knee, then stands up. "Let me check on the coffee and get Bruce back in here, and we'll get down to it."

He's halfway to the kitchen when he turns back to me. "For the record, you always have a choice."

Not true. I had lots of choices once, several of which led to the defining choice of my life. But right now, the path is laid out in front of me. For the next however many days, Bruce and other cameramen like him will be my new constant companions, documenting my every move, including my reunion with my daughter.

When Rick comes back, he's got a coffee mug in one hand and is holding Ranger's collar with the other. "The dog will help you come across as warm and accessible."

"I am warm and accessible."

He laughs as he sits and hands me the mug. "Of course you are. And we want everyone to see that."

Ranger hops up onto the couch between us and puts one paw and his head in my lap. Rick was right, having him with me is much better. On the other side of the coffee table, Bruce hoists the camera onto his shoulder and resumes his position.

"Are you ready?" Rick asks.

The question broke me moments before, but not now. I gulp in a breath and nod sharply. "Let's do this."

One more decision taking me one step closer.

CPSIA information can be obtained at www.ICGtesting.com
Printed in the USA
BVOW07*2146270415

397962BV00003B/11/P